THE SQUID FLESH TINGLED IN REMO'S HANDS.

There was no pain. It wasn't directed at hurting him, but the half carcass was trying to pull out of his grip. Remo grunted as he tossed the half carcass as far as he could throw it.

It landed in the gravel with a sickening liquid sound, just beyond the flock of business associates from Jackson. They were dumbfounded, but they had enough sense to part ways when the bolts of energy reached out from the carcass in Bedders's hands and sought out the other half.

Remo's foot slammed into Bedders's head with enough force to snap his neck, but the neck healed in an instant.

Bedders tossed the half squid carcass in the general direction of its other half and raised both arms to block Remo's next blow. His forearms snapped and folded, then straightened out and fused solid, but Chiun was there, coming down on his shoulders, and Bedders was driven down into the gravel in a spineless heap.

D0029266

Other titles in this series:

CREATED BY MURPHY & SAPIR

THE DESTROYER

FRIGHTENING STRIKES

A GOLD EAGLE BOOK FROM
W✷RLDWIDE®

TORONTO • NEW YORK • LONDON
AMSTERDAM • PARIS • SYDNEY • HAMBURG
STOCKHOLM • ATHENS • TOKYO • MILAN
MADRID • WARSAW • BUDAPEST • AUCKLAND

First edition October 2005

ISBN 0-373-63256-8

Special thanks and acknowledgment to Tim Somheil
for his contribution to this work.

FRIGHTENING STRIKES

And for the Glorious House of Sinanju,
sinanjucentral@hotmail.com

Prologue

The creature in the tank was looking at Mary Ordonez. It hated her. It knew she was responsible for its imprisonment. Maybe it knew she was to blame for killing it.

The giant squid was dying. Ordonez, a marine biologist, had no doubt of this. She was the one who had engineered its removal from the Pacific Ocean and its rapid transport across the country. She'd created an environment for its survival—without knowing what it needed to survive.

Even by the standards of the world's great oceanariums and aquariums, the tank was massive. It cost millions of dollars for the water filters, for the chemicals used to treat the water, for the electronic systems that continuously analyzed the water and adjusted the chemical balance to match the waters from which this creature had come.

The squid had survived the change in pressure, the journey from the Pacific and the humiliation of being on display for thousands of gawking human beings. People came in droves to view this unique specimen, and for weeks it had thrived. Now, for some reason, it was dying.

Called the Chicago Giant, it was the only giant or colossal squid that had been captured alive within human memory. Until recently, it was the only giant squid even *seen* alive since the nineteenth century. Sometime in the late 1800s, a giant squid was reportedly beached on the East Coast and snagged by some fisherman with a boat anchor while it was still writhing. It didn't live long, and the fisherman eventually chopped it up for dog food.

Until the very recent past, that was the only reliable account of a giant squid being seen alive by man. Then came the time of the turmoil, when the oceans were in flux. At the same time the unexplained water geysers had sprung up around the globe, the global population of cephalopods entered a bizarre behavioral state.

They swarmed to the surface and to the shores and clustered around ships at sea. Not just the tiny hatchlings and microscopic krill, but the cuttlefish, the large-tentacle sea creatures and even the giants. The giants came to the surface in numbers scientists hadn't even guessed existed. They were powerful enough to battle whales. They were aggressive and seemed to act with a strange instinctive agenda that the experts couldn't even begin to understand.

There were reports that they had attacked sailing vessels. This was nothing new. Such attacks had been reported since man took to the sea. They inspired the tales of Kraken and the South Seas squid gods and who knew what else. Still, it seemed unlikely that they had attacked in pods and dragged cruise ships to their doom, as some recent reports claimed.

But the strange behavior was a stroke of luck for Mary Ordonez. The marine biologist happened to be on a trip to collect marine mammals for the Chicago Aquarium when the turmoil erupted. She witnessed the behavior of the cephalopods firsthand—and she was there when a colossal squid surfaced. Her team had all the right equipment on hand to snare the thing without killing it. She knew how to raise the emergency funding for the special aircraft needed to get it home to Chicago.

Technically the Chicago Giant was a colossal squid, but the distinction between a giant and a colossal was controversial, and the marketing department deemed that the term "Chicago Giant" could be more effectively imprinted on the minds of advertising victims than the term "Chicago Colossal." They could call it a giant llama for all Ordonez cared. In the world of the marine biologic sciences, she had made the find of the century.

With almost no promotion prior to the event, the squid was revealed to the world. The world didn't pay much attention, since it was involved in the agony of its own destruction. When the waterspouts vanished and the threat of imminent global destruction receded with them, the world felt safe again.

The geysers left only minor bruises on the planet. There was a great swath of decaying, steam-cooked jungle in South America. There was a crater filled with fresh ice where a Rocky Mountain ski town once stood. The waterspout that rose from the oceans of the South Pacific had vanished without a trace.

Millions of cubic tons of seawater remained frozen around the remains of the two Antarctic geysers, and would likely remain locked there forever. The continual displacement of seawater could have affected the climate or shifted the global rotation or who knew what. But that danger had now passed, and the ice fields were far away and unseen and already forgotten by most.

The world went on existing and people were ready for new amusements, like the Chicago Giant. The Chicago Aquarium heavily promoted the new attraction, with T-shirts and a Web site and fast-food plastic toy giveaways. The aquarium brought visitors by the thousands into a new exhibit space that included a highly realistic aquarium home for the colossal giant squid. This included coral, plants, fish, all chosen for their small size so they would enhance the gigantic squid even more.

Marine biologists who specialized in studying large cephalopods were eager to get their probes into the Chicago Giant, to take their samples, make their tests and observe its behavior. From the very start the researchers who were not attached to the Chicago Aquarium complained about how the find was handled. Most of the scientific community was unaware of the specimen until the public unveiling. After the squid went on display, access for serious study was severely restricted. Some researchers even accused the Chicago Aquarium of sacrificing scientific advancement in favor of providing a spectacle to the masses.

An alliance of researchers made a public appeal to Chicago citizens, asking them to stay away in protest. One of the scholars made the mistake of saying at the press conference, "We in the scientific community shouldn't have to buy an admission ticket like regular people. What I mean to say—"

What he meant to say was irrelevant. What he did say alienated the public instead of garnering its support. Nonaquarium researchers were kept away in droves, and the people approved.

The aquarium used special lighting to keep the giant's tank dimly lit. This was for the benefit of the people, not the squid, and it was just one of the practices targeted by the outside researchers.

"It's a deep-water dweller," explained the famous and irate marine biologist Philip Sylvie. "It lives in a lightless environment. The Chicago Aquarium should be keeping its holding tank in darkness, for the good of the animal."

"But," asked a reporter, "wouldn't that mean the people wouldn't be able to see it, either?"

Professor Sylvie didn't see the point of the question. "Of course."

"The public's not going to pay to see a dark tank."

"That's irrelevant. What matters is the welfare of the

animal, which means giving it the proper environment. It's clear the Chicago Aquarium doesn't have the expertise needed to care for this magnificent specimen. Which isn't surprising. After all, how can a Midwestern aquarium be expected to have a good understanding of ocean dwellers? No offense intended, but they shouldn't even be allowed to have the creature."

"Offence taken," shot back the eternally rumpled mayor of Chicago in a press conference hours later. "Just try to take it away. That fish is the pride of this city."

The Alliance of Concerned Marine Biologists kept complaining. They claimed the data that was being shared by the aquarium proved its inability to properly care for the creature.

"They're feeding the animal fish," said an exasperated Professor Sylvie, trying to redeem his cause in the eyes of the people. He didn't like the public, but he knew he needed its support this time. "This is entirely unsatisfactory. In order to keep the animal healthy it must be provided with live food of the same type it would eat in its natural environment."

"That would be kind of cruel to the poor fish, wouldn't it?" asked a radio talk-show host. He was giving the much-maligned professor the chance to reverse some of the negative publicity his former comments had created.

"I'm not talking about fish at all," Professor Sylvie said. "*Mesonychoteuthis hamiltoni,* or the colossal squid, eats sea mammals. Dolphins. Orcas. Whales."

"Dolphins? You want them to feed live, air-breathing, intelligent dolphins to that slimy beast?"

"And why not? In fact, the aquarium has an overpopulation of Pacific white-sided dolphins and more beluga whales than its tanks can comfortably accommodate."

The radio host gasped audibly. They heard him all over northern Illinois. "Are you suggesting we let Bayuka the baby beluga be eaten alive by that thing?"

"Or one of its parents."

"Do you know we had a vigil in this city when baby Bayuka was sick with the flu last year? So you know the aquarium received two thousand get-well cards from local schoolchildren? Drawn with crayons?"

"I'm not following you," Professor Sylvie said.

"You want us to put that precious little creature into a tank with that monster? Maybe we should take some video of his reaction when the squid fangs sink into his baby-white flesh?"

"Well, actually, the squid doesn't have teeth at all." Sylvie really warmed to his subject. "Squid have beaks, made of a very tough horny material. The rows of swiveling hooks on the ends of its two tentacles make the colossal unique. The more the prey struggles, the more tightly the hooks sink into its flesh and hold on. The arms have suckers with more chitinous hooks around them. Once the colossal's got him, the prey is doomed. Then it's drawn to the beak, which is used to chomp the prey into chunks small enough to swallow. The radula is the squid tongue, covered in sharp scales, and it crams the food into the squid's throat."

Commuters, too furious to drive, were pulling onto the shoulder in northern Indiana. Outraged listeners were flooding the radio station's phone banks from as far away as central Wisconsin and eastern Michigan. Half of Chicagoland was in a fury.

"You're talking about Bayuka the baby beluga," the radio host tried to explain. "I still have a T-shirt somewhere. Here it is. See?"

"I see," the professor was heard to say. "How long ago was that photo taken?"

"It's from our Name the Baby Beluga promotion. Two years ago, maybe two and a half."

"Ah. No problem, then," Sylvie said happily. "Bayuka will be quite mature enough to provide a good meal for the colossal squid."

"I don't…know quite…what to say," the host stammered. "How about if we take some calls?"

"I'd love to," Sylvie said. As far as he was concerned, the interview was quite successful so far.

"You evil, heartless, despicable man," hissed the first caller, choking with emotion.

It went downhill from there.

PROFESSOR SYLVIE was removed from the role of spokesperson for the Alliance of Concerned Marine Biologists, but the damage was done. The public wouldn't listen to the alliance any longer, even after the hiring of a public-relations professional specializing in cata-strophic-event management. The PR pro had done an excellent job for a downstate chemical company that was found to have leaking storage tanks in a town where eight out of ten people had been diagnosed with pan-creatic cancer.

The PR pro was helpless against the well-known image of a smiling whale. The TV footage showed Bayuka laughing with visiting children, or approaching a viewing window to peer at the open pages of a book being held to the glass by an aquarium patron.

The director of the aquarium went on every radio sta-tion, every news program, promising he would never allow any of his intelligent, people-loving marine mam-mals to be fed alive to the colossal squid.

Attendance went up. Special admission fees were charged. Not just for the squid, but for precious Bayuka, as well. Professor Sylvie and his alliance faded back to California, or wherever it was they came from.

Dr. Ordonez was hardly aware of any of it. She was too busy monitoring her baby, her own precious *Mesonychoteuthis hamiltoni*.

Professor Sylvie was right about one thing: the aquarium didn't know much about taking care of a co-lossal squid. But neither did Professor Sylvie or any human being on this Earth. Dr. Ordonez would simply have to use her own best judgment—and she was as qualified as any other marine biologist to do so.

But her best wasn't good enough.

The colossal squid became less active, then lethargic. Dr. Ordonez would never know why her colossal squid died.

Dr. Ordonez was keeping her vigil at some point after midnight when she sensed her beautiful squid was dead, although the instruments had not yet recorded it.

She didn't want to consult the computer display yet. It was too impersonal and clinical. She wanted to just stay there in front of the glass tank, guided by her instincts about what was alive and what was dead, and watch the big beast.

The color was changing in its body, just as it did when it was alive. The skin hue of a squid could keep altering for hours after it died, until it finally became pale gray forever.

Its ten limbs hung limp in the water. Science called eight of them arms. Only the two longest limbs were truly considered tentacles, and these looped through the water in graceful arcs with the tips barely touching the gravel bottom of the massive display tank in what was now called the Squidarium.

Mary Ordonez's colossal squid didn't move. The flesh didn't pulse. The beak was frozen partially open.

She wondered why her instruments weren't sounding audible alarms—they should have, when the vital signs stopped. The monitoring terminal she used was on a rolling cart, which communicated with the main sensor station in a room above and behind the tank. She leaned over the laptop display and noted strange readings. There was some activity in the body. Nerve activity, maybe causing muscles to contract. Maybe it took a long time for all the extremities of a creature this huge to understand that the mantle, the torso of the squid, was truly dead.

An alarm beeped finally, but the reading wasn't what she expected. Sensor error. The system thought a sensor was no longer sending its signal, but even when the thing was dead the sensors should continue transmitting some sort of a signal.

Another beep. Another sensor stopped functioning.

Ordonez looked back at the tank, as if that would tell her anything, and was just in time to see a spritz of light flicker across the bottom of the tank. First she cursed—the sensors in the bottom of the tank had to be shorting out for some reason. Then she realized the spark had come from the tip of a long tentacle where it had drifted into a pile of rock. There sparks had disturbed a layer of sediment that blanketed the rocks.

There was something under the little cloud of sediment.

Mary Ordonez walked alongside the front of the tank, where once a thousand attendees had lined up to view the marvelous colossal squid. Then she started running.

"Oh, God." She didn't know what else to say.

Another little shower of sparks came off of the tip of the dangling tentacle, stirring up more waste on the floor, and the disturbance revealed a spherical object nestled amid the rocks.

"Oh, God!" Ordonez blurted.

What caused the electric sparks? Were they coming off the squid itself? What was the object in the rocks—an *egg?* That was not possible for a hundred reasons. Squid produced gelatinous masses containing thousands of eggs. Even the colossal squid was thought to produce tiny eggs, just a few millimeters in diameter. This object was as big and round as an ostrich egg. *But what else could it be, if not an egg?*

Ordonez pressed her face to the glass and she spotted another object in the tank. And another. If those were eggs they would have had to have been fertilized before the thing was captured, months ago. A female squid could store and mature eggs in an oviducal cavity in the mantle but not for months. And what was the electrical activity? It came from the very tips of the tentacle—there, it was happening again. The tentacle drifted away and now a shimmering shell of yellow energy enveloped the eggs and reached up to the tentacle. What *was* that?

What kind of electrical discharge came from a dead squid? What was the connection to the eggs—if they were eggs? None of this made any sense.

Then one thing did make sense to Dr. Mary Ordonez—the eggs, if they were eggs, were in danger. The water in the tank would quickly become poisonous as the carcass of the giant squid began to decompose. The body would already be disgorging internal fluids directly into the closed environment of the tank. The filters would be overwhelmed by the concentration of poisons in the water. The eggs—if they were eggs—had no protective gelatinous carrier and thus were likely porous, so they would be fatally injured. The aquarium staff could remove the carcass from the tank with the use of the overhead crane, but it would take hours to assemble everyone to do it. The eggs might be in jeopardy in a matter of minutes.

Dr. Mary Ordonez acted fast. She jogged into her office, tore off her lab coat and clothing, and pulled on her swimsuit. She grabbed her mouthpiece with a small compressed-air tank. In no time she was ready to dive.

She jogged back to the Squidarium exhibit hall. Her bare feet slapped on the floor. The place was so big and so still. She considered calling for help—but the call could wait until after she saved the eggs.

Not eggs, she told herself. They couldn't be eggs. But if not eggs, then what?

She scaled the stairs alongside the Squidarium tank, in a maintenance section that was usually closed off from the viewing public. There was a maintenance and observation platform at the top of the tank. Mary Ordonez stepped into the water and allowed herself to descend the ladder inside the squid domain, barely holding on to the rails. Her feet landed on the gravel bottom of the Squidarium.

She barely glanced at the squid carcass. It hung above her, huge and still, its underside tickled by the bubbles from her scuba breather. She walked across the gravel bottom to the rocky place and she found the spherical objects.

They *were* eggs—she could see fully formed para-larva moving inside the translucent shells, like miniature replicas of the parent. She reached for a little snap-on net on her dive belt, but she didn't unsnap it. Her attention was drawn away from the miracle babies by the movement of the mother squid.

The arms were coming together. The extralong tentacles were closing on Dr. Mary Ordonez, and what truly dismayed her was that the squid was undeniably still dead. How did it move? She tried to get away but the tentacles closed in on her. It wasn't by chance that the arms caught Dr. Ordonez; something external from the carcass was directing the arms' action. What and how?

The colossal squid's tentacle suckers, equipped with tiny barbs to better grip its prey, pierced Dr. Ordonez's flesh.

She saw the glimmer of yellow charges dancing from the tentacle tips, piercing her body more deeply than the barbs. She gasped from the pain. More arms were holding her in place. Yellow bolts of energy shocked her and sizzled across the water, to the eggs.

Ordonez felt her body give up its strength. Ah, she was being drained of life and the life was being spoon-fed to the eggs. They were nursing on the indefinable forces that gave her life. The pressure in her chest cavity was excruciating. The bubbles from her own breather were billowing all around her. She felt her ribs yield to the pressure, and Dr. Ordonez burst apart.

SHE WOKE UP.

It was a dream, right?

She focused her vision and found herself looking at the underside of the squid carcass. She was right where she remembered being, on the bottom of the squid tank. There were no bubbles. She gasped for air, but there wasn't any air. The scuba breather was empty, which meant she had been down for longer than fifteen minutes.

The squid wasn't holding her now. Her chest hurt. When she looked at her chest, she tried to scream. Her swimsuit was ripped to shreds. Her stomach was caved in, and half her rib cage looked as if it had collapsed. There was no blood, but her body was mangled under sickly, pale new skin.

The impossibility of all this was enough to be disabling. She had to stop thinking and just get out of the water. Maybe this was all an hallucination caused by bad air. She got to her feet—then the yellow energy danced across the gravel floor and cut her legs out from under her.

The energy came from the eggs. The colossal squid was moving again, closing in on her, but was still dead. She didn't understand any of this. Her chest filled with pressure even as the energy that kept her alive was channeled out her body and across the rocks, to be absorbed by the nest of eggs.

The pressure was too much. She hoped it would end soon—and end for good this time.

Prologue

They called in Oscar Bedders, renowned as the most skill-ful diver in the Midwest. He declined the assignment, it being his day off, and a Sunday. He had plans to spend his day in a buddy's media room watching women's beach volleyball on the plasma screen and sucking down beer.

Various favors were called in at levels of importance far above the head of Oscar Bedders. It started with the Chicago Aquarium director, Horace Vouzu himself, convincing the chief of the Chicago Park District Police to have Bedders summoned for duty on his day off.

Oscar Bedders didn't *have* to come in if he didn't want to. There were other divers on the clock, just sit-ting on their butts, and they were competent enough for a no-brainer, easy-water recovery job like this one. Still, Bedders knew better than to turn down an assignment veiled as a personal request from the chief—and Bed-ders really needed to keep this job for a while.

Bedders arrived with a scowl etched in the hard lines of his leathery skin. Aquarium Director Vouzu inter-cepted him in the rear corridors and tried to make nice.

"We're very distressed, all of us. We lost our best researcher and our most prized exhibit."

"Your biggest cash cow, you mean."

Director Vouzu darted his eyes around, searching for a response, and couldn't find a good one. "It was quite a blow when I got the phone call."

Bedders just kept walking fast, lugging a duffel bag with his equipment. It didn't weigh him down much. The man was all muscle and gristle. Vouzu almost skipped to keep up.

"I'm sorry you had to come in on your day off." Vouzu sounded like he really wanted Bedders's cooperation.

"You could at least tell me why."

"Oh, well, the nature of the situation. It's a salt water tank. You've dived in salt water."

"So's every diver in the unit. And there's nothing special about this dive."

"We've always used you in the past, Officer Bedders."

"It's a short dive, there's no dangers in the tank. You could have used anybody. You must have a hundred people on your own staff capable of going in there."

"Not to retrieve a body. They're calling this a crime scene."

Bedders made a wry line out of his lips. "Yeah, right."

"That's what they're saying."

"The world is full of morons."

Director Vouzu felt his face get hot, knowing he was one of the morons in Bedders's view, and he let the diver get ahead of him. The man knew the way to the Special Exhibits Seascape.

When Bedders pushed through the double doors, he was greeted with a new banner that informed him it was now called the Squidarium.

The bang of the doors was like an assault in the somber Squidarium. All eyes turned. Bedders ignored the ugly looks from the people just as he ignored the ugly thing in the tank.

Bedders wanted nothing to do with the smart-ass scientists who did God-knew-what in this place. It didn't bother him one iota that a researcher was pulled to pieces by one of her cage animals. There was nobody here that he respected enough to act as if he cared.

The cop in charge of the scene didn't have to introduce himself. Bedders knew and disliked the man. The feeling was quite mutual.

"Good morning, Officer Bedders," Detective Orson said, not even trying to sound cordial.

"Who's it good for? Not me. You having a good morning?"

"Not anymore."

"What's the problem here?" Bedders demanded as he dropped his duffel at the base of the metal stairs that led to the top of the tank. It was situated in a causeway that was normally sealed off from the public sections of the Squidarium by forty-foot, rolling wall sections.

"I'm supposed to be sitting in front of my buddy's plasma watching beach volleyball in a couple hours."

"Keep your voice down," Orson said.

"You ever see them bikini babes spike a ball in high-def? It's sweet. And I'm missing it."

"Show some respect."

"Why you dicks think this is a murder?"

"There is a body."

"In a tank with a great big fishy. That ain't murder. I'd be surprised if she weren't dead."

Detective Orson was counting silently to ten before each response. It was one of the tricks they taught in anger-management class. He was doing surprisingly well, he thought, since Bedders was one of the most abrasive individuals he had run into at any time in his career in law enforcement—and that included a few unrepentant serial killers.

But really, not many people lost their cool around Oscar Bedders. There was plenty of grapevine talk about what happened to people who pissed him off.

"The thing is, the squid is dead, too," Detective Orson explained.

"I heard they were both alive last time anybody checked."

"Right. The squid was sick and Dr. Ordonez was nursing it."

Bedders yanked off his boots, then dropped his trousers without warning. There was a gasp from one of the women in the sad group. Bedders gave her a leer as it was revealed he was wearing his swim trunks. The mourners shuffled uncomfortably to the rear of the Squidarium.

"I still don't see a reason to think she was murdered." He began dragging on his full, official quarantine dive suit. "Or why you're making me wear all the extra shit."

"It might be that the squid was poisoned, since all these good scientists couldn't find a cause for its malaise."

Bedders sneered as he pulled on the dry suit. "Its malaise? You mean it was sick?"

"That's what I mean."

"Then why don't you just say it was sick?"

Detective Orson silently counted to five.

"I'll tell you what happened," Bedders interrupted, speaking loud enough for his voice to carry from one end of the exhibit space to the other. "These dumbfucks put the big fishy into a tank without the slightest clue what they were doing, and it died. They're gonna lose millions and a lot of people are going to know they screwed up, but they want to make it look like they did everything they could do."

Bedders thrust a thumb over one shoulder at Director Vouzu, who was uneasy and couldn't seem to figure out where his hands should go. "Because this guy's trying to keep his job, I got to get up an hour early and I don't get to see babes with their swimsuits riding up their cracks. All so you can make it look like some mysterious circumstances."

The detective couldn't make himself wait before he said, "Look at the body, asshole. Her arms and legs are torn off."

"Wonder what could have done it?" Bedders hoisted on the suit.

"It is probably true that the squid died of natural causes. And Dr. Ordonez probably went into the tank to look for the cause or administer the creature somehow. Maybe she thought it was already dead. Then it revived enough to mutilate her."

"That's what happened, all right."

"Probably. But there's a slight suspicion that the water has foreign agents in it. It'll be a couple of days until the tests tell us for sure. Until then, we treat it as a homicide. You want to go in there without a haz-mat suit, you go right ahead."

Bedders zipped up the chest seal on the dry suit. "I'm not stupid enough to disobey orders just like I'm not stupid enough to think it ain't a waste of my time. But at least I get to see a babe in a swimsuit, after all." He nodded his head at the tank and the remains of Ordonez.

Orson was aghast. Bedders smirked and hoisted his headgear over his shoulder and scaled the ladder alongside the glass corner of the aquarium. At the top was a small dive platform, where he sat and checked his gear. He didn't need flippers. He wasn't going far and he could just walk on the tank bottom. He started the flow of breathable gas from the tanks and the pressure gauge told him the suit was sealed.

Below him, the bloodless mass of the giant squid bobbed in the water, tentacles swaying gently. The carcass was anchored against the rear of the tank with long hooks and chains, under the maintenance dive platform. Another small knot of brainy types in long lab coats reached down with metal rods and pinched flesh samples off the creature.

Officer Oscar Bedders of the Chicago Park District Police ignored their wan smiles of encouragement as he stepped off the platform and sank into the aquarium tank.

SURROUNDING THE SQUIDARIUM were police officers and senior aquarium staff who had been colleagues of Ordonez. Their fascination was greater than their repulsion, and they came forward to view the recording of the crime scene.

"That guy is the biggest asshole I know," the detective said. "He ought to be kicked off the force."

"He's the best diver in the city," the aquarium director said. "He's got impressive credentials."

"Oh, sure, great résumé. Ask him why he's not in Lauderdale anymore. Or D.C. or Boston. He's been kicked out of every respectable marine police recovery unit on the East Coast. You think he came inland because he likes Chicago?"

Vouzu said nothing. He felt nothing but loathing for Bedders personally, but he knew the man had a reputation as one of the strongest, most fearless police recovery divers in the country. Bedders had performed extraordinary recoveries, including the deep-water retrieval of the body of a Japanese diplomat and the three prostitutes who were with him when his fuel tank exploded and sent their small pleasure craft to the Atlantic floor off New Jersey. It had been a race against time before the networks got their own divers into the water to photograph the body and confirm the scandal, which would have been a major embarrassment for the U.S. Bedders had gotten credit for keeping the scandal from breaking.

He was also renowned for bagging six bodies from a drug boat that went down off Miami and had lain there rotting for three months. Other divers, even those experienced with recovery, were too repulsed by the conditions to function. Only Bedders was able to crawl through a shoulder-wide entrance port into what had been a hidden compartment on the boat. A ton of narcotics and all those swollen cadavers packed into a space the size of a broom closet.

Every police force that hired and eventually fired him gave the same reference: "Oscar Bedders was the most skillful diver we ever employed, and we would never employ him again."

BEDDERS'S WEIGHT BELT PULLED him easily to the bottom of the tank. His arm brushed against the trailing end of a tentacle and he ignored it. Dead squid didn't bother him. Dead people didn't bother him, either. He didn't see what the big deal was about dead bodies. They were just junk. He didn't even see the need of getting them back. Why pull a body out of the ocean just to bury it somewhere else?

Whatever, it was his job. Even if he didn't see the point half the time, he liked the diving part of his job. The money was good, too—or it used to be. Lots of hazard pay when you were working ocean recovery. Not so much here in Chicago. He hated this Podunk city. Soon as a position opened up on either coast, he was out of here. He just had to wait for the flack to die down from the trouble in San Francisco. He'd slugged a fellow officer, and it wasn't the first time. Now his reputation as a trouble-maker covered both coasts, rivaling his reputation as a fearless diver.

He still couldn't believe he was rotting away in the middle of nowhere, and doing gofer work for the aquarium suits, no less. All to make them look good. All so they could say they called in the best diver in the state of Illinois, so no mistakes would be made. Maybe he could turn this to his advantage, take a little of the publicity for himself, get noticed by one of the coastal departments in need of a good diver.

Bedders didn't look at the squid. After all, it was just a squid. He'd seen lots of them. This was just bigger than the others.

He didn't spend much time examining the body. He just started taking pictures. He snapped twenty shots from a distance, then moved closer to extend the tape measure and lay it beside the body.

The dead doctor had actually been nice-looking. Cute face, if you got rid of the breathing unit and closed the wide, horrified eyes. Nice hair. Really nice body, what was left of it. Lucky for him, when her arms had come off, the straps of her bathing suit had slipped off her shoulders. Bedders took a few close-ups of her upper body, for personal use.

Then he stopped and lowered the camera. He stepped alongside the torso and waved at the woman's shoulder stump to clear a cloud of swirling water debris.

The arm didn't look right. It was as if the stump had healed over. It wasn't a clean, smooth knob like a healed surgical amputation. It was messy, uneven, but covered in flesh. There were a few signs of black scarring. Burns? Were the stumps cauterized after the delimbing? What could have caused that?

Maybe there *was* more going on than met the eye. Maybe this wasn't just a simple death-by-squid situation. He saw something moving.

"WHY'S HE DOING THAT?" the aquarium director asked Detective Orson.

"He's got to take pictures of the crime scene. That's his job."

"He could show some respect for the poor woman. He doesn't have to act like this is just another day on the job."

It also seemed to Vouzu that the diver was taking more pictures than was strictly necessary. He wished the man would hurry it up and get a cover over the corpse.

He couldn't stand looking at her like that, eyes wide and staring into the heaven. Lying there so exposed was a continuation of her violation. Vouzu wanted this to be over with.

"What is he doing now?" the aquarium head demanded. "Why doesn't he leave her alone and get out of there?"

"Marking the body for scale," the detective said. "This isn't like a regular crime scene, you know. We can't have all kinds of field technicians to evaluate the victim. Our diver's got to do it all himself. Measurements, photos, crime-scene samples. This is our one and only chance to preserve all the information we can about the crime. As soon as we move her, it compromises our data."

"She's not data. She's a human being. Give her back her dignity."

"I'd prefer to give her justice."

Their diver straightened, then took a step away from the body. It was a careless step, and his foot slid out from under him on a slippery rock. Bedders sat down on the gravel floor.

Director Vouzu cocked his head.

Orson saw it too and pushed his face close to the glass. He had just seen a movement in the rocks a few feet from the remains. If the lady professor still had arms, she would have been able to reach out and touch the place where the thing had moved.

"We were told there were no other display animals in this tank."

"There's not," Vouzu said. "There can't be."

"You just saw it and I saw it and my diver saw it. You want to make this even worse?" Detective Orson waved at the glass, at the body of the woman and the carcass of the colossal squid. "If my diver is in danger, this could become a lot worse. Maybe you should try to find out what is in the tank."

Director Vouzu saw the wisdom in it and shouted at one of the aquarium staffers. "Martin, what the hell is in there?"

Dr. Martin Suut was in a lab coat and his goatee was matted with tears. He was Dr. Ordonez's assistant and had never had the courage to tell Dr. Ordonez, or anyone, that he was in love with her. Now it was too late and he could scarcely contain his grief; he was slow to understand the question.

"In with the squid! What else is in there? What specimens?"

"Not a one," Suut said.

"Feed fish?"

"No. The squid was on pudding."

"Pudding?" Orson snapped.

"Fish meal and rendered fat, cooked in edible casings. Like a sausage or English Christmas pudding," Suut explained.

"There's a specimen or something in there, Martin. Get the team on the top deck to search it out with the tank scanners."

"What I want to know is, should I pull my diver?"

the detective demanded. "What are the chances it's dangerous?"

"I doubt there is a danger," Director Vouzu said.

"How do you figure, seeing as how you don't know what it is?"

"It's small—we know that. And quick, so it's not a jellyfish specimen. Not many small specimens besides jellyfish are going to be dangerous."

Bedders was back on his feet, peering into the tumble of rocks beyond the victim but unalarmed. Detective Orson decided he'd let the diver make his own call in this case. Bedders could take care of himself.

Orson found himself focusing on the great, pale mass of gelatinous flesh that hung at the top of the water, its arms and tentacles swaying in the gentle circulation of the tank. Orson had avoided looking at the thing. It was disgusting enough when it was alive, and now it was utterly repulsive, more so than any human remains he had ever lain eyes on.

The squid was moving.

He rubbed his forehead and looked again, but his eyes still told him that the squid's ten slimy limbs were stiffening and contracting.

"What are they doing to that thing?" Vouzu asked. He sounded irritated and impatient, which snapped Orson's irrational horror. The staff on the platform above the tank—that's what the aquarium head was talking about. Those people were manipulating the carcass for their own esoteric reasons. Maybe using a crane to begin hauling the squid out of the water, against police orders. Maybe the death-hardened limbs were being drawn down as a result. But the effect was terrifying.

"Martin, tell them to leave the carcass alone. Stop whatever it is they're doing."

Suut looked up from his cell phone. "They're not doing anything to it. Oh, my God."

The others saw it now. The squid's arms were as stiff as bone, bent at fingerlike joints, and closing deliberately on Oscar Bedders. One of the women shrieked. There was a hubbub of voices.

"It's still alive," one of the police officers wailed.

"No, no," Suut said. "Look at the color. It's dead. The nerves are just acting up."

"Signal Bedders to get the hell out," Detective Orson ordered, then turned to Suut. "Like a postmortem galvanic response in a human cadaver?" The explanation was for him and everybody else.

"Yes." Suut was distracted by the squid. "But I don't know what *that* is."

The electric activity started as tiny shimmering threads of yellow, so faint they were almost tricks of the eye, but then became visible streaks of energy dancing across the flesh of the carcass and along its tentacles. Orson didn't know where the electrical pulses were coming from, but he knew that they were responsible for the carcass's movements.

"You people have some sort of an electric current in the water!"

"That can't be," Director Vouzu murmured.

"Those are static discharges," Suut said in wonder, his scientific curiosity overcoming his grief and alarm. "It's not from an applied current but from the animal itself. I've never heard of such thing."

Oscar Bedders wasn't making his exit. Orson grabbed a radio from the recovery support officer, flipped it on and said, "What are you doing? Get out of there."

The support officer pulled his gaze away from the tank. "He's not wearing a radio. We couldn't see a need for it."

Bedders stood beneath the slow-moving carcass of the squid and didn't even notice the stiff tentacles closing on him like pincers. Orson pulled handcuffs from his back pocket and rapped the glass, shuffling along it and waving his arms to get Bedders's attention.

The diver was oblivious. The fractured relief of light and shadow painted the floor of the tank from the flickering energy, but Bedders was just standing there, eyes fixed on the tank floor. What was wrong with him?

"He's paralyzed," Orson decided. "The electricity zapped him. He'll drown. We need to get him out of there!"

Nobody acknowledged him, and Bedders proved he wasn't paralyzed by backing away from the corpse. He dropped his camera. Whatever he was trying to get away from, it was enough to keep his eyes riveted on the tank floor just beyond the body. The famously fearless Oscar Bedders was afraid of what he saw in the rocks.

The rocks were producing their own charges. The pulses originated in the rocks, tracked across the gravel and nailed the head of the dead woman.

Director Vouzu made a hopeless sound and crossed himself. The remains of Dr. Ordonez jerked from the bolts of tiny lightning. Her wide eyes bulged in their sockets. More bolts came from deeper within the tumble of rocks, shaking and jittering the body, disturbing the gravel and swirling the cloudy water.

But Bedders moved slowly, as if he were wading in sludge. Or as if he were hypnotized. The discharge from the squid increased in intensity and reached out for Bedders. Bedders stiffened in midstride as the energy flowed into him. Orson half expected his body to be surrounded by an aura of energy, but this was no cartoon electrocution.

Bedders turned his face to the glass, rolled his eyes into his skull and screamed underwater.

Something splashed down into the surface of the tank far above and descended. It was a metallic basket on a crane line, and it attracted energy from the squid carcass, which it then deflected back at the creature. Errant energy waves careened across the surface of the squid, interrupting the energy buildup. The finger of static impaled in Bedders's head now flickered.

Bedders lunged aside, and the energy released him.

"Tell him to get to the basket," Suut instructed, keeping a cell phone glued to his head.

"Are you crazy?" Orson returned. "It's attracting the current."

"He'll never make it up the ladder," Suut said. "He can barely walk."

Bedders was indeed struggling to get to his feet again. The interruption in the charges on the squid carcass had stopped the movement of the tentacles, and the boiling charges in the rocks had decreased to a low-grade sizzle. The disharmonious energy waves faded on the squid, then brightened again.

"Listen to me—my guys are back on the platform. The crane's electrically grounded. They'll get him out."

"And fry him all the way to the surface."

"How else will he get out?" Suut demanded.

Detective Orson was looking everywhere and nowhere, hoping for inspiration. "Do it," he said quickly. "Have them get anything else metallic onto the platform. Anything big and metal that they can find—dump it in the tank to attract the current."

Suut understood the strategy and began explaining into his cell phone. Detective Orson pounded his handcuffs on the glass and managed to attract Bedders's attention. He pointed at the retrieval basket, which was coming to a rest on the floor of the tank. Bedders wouldn't understand. He would see the basket as a death trap, just as Orson had. And maybe it would be. But it was the only chance of getting him out of the water alive. He had to go for it.

Bedders rolled his face mask at the detective. His unfocused gaze was asking the all-important question. "Are you sure about this?"

"Go," Orson mouthed.

Bedders walked unsteadily into the center of the tank, to the basket. It was a brave decision, and a trusting one, the detective had to admit. It took a hell of a lot of nerve to not make for the ladder—a closer escape and more distant from the intensifying fields of energy. Bedders paraded into the field of electrical charges, pushing the water with his hands, and he seemed to gain strength by the time he got to the basket.

The water filled with movement as the energy discharge shot from the squid, penetrating the gravel like an iron spike. Again. Again. Homing in on Oscar Bedders. The ground cover of energy in the rocks was rattling Ordonez's body again. The Squidarium was a maelstrom.

Bedders disconnected his weight belt as the energy spike located him, making him go stiff. The belt landed in the gravel. Bedders managed to kick against the ground—just enough to deflect his fall so that he collapsed inside the retrieval basket. The energy charges crisscrossed from the wire weave of the basket and the diver, who quivered like a convict in an electric chair.

"Tell them to lift the basket and throw in whatever they've got," Orson called to Suut, who relayed the message. It took a few endless seconds before a steel cart splashed onto the surface far above. Then several

CRT monitors plopped in, one after another. The energy was sucked up to the table and small residual charges reached for the CRTs, which burst in clouds of glass.

It wasn't enough. The energy continued torturing the diver even as the basket rose one agonizing foot a second.

"Tell them to throw in more stuff," Orson shouted. "Something grounded but not on a live current."

"Like what?" Suut demanded, then answered his own question. "Environmental control station for the tank. It's the remote one."

"It's on 220 volts," Vouzu said.

"The circuits will break when it hits the water—it's designed for use near the tanks."

"It cost 1.2 million."

"Throw it in!" Orson demanded.

"There's safety rails designed to keep that from happening," Vouzu protested.

"Roll it against the stops hard as you can—it'll go over. Just do it fast."

Police diver Oscar Bedders was being cooked alive in front of their eyes. The distance to the surface seemed immense. There was a fragment of shadow above the surface, then a complicated-looking control panel was crushed below the surface by its own weight. It created its own electrical display for a heartbeat, then grew dark, only to be attacked by a torrent of energy bolts. The discharge from the squid was stronger than ever, but the pull of the dead control panel was immense. It seemed to be attracting the stiff tentacle tips toward it.

The basket was attracting none of the lightning bolts. It ascended in sudden peace, Oscar Bedders limp inside of it.

Then the ground-hugging energy from the rocks reached up and took the basket into its grasp, giving spastic animation to Bedders once again.

The 1.2-million-dollar Squidarium Environmental Control System burst apart, then the colossal squid's energy went back to Bedders as if with new determination. Detective Orson was about to shout for more metallic items to be tossed in, but by then it was too late.

Like the control panel, Oscar Bedders was ripped to pieces by the greedy claws of energy. It was more like an explosion than a disintegration. Pieces of him flew everywhere, turning the water to stew. Orson glimpsed the basket flipping over in the commotion, and saw the dim shape of the torso tumbling back to the tank floor.

The detective stepped back from the tank, but he couldn't tear his eyes away.

He was watching when he saw more movement that was not the settling of Oscar Bedders's many fragments. Something was scurrying along the floor, snatching at the fragments of human and pulling them in.

"Christ, what's that?"

"I don't know," Suut said.

Almost immediately, the water began to clear. The movement was gone in a flash. Oscar Bedders was flat on his back, just like Dr. Ordonez. Ordonez had suffered further damage, with pieces of her abdomen and chest chopped out.

Bedders was surprisingly intact. In fact, the detective could swear that through his turmoil he was seeing chunks of Bedders falling back into place, as if magnetically attracted to his body.

He turned away, squeezed his eyes shut and turned back. The water was noticeably clearer.

The onlookers were stunned to silence until someone in a lab coat choked on his own words. "Oh, God, he's not dead."

This could not be true, and yet it was true. Bedders was raising his head. His mask was gone and his jaw was gone; somehow the breathing apparatus was still clinging to the upper teeth and releasing churning bubbles. Bedders gulped at the airflow.

Orson realized the energy was gone. He snatched the phone from Suut and identified himself. "We're going to have to maneuver the crane to him."

"These things don't work like that," said somebody from the observation platform. "They just sort of swing back and forth."

"You will make it work," Orson said. Where was he getting his cool in all this mayhem? "Move it to your left forty feet."

The crane operator complied. The cable cut through the water on the surface. The basket swung along with it after a long delay.

"Back ten feet. Extend the crane six feet. Lower it now. Two feet back."

It was an eternity, but then the basket came to rest in the sand just inches from the wounded diver.

Bedders's fingers closed on the mesh wire basket, some of them turning backward on broken knuckle joints.

Funny thing. A minute ago, Orson saw Bedders's fingers reduced to stumps—or that's what he thought he saw. Both hands were more or less intact now, but scrawny and emaciated.

The diver fell in the basket and curled into a ball, then straightened and clamped down on the air supply.

A moment ago, Orson had seen Bedders missing his lower jaw. Now his teeth were locked on the remains of the air tube and sucking at the bubbles.

It seemed wrong for Bedders to be alive, and Detective Orson stifled his revulsion to take hold of the basket that was dangled out over the viewing area and lowered to the floor. Paramedics had been on hand as a matter of procedure during what might turn out to be a high-risk recovery. These were not the dangers anyone had anticipated.

Orson bent over them as they examined Bedders. They tore away the clinging remnants of his suit, exposing the pits where his wounds were. The flesh was closed.

"I guess the skin was cauterized by the discharge," the paramedic reported.

"Doesn't look cauterized," Orson said. In fact, the flesh covering the indentations of the wounds was surprisingly unblemished.

"You got me," the medic said. "Pulse is good. Respiration labored but strong."

Detective Orson had a funny feeling that reality was slipping out of his grasp. Bedders should not be alive. Pulse should not be "good" and respiration should not be "strong" and none of this should have happened in the real world.

"More of him should be missing," Vouzu muttered. Orson knew that the aquarium director, for one, was even more out of it.

"He has his jaw," agreed one of the lab techs. "I saw his jaw come off but now it's on again."

"What was it in the tank?" Suut said. "What the hell was it?"

"I was going to ask you that," Orson said,

Suut had seen too much. His eyes were wide as soupspoons. "Damned if I know," he said.

"Something god-awful," said a cop.

"The tank was cleaned three weeks ago when the squid's symptoms appeared." Vouzu was trying to state his case to no one in particular. "We introduced only heat-sterilized feed to keep bacteria from entering its environment. Our environmental-control systems are the best in the world."

"Horace," said an elderly woman with a Ph.D. on her name tag, "we all saw something in there."

"They looked small," the detective pointed out. "Like piranha or something. "

The director laughed harshly. "Piranha don't even live in salt water."

"Then you tell me. It was *something*." Orson noticed they weren't even mentioning the electrical incident. Trying to come to grips with one inexplicable phenomenon at a time.

The paramedics were helpless. They took Bedders's vitals, then radioed the hospital for consultation with a physician. There were no wounds to bind or bleeding to stop. Bedders made gargling sounds in his throat, then went into convulsions before he finally slumped dead on the gurney.

"So what do we do now?" asked the aquarium director as the gurney was wheeled away.

Orson's eyes followed the long steel cable from the floor to the crane mount far above. "You have a mechanical claw for that thing?"

Vouzu was stricken. "You want to fish Mary Ordonez out with some big salad tongs?"

"You got an any better ideas?" Orson said. "We sure can't send in another diver. Unless you're volunteering."

2

His name was Remo and he was conspiring to commit insurance fraud.

"Try harder," said Conner Shipmen. "You have to really *sell* the idea."

Remo thought about it, then begged in Korean, "Please, can I break your leg?"

"No," said Min Su, a homeless Korean prostitute. "Are you a lunatic?"

"Hey, this isn't my idea. It's his scheme. He thinks we can make insurance money if I talk you into letting me break your leg."

Min Su had lived for months on the streets of Annandale, Virginia, a few miles from Washington, D.C., and now she understood. "He's Bonebreaker Shipmen."

"I thought his first name was Conner," Remo said.

Min Su shook her head. She was afraid now. "They call him Bonebreaker. Everybody knows him on Hummer Road, but I never heard of him working in the Koreatown neighborhood."

"He never had somebody who spoke Korean before."

"But now he has you."

"Pretend you think it's a really good idea for me to break your leg."

The woman stood up straighter. "Never. It's wicked."

Conner Shipmen was getting impatient. "What's the problem?"

Remo switched to English. "I don't get it. For some reason she doesn't want to have her leg broken."

"Then you ain't being convincing."

Remo asked Min Su. "Are you really, truly sure you don't want to have your leg broken? You'll get a lot of money from the insurance."

"Liar!" Min Su snapped in Korean. "He promises money, but the money never comes. I know street people from D.C. who have gone along with Bonebreaker's schemes. Poor people, sick people, always people without a place to live and desperate for food or money to get their next fix. They suffer horribly and never do they get what they were promised."

"Really?" Remo said. "That's not the Bonebreaker I know." He switched to English. "This lady says you reneged on your deals with the homeless folks in D.C."

Min Su understood English. When she heard Remo rat her out, she knew she was dead. Bonebreaker would kill her.

"Bitch. Whore. I'll break your head, that's what I'll do. Come here." Bonebreaker lunged at Min Su.

Min Su saw the end coming. She was on a dark street

in the middle of the night. Nobody else in sight. She was a dead woman.

But before he could latch on to her, Bonebreaker broke.

"Oops," Remo said.

"Son of a bitch." Shipmen hopped on one leg and grabbed his knee, then hopped across the sidewalk to lean against the brick front of the Korean grocery. "My knee's busted."

"Sorry. I guess I got nervous. I was all pumped up to break *somebody's* leg."

Min Su stared at Remo. She had seen him do the breaking, but she couldn't see what he'd used to do it.

"I'll kill you," Shipmen howled.

"It was an honest mistake."

"Call an ambulance."

"See. It doesn't look that bad, does it?" Remo asked Min Su. "It's not that bad, is it, Conner?"

"I'll kill you."

Remo whipped a rolled, multipart form from the front pocket of his chinos. "So, you just sign for health coverage on the line, then I break your leg, the insurance pays off and everybody's happy. Okay?"

"No, thanks," said the homeless sex-industry professional.

"I will fucking kill you," Conner groaned. He rested his broken foot on the sidewalk and hoisted a handgun from the inside pocket of his blazer. Min Su screamed.

Remo tapped the form with Conner's handgun. How

he came to be in possession of the handgun, Conner and the Korean woman couldn't say.

"I can see you're tempted, but you are still not convinced that maiming is right for you," Remo said. "What if we customize the deal to fit your particular needs? Maybe you think a broken leg would be an inconvenience, so I could break your arm instead. Getting your arm broken is *nothing*."

She looked at Remo as if he were growing antlers.

"See?" Remo broke Shipmen's left arm. "That doesn't hurt, does it?"

Shipmen screeched wordlessly.

"How did you do that?" the prostitute asked.

"Just for you, I'll demonstrate. Watch closely." Remo broke Shipmen's right arm by giving the man a quick, flat-handed poke to the elbow. "Did you see?"

"I saw," she said.

"Interested?"

"No, thank you."

"Last chance to get in on this ground-floor opportunity."

"I'll pass." Min Su was no longer afraid. In fact, she smiled. "You're cute."

"Aw, shucks, ma'am. I'm supposed to be buttering you up, not the other way around."

"And yet, you are a first-class weirdo," she added, still smiling.

"Naw, I'm Master of Sinanju."

"Whatever that is."

"Ask your grandparents next time you go visit. Look, you seem really nice, but it's my first day. I have to make at least one sale or my boss is gonna be pissed off." He glanced meaningfully at Bonebreaker, who was moaning and trying to hold on to all his busted limbs.

Remo gripped Conner Shipmen by the neck and helped him hop on one leg. Every landing elicited screams. "C'mon, be quiet, man," Remo said. "You're driving off the customers." He found an old Korean bum sitting on a bench at a bus stop. Even leaning on an old wooden cane, the old man was about ready to fall over.

"Want to make some easy cash?" Remo asked. "Easy as one, two, three."

The old Korean man stared at him with watery, red eyes.

"One, you sign your name on an insurance form. Two, I break your leg. Three, you and me and Conner here, we laugh all the way to the bank."

The old man began trembling.

"I know what you're thinking. Break my leg? Ouch! But let me show you how quick and easy it can be." Remo broke Conner Shipmen's only good leg, and Shipmen's screams echoed up and down Hummer Road.

"So, want a piece of this action?"

"Do I have a choice?" the old man asked tremulously.

"Sir," Remo exclaimed, "I'm not going to force you to have your leg broken if you don't want to."

The old man nodded and doddered off down the street.

"Dude," Remo told Shipmen, "your loud mouth is queering my deals."

"Get me to the hospital," Shipmen gasped. "Then I'll kill you."

"You promised me the Koreatown territory, remember? Now I'm gonna collect some of that easy cash you were talking about." He pointed to a Korean teenager who emerged from a walk-up apartment and was riveted by the spectacle of the wounded Bonebreaker. "I bet she'd like some easy money. Miss? Oh, miss?"

REMO WAS BATTING zero. Not one sale—and he was really giving it his all.

"I'm sorry, Conner." He propped Shipmen against a No Parking sign. "I guess I really let you down."

Bonebreaker managed to wiggle his cell phone out of his blazer pocket, every movement a heroic effort. He flipped it open and shouted at it. "Call Smiley."

The phone ignored him.

"*Call* Smiley. Call *Smiley*. Kill Smelly."

"I'd offer to help," Remo said, "but I'm not good with gadgets."

"Cold Slimy."

The phone finally understood the command. It lit up and rang, then a faraway voice said, "What's up, Con?"

"I'm in Annandale. Hummer and Fairfax. Bring all the boys you got. I'm hurt. Hurry the fuck up."

"We're coming, Con."

Shipmen groaned. "Now you're dead."

The Lincoln purred up Hummer Road minutes later and chirped to a stop at the curb. Four brawny men jumped out.

"I guess this means I'm not getting the Koreatown territory." Remo was despondent.

"Oh my God, Con," gasped a barrel-chested giant with long waves of black hair that glistened in the light from the street lamps. "What happened?"

"Kill him. He's a lunatic. *Kill him dead.*"

Smiley Shipmen pulled a mountain-bike chain from his front pocket and took a swing at Remo. Remo stepped aside and held up a finger. The chain wrapped around it twice, then Remo swung the chain around the head of Smiley Shipmen.

"I know you," Remo said. "You're Conner's brother, Smiley Shipmen. They say you collected more than a million bucks in insurance claims from putting homeless people in the hospital."

Smiley was staggering into the street and holding his head. A long scarlet weal crossed his face. Another man threw a punch at Remo, who stepped aside and gave him a nudge in the backside. The attacker flew into the gutter on the outside of a Korean café. The aluminum gutter was dented. The attacker rebounded.

Two more thugs pounced on Remo. They were just

hired muscle. He swung them into one another with just enough force to stop them but not enough to knock them out.

Remo wanted everybody to be awake and alert for what came next.

He started breaking bones.

3

In the end, they couldn't get Dr. Ordonez out even with a mechanical claw.

It was as if the dead squid couldn't bear to give up its former caretaker.

The claw was a scary-looking contraption. In fact, Vouzu explained, it was often used for retrieving large dead specimens from display tanks. When Suut overheard this, he threw up in the corner.

The claw descended through the limp tangle of squid arms and the control cable opened the toothed scoops. It touched down in the gravel like a crocodile mouth stretched wide around a duckling. Orson was surprised how gently the claw closed around Ordonez.

The claw retracted ten feet, then the energy discharge struck abruptly. It came and then it was gone. The crane's electrically grounded, moisture-insulated power system was disabled and the jaws snapped open. Dr. Ordonez tumbled back to the bottom and the crane hung still in the water.

Orson heard the commotion from the platform. The

brief whoosh of a fire extinguisher and the smell of a burning servomotor. The crane was out of commission.

"I guess," Detective Orson said, sighing, "we drain the tank."

THE ADMINISTRATIVE CORRIDORS of Folcroft Sanitarium in Rye, New York, were dark and deserted in the pre-dawn hours. Any doctors that were on duty were below in the patient housing wings. No one was needed on duty in the upstairs administration offices.

Only Harold W. Smith was at his desk, and he wasn't at work on sanitarium business.

To the public, Harold Smith was the longtime director of the sanitarium. Folcroft was known to be a professional and efficient establishment. It hired skilled staff and kept beautiful grounds, made scenic by its proximity to Long Island Sound. As a private hospital it treated ailments and injuries both mundane and highly unusual. It was operated with great competence and discretion. The accounting was impeccable.

Smith got the credit for running a tight ship, although he was an odd bird who might hole up in his office for weeks at a time. His assistant was a young man named Mark Howard, who came to Folcroft with suspect credentials. But Howard turned out to be friendly and had come to be liked by the Folcroft staff in general. Still, Mr. Howard was turning out to be an eccentric, like his boss.

Mark Howard was also known to have mysterious health problems.

"Drugs," one of the old biddies in long-term residence whispered.

"Pshaw," protested another old biddy.

"My great-grandson's on drugs, and I can tell you our Mr. Howard doesn't act like that at all," declared Lois Larson, the grand dame of long-term residents. She'd lived at Folcroft forever, and she was only incoherent one or two days a week. "People on drugs don't get sick the way he got sick. I think our Mark has a malady. I think he has, you know, attacks."

"What kind of attacks?" demanded Agnes Beagle. Agnes was a busybody and buttinski, who had been at Folcroft just ten years but considered herself just as experienced and knowledgeable as Lois Larson—and she was only eighty-eight.

"How should I know what kind of attacks?" Lois said with a little raspberry sound that indicated it was a silly—maybe even senile—question. Agnes colored. "Besides, he's too nice to be on drugs."

Mrs. Beagle humphed. "Lois, I've met your great-grandson, and he's nice, too."

"He's a jerk."

"I found him quite pleasant."

"If you knew him like I did, you'd say he's a spoiled brat," Lois declared.

The general opinion of Mark Howard fell dramatically when he had yet another of his bouts of mysterious sickness. They even said he was in a coma for a while. What else could it be but drugs?

Then he brought home a girlfriend. A Ms. Sarah Slate. Scandalously young, even for young Mr. Howard—why, she looked like a high-school girl. But Mark was lucky enough to be grievously wounded, which garnered high levels of sympathy. Unlike his mysterious comas, a gashed leg could never have been the result of addiction. Still, there was no good explanation for what had caused the leg injury.

Ms. Slate turned out to be several years older than the gossip claimed and quite likeable, taking an interest in the residents and patients at Folcroft. She won their hearts. After that, Mark Howard and even the strange old Mr. Harold W. Smith gained a higher degree of acceptability.

That didn't mean the gossip mill didn't keep churning. Smith and Howard were just so *strange.*

THE TRUTH WAS wilder than any gossip. In addition to operating Folcroft, Smith and Howard secretly ran CURE. This was what kept them locked up in their offices for hours and days at a time. If the gossips only knew.

CURE was a tiny, powerful, supersecret federal organization. The staff consisted only of Smith and Howard as directors and Remo Williams and his mentor as the enforcement arm.

Smith was chosen as director when CURE was created. He was ex-CIA, with a brilliant intelligence career behind him and on the verge of retiring from intelligence when the role of director of CURE was offered to him by a young, brash man who was President of the United States of America.

This President had seen the writing on the wall for the nation he loved. The country was being eroded from within by the very freedoms it embraced. Those who were corrupt used their constitutionally guaranteed rights and freedoms to bypass the rule of law. Criminals were turning the law against the law enforcers, bogging down the courts in legal maneuvers and generally deflecting the hammer of justice. The crooks weren't getting nailed. Justice was losing ground.

The only way to combat such injustice was to ignore the constitutional protections that made it possible—but repealing the Bill of Rights was a guarantee of national anarchy.

So there had to be a secret group that was charged with bypassing the rights set forth in the Constitution for the good of protecting the Constitution. The President would sanction such a group at grave risk to his political career. If the group was ever revealed, it would be grounds for his immediate impeachment. The group had to be highly secret.

Although created under the sanction of the U.S. President, the organization would not be under his control, or the power would almost certainly, eventually be abused. Presidents were only human.

The man who wielded the authority over this group had to be highly intelligent, unquestionably loyal, devoutly ethical and maybe a little dull witted in the imagination department. This description was a paraphrase of Harold Smith's CIA personality profile.

The President, not long before his assassination before the eyes of the world, chose Smith to head CURE. Smith could not refuse; his loyalty to the country would not allow him to refuse. He chose one trusted CIA friend to be his right-hand man, and together they launched the intelligence-gathering agency called CURE. They hired agents around the world, agents who thought they were working for the FBI, the CIA, newspapers, foreign embassies. The data began to come into CURE headquarters at Folcroft Sanitarium in Rye. Even within the walls of Folcroft were data-crunching intelligence experts who helped collate the data without knowing that an agency called CURE even existed.

CURE provided information to federal and local law enforcement. The information was illegally obtained, but it helped nail criminals in unprecedented numbers—and still it wasn't enough.

Smith reluctantly took the next step; he hired an enforcement arm for CURE. It was to be just one man, but that man would have to be a ruthless assassin, incredibly skilled, to carry out the blatantly illegal actions dictated by CURE. The world couldn't know this man even existed.

To achieve this end, Harold Smith commissioned the frame-up and electrocution of a young New Jersey beat cop named Remo Williams. The plan worked.

Remo the cop was convicted and electrocuted. There was a gravestone placed where his body was said to be buried. The world forgot Remo Williams.

But Remo wasn't actually killed in the chair. He woke up in Folcroft, endured his training and started work as CURE's assassin.

Remo did his job well. His mentor, the old Korean martial-arts master named Chiun, was an unplanned addition to the team, but also a useful one. Soon after Remo joined, Smith's old CIA friend was killed in action.

Most of the old network of intelligence agents was decommissioned as Smith's electronic gathering systems became more sophisticated. For years, CURE was just Smith, Remo and Chiun. Again it was an American president who shook things up by assigning Smith an unasked-for assistant.

Mark Howard turned out to be a useful asset. He exhibited intelligence-gathering skills that might someday rival Smith's, and he had the technical savvy of a man who had grown up in the dawning decades of the digital age.

Mark Howard had something more to offer, too, a sensitivity that couldn't be classified as precognition or mind reading or psychic power. It came and went, provided accurate insight into some of CURE's most puzzling problems—and made Mark Howard the target of psychic attack.

He also had a most inconvenient, know-it-all girlfriend.

Sarah Slate came to Folcroft to nurse Mark Howard after he sustained a leg injury while protecting her. Within a matter of days she had ascertained most of what was going on—what sort of an organization Mark Howard worked for and Remo's role. She even knew something of the existence of the Sinanju Masters.

Harold W. Smith had a common solution for outsiders who learned too much about CURE—but not this time. Sarah had earned the affection of Chiun himself when she helped him save the life of Remo Williams. Smith was never totally clear how this all came about, but he understood, in very practical terms, that putting Ms. Slate in the old Folcroft incinerators would do more harm than good in terms of protecting CURE security. Chiun would be angry, and an angry Chiun was quite a dangerous thing. He would wreak havoc. CURE would likely be obliterated, along with Smith.

Two options remained: Sarah could join CURE or CURE could fold. Luckily for the world, Sarah chose to join CURE as Mark Howard's executive assistant.

Harold Smith had an assistant himself. Old Mrs. Mikulka was a true godsend. It was she who deserved the credit for Folcroft's day-to-day functions for all these years. She churned out reports that Smith only had to sign—and the reports were always correct. She handled each crisis exactly as she knew Smith would handle it. What else was she to do, when the Folcroft director kept his door closed for days at a time?

Somehow, the good lady had managed all these years to mind her own business. Whatever she suspected Smith was up to—surely she suspected something—she ignored it. Looked past it. Pretended it wasn't there. And she kept Folcroft running like clockwork.

There might come a time when Mrs. Mikulka decided to retire for good. She was already cutting her hours down to six, then five a day. Who would handle her duties after she left? It was logical that there be a secretary for the assistant director just as there was a secretary for the director. Sarah Slate filled the role well—and it was much easier, Smith was forced to admit, to operate without the need to constantly guard his activities from the person in the next office.

At first, Smith had been reluctant to admit that Sarah Slate would even stay around long enough to truly become a member of the Folcroft-CURE team. She was too young, too peppy. Initially he mistook her exuberance for a lack of maturity. He was beginning to change his opinion. Sarah had intelligence, consideration and people skills that Mark—and even he himself—never had. She was more friendly with the Folcroft medical staff, patients and long-term residents than Smith had ever been. Sarah Slate, he decided, if she continued as Mark's assistant, might turn out to be an ideal manager of Folcroft's operations.

But this was all just speculation. Mrs. Mikulka had no wish to become a full-time, do-nothing retiree. Smith certainly wasn't going anywhere. He worked fewer hours overall, but in times of crisis he was behind his desk, day and night, come what may.

RIGHT NOW IT WAS very early in the morning, and Smith peered into the many windows on the LCD display mounted under the glass of his desk. Hidden speakers channeled radio communications on the Chicago, Illinois, emergency radio bands.

A few minutes ago he had wondered if it was a foolish waste of his time to monitor the activity at the aquarium in Chicago. Soon he knew he was listening to a catastrophe in the making. Although the facts were far from clear, *something* was happening in Chicago. The police were being careful not to reveal too much on the public radio waves, and the briefs being transmitted over the emergency-response text-messaging systems were confusing and contradictory. Nobody seemed to know what was really going on.

Smith detested uncertainty.

The hard facts were these: the colossal squid in Chicago, in which Smith was quite interested, had sickened and was probably dead. The marine biologist who had caught and cared for the squid was dead, too— both discovered in the squid tank a few hours ago. A police diver had attempted recovery of the biologist's body and was killed in the attempt.

Everything else was conjecture or based on noncredible information. How had the recovery diver died? How had the marine biologist died, for that matter?

More than once, the police slipped during their radio exchanges and used the word *attack*.

This suggested an attack by the squid. A squid could look dead and not be. It took hours or days for a dead squid to stop changing color—was there a presumption the sick cephalopod was deceased when it was not? If it was motionless in the water, perhaps it was assumed to be dead, only to strike at those who came into its domain.

But the marine biologist wouldn't have been fooled by a motionless animal, and she had to have sophisticated instruments to monitor its metabolism. So what killed her?

Even in the communications out of Chicago, there were few indications that anyone blamed the squid for the deaths. Directly.

There shouldn't have been other animals in the tank with the squid. If there were, why would the scientist or the diver venture in? If there weren't, what had "attacked" the recovery diver?

Smith got the impression that the police in Chicago were as baffled as he was.

Normally, Harold Smith took no interest in matters of marine biology, zoological assaults or squid fatalities. This case was unique.

He learned the police were now draining the massive tank to allow recovery of the scientist and scattered body parts.

Smith weighed his options. He was not being indecisive, as indecision was alien to his nature. He was thinking ahead a hundred moves, like a skilled chess player. But the chessboard offered limited variables. For Smith the game board was vast and the players had unknown capabilities. There were also more possible outcomes than simple checkmate or a draw.

Those were possibilities he could not fathom. As great as his intellect was, Smith had no real imagination to speak of.

This was where he hesitated. Even with what he suspected about the squid in Chicago, he didn't have the creative capacity to conjure up the scope of its potential danger. Maybe it posed no danger whatsoever. The squid in Chicago might be nothing more than another deceased sea creature. Smith's common sense insisted that a big dead squid was not a threat to the world or to the United States of America.

But Smith knew some squid-related facts that defied logic and didn't fit into any comfortable sense of order.

He couldn't ignore these unsettling facts. He couldn't dismiss how they might bear on a dead squid in Chicago.

Smith was startled when he realized someone was standing in front of his desk.

"Morning, Smitty, " Remo said, hands behind his back, bent far over the desk to see what was on the desk display.

"Remo," Smith asked sourly, "how did you get through the door without setting off the alarm?"

"I didn't know you had an alarm."

"That is no explanation."

Remo straightened. "Why ask me? It's your alarm."

Smith said nothing more about it, but made a mental note to have the alarm system checked. Even Remo should not be able to get into his office without sounding the alerts tied into the desk monitor. They were designed to blacken the screen if the office door was opened unexpectedly.

"You want to know about my trip to D.C.?" Remo asked.

"Not especially."

"The Shipmen Insurance Associates are out of business."

"I assumed you would handle it. Something else has come up."

Remo appeared behind the desk at Smith's side and jabbed a finger at the display. "This?"

"The colossal squid at the Chicago Aquarium has sickened and died," Smith said. "Last evening."

"That's a good thing."

"No. Something went wrong," Smith said.

Remo returned to the front of the desk and sat in a guest chair, which was of cracked leather older than him.

"The squid is still alive?"

"No. As I said, the squid died."

"But then you said something went wrong. About the only thing that can go wrong with something dying is that it doesn't die."

Smith had a hard time telling when Remo was toying with him. He explained the sequence of events as he understood them.

"A Chicago Park District Police diver was deployed into the tank to recover the body," Smith said. "Something killed him."

"Something?" Remo said. "Something, but not the squid?"

"Correct. The latest reports allude to some sort of electrical activity in the tank. There has been mention of significant tissue damage to the diver. There have also been mentions of some sort of an attack, which would seem to contradict electrocution. The danger of electrocution made recovery of his body problematic. This is all I pieced together from emergency radio traffic in Chicago. I do know the situation was chaotic, and that the diver was still alive when pulled from the water finally. Paramedics on the scene reported significant damage to the body, but reported no bleeding. There was some speculation that the electrical activity cauterized the wounds."

"Yeah, right. So where'd the electricity come from? Somebody accidentally drop their dryer in the tank?"

"No." Smith pursed his mouth. "There has been no cause assigned to the electrical activity. I've investigated reported electrical discharges coming from dead cephalopods. There is no evidence of this occurring on any significant level."

Remo considered that. "You mean, strong enough to kill people."

"Or even to be noticeable without sensors," Smith clarified.

Remo nodded, but he wasn't happy with what he was learning.

"This is strange."

"Yes," Smith said.

"I've met squid just like that one. They were aggressive, but they didn't try to shock us."

Smith nodded. He had heard their reports of Remo's and Chiun's interaction with giant squid in the Pacific Ocean. "Remo, this may have a bearing on Mark's recent reaction."

"How is Mark?" Remo asked. It wasn't a casual question. Remo sounded dead serious.

Several days before, Mark Howard experienced a reaction to a news item that reported that the Chicago squid had fallen ill.

Howard had been known to be sensitive in the past to certain threats, including specific threats from a source linked to the world's cephalopods.

"He has been under the weather but will be back at work in a few hours. Our doctors diagnosed a viral infection."

"But it wasn't," Remo said. "It's Sa Mangsang."

"We don't know."

Remo got to his feet. "You can pretend not to know if you want to. I do know. It's him. It. Sa Mangsang. Ah, shit." Remo strode to one end of the room and back to the middle. "What's he up to? I thought he was out of commission. I thought he was in recuperation mode. I thought I was leaving the Sa Mangsang problem for some Master of Sinanju in the twenty-third century."

"We don't know it is him."

"It's him. Deal with it." Remo stopped and stared out the wide picture windows. "But I don't understand what he's trying to pull. Where's Chiun?"

Smith said, "Traveling. He's on a road trip in his camper trailer. He departed Rye not long after you left for Washington."

Remo screwed up his face. "He could have let me know he was going. I need him, Smitty. I don't have a clue what's happening here and Chiun might."

Smith nodded. "He is in Detroit at present. I contacted his driver and left a message on his machine. Master Chiun has not yet responded." Smith was clearly displeased by this. "It would be best if you went to Detroit first, to ascertain his status."

"It's more important to figure this out," Remo declared. "Leave another message and let him know what's going on. Once he knows this is somehow linked to Sa Mangsang, he'll call you back in a big hurry."

"And if he doesn't?"

Smith was talking to himself. The office was empty. Remo had departed without a sound, and again the alarm had not activated.

4

The examination room was crowded. The chief medical examiner for Cook County was on hand to observe. Representatives from the Park District Police, the Chicago Aquarium and the mayor's office were present. There were students from the ME's internship program, and students from the police academy.

The examining room was plenty large enough to accommodate the guests. It was the biggest ME facility in the state. All the popular and high-profile autopsies happened here.

Dr. Seth Sanders would do the hands-on, slice-and-measure work under the supervision of Chief Medical Examiner Marvin Kara. Kara hadn't cut a cadaver in years, but he was always close by to offer consultation and leadership to his staff.

Sanders had four gurneys to work with. Two held body bags. Two had plastic tubs of parts.

"An estimated seventy percent of the victims was recovered," Sanders told the digital voice recorder.

"Approximately seventy percent recovery rate," Kara announced.

"How'd you know?" asked a man from the mayor's office. The mayor and his office were not pleased with any of the day's events. The mayor's representative looked Kara right in the eye.

"You're asking how we know the recovery rate is seventy percent," Kara said.

"That's what I'm asking."

"It's an estimate based on the body weight of the recovered pieces and the known body weight of the victims," said the hands-on man, Sanders. "With some adjustment made to accommodate water weight."

"Seventy percent the best you could do?" the mayor's man asked.

"We didn't do it at all," Sanders said. "We're simply working with what was delivered to us."

The mayor's man was deeply unsatisfied with that. He needed a guilty party.

"This is my turf," Kara informed him in a low voice. "Maybe you should back down."

"The mayor's office has a high level of interest in the outcome of this examination."

"But don't throw your weight around in my office," Kara said. He nodded to Sanders.

"More pieces may be found, as I understand it," Sanders added.

The tank was drained to four feet, using an emergency water-evacuation system. The drainage went into

one of the aquarium's underground quarantined holding tanks. The smallest body parts were caught in the
fabric drain filters. Other parts were scooped from the
tank using nets on wooden dowels. Dr. Ordonez was removed using a plastic rope one of the cops managed to
lasso around her torso.

All the recovery tools were electrically nonconduc-
tive—and still the static charges jumped and jittered up
the dowels and the nylon lines and managed to zap
members of the recovery team. Two people were in the
hospital, brain-dead, and now the Squidarium was off-
limits while engineers tried to isolate the source of the
electrical emissions.

Technicians busily set to work opening and removing the contents of the body bags, which included the
largest sections of the bodies. Assistant ME Sanders set
to work on the diver, while a medical examiner with less
tenure took Ordonez.

The mayor's man turned away, getting nauseous.

Aquarium Director Vouzu frowned at what he saw.
"I did my share of postmortems in med school and during my residency. It's been years and I know I'm rusty,
but I never heard of anything like that."

"This is unlike any electric burn scarring I've seen,"
Sanders agreed in a library voice. "What sort of machinery were you people operating in that tank?"

"Nothing that would have leaked current. And I
mean nothing. We chose top-of-the-line filters, circulation, aeration, but nothing that wasn't a proved de-

sign. You wouldn't believe the redundancies we put in the circuit-breaking systems between the power mains and the exhibits."

"And this isn't electrical scarring after all," the assistant ME added.

"Whaddaya mean it isn't electrical?" demanded the mayor's man, who was swallowing frequently. "Everybody said they saw electric shocks in the tank. I told the mayor it was electrical."

"We said it looked like static discharge, but it behaved like no electrical emissions we were familiar with," the director maintained, sounding weary.

"You also told me it was comin' from the big squid, right, smart boy? Like an electric eel or something?"

"It appeared to come from the carcass, as well as from the floor of the tank, but there's no way to know the source as of now. Appearances are deceiving when you're talking about static charges. Like lightning that looks like it comes from the clouds to the ground, but it really starts from the ground and travels up."

"Lightning comes down, you moron," said the mayor's representative.

"As any high-school graduate can tell you, lightning can travel from the ground source up," ME Sanders said. "And I'll say again, these are not electrical-burn scars. I wouldn't even call these scars if I didn't know the circumstances of the subjects' death."

"Then what?" the mayor's man asked, feeling stupid.

"Look." The medical examiner gestured across the

four tables to the limbless torso of the marine biologist. "Dr. Brill, show him the left-shoulder detachment point, please. See any damaged dermis there? See any evidence of burning? Now look at this." The ME grabbed a lump of flesh from a leftovers bin and thrust it to the stump. "Look at the contours. This is part of her upper arm. See how it fits? You ever hear of anything that causes massive tissue removal and then closes the wounds so perfectly that it looks *healed?*"

The fragment of upper arm was pitted and gauged, like worm-eaten wood, but there was no blood. The skin had closed and knitted together.

The mayor's man tried to speak, but gagged instead.

The aquarium director put the back of his hand to his mouth. "Oh, God. Look at her chest."

The assistant medical examiner pulled the sheet back up to cover Dr. Ordonez's upper chest.

"I mean, she had her breasts."

"Horace, get ahold of yourself," ME Kara growled quietly.

"No, I'm right about this. Her breasts were exposed when we found her. There are ten senior staffers who'll bear me out on this. I wanted the diver to cover her up, give her back her modesty. They must have been destroyed in the attacks on Bedders."

Chief ME Kara nodded. "So?"

Sanders threw off the sheet again. "I see what you're saying. These wounds are closed like all the others, even though they occurred hours after her death. Whatever caused the wounds to close could not have been using the body's own restorative systems to cover the wounds."

The ME was startled by the idea. "You were thinking the energy discharge was causing the wounds to *heal?*"

"Of course," Sanders said. "I thought maybe the body's healing mechanism was being hyperstimulated. It's outlandish, but what else makes sense?"

The ME said nothing, then forced words from his mouth. "It's an outlandish notion, Dr. Sanders. As you've said, it can't be. Unless your Dr. Ordonez was still alive in the tank when Bedders went in after her."

Dr. Ordonez's eyes flew open.

"God in heaven!" the mayor's liaison whispered.

"Normal response," Sanders said offhandedly. "Just dead nerves reacting to the breakdown of the body." He used the tips of his rubber-gloved fingers to push her eyelids closed again. "What appears to be new growth might actually be some sort of breakdown of the skin into a semiliquid state, causing the flesh to flow over and adhere to the surface of the fresh wound."

The mayor's man made a sound like a goose with a feeding funnel in its gullet.

"It's too complete," one of the interns protested.

"I agree," Sanders said. "It's unbelievable. But it's the best explanation I can come up with at this time. It's surely more reasonable than the near-instant growth of fresh dermis. The skin is a bodily organ—it can't grow

if the body is dead. There's no way at all that Dr. Ordonez was still living when the attack occurred on the
diver."

"Guh," said the mayor's man as Ordonez's eyelids
opened.

"She was submerged two to five hours," Sanders
continued, pulling the lids closed.

"Her eyes moved!" the mayor's man gasped.

"Just the nerves causing them to open," Sanders said
gently.

"Her eyeballs, too."

"Have some respect, would you? She was a friend
of mine," Director Vouzu snapped at the city-hall suit.
"She would have drowned even without the bodily injury long before Bedders got to her."

"Oh, God!" the mayor's man almost sobbed. Ordonez was looking at him again.

"She really wants these eyes open," Dr. Brill said,
chuckling.

"Wasn't the water cold enough to support thermal stasis?" an intern piped up. "I thought the giant squid was
found in Antarctic waters, which meant the tank would
be maintained at less than zero degrees centigrade."

"No," Vouzu said impatiently. "Dr. Ordonez found
the animal in Pacific waters at 25.5 degrees centigrade
and that's exactly where we kept its environment."

Sanders was ready to get beyond the topic and get
on with his job. "Then I promise you, there was no
thermal stasis and Dr. Ordonez was very, very dead."

"Uh!" said the mayor's man, one finger crooked at the corpse. All eyes turned to Dr. Ordonez just as she took a deep and ragged breath.

Her eyeballs rolled toward them and the air flowed out of her mouth in a deep, spook-house moan. It sounded like words. It sounded like, "I'm alive."

The assistant ME took hold of her neck as the eyes closed and the body grew still. "There's no pulse," he announced. "Did you *see* that?"

"Did she speak?" the director cried. "I heard her speak."

The ME took a stethoscope from one of the technicians and pressed it against Dr. Ordonez's chest. "There's no pulse."

"She spoke," the director insisted. "She's alive."

"There's no pulse. You said yourself she was under the water at least two hours." The ME glared at the torso. "She's dead."

Mary Ordonez had something to say about that. She stiffened, rolled her eyes to the ME and took another gulp of air into her bubbling lungs. "I am alive."

"She's alive!" the director said. "Get a resuscitation kit!"

The mayor's man didn't know if he should scream or vomit as the medical team worked on the hideous thing on the examining table and the enthusiastic interns jockeyed to watch.

When he glanced at the other table, he decided vomiting and screaming were both in order.

THE SLURPING SOUND CAME from Oscar Bedders as he tried to make his lungs work, and when he inhaled he drew the dangling remnants of his tongue and face into his windpipe. He managed to suck in enough air to make words and he said, "Hurts."

He was trying to sit up. There were more cries of disbelief. An intern put an oxygen mask over his face and turned the spigot on the steel bottle. Bedders felt cool air enter his tortured, water-logged lungs. He grabbed the mask, holding it in place on his mouth, trapping the intern's hand.

Bedders knew what to do. Instinctively, he extracted what he needed from the intern.

"Not again," moaned Vouzu as the nightmare restarted. The corpse of Oscar Bedders was embracing the young medical intern, and the space between them was filled with sizzling energy of a sickly yellow color.

The intern was breaking up. His parts were flowing into Oscar Bedders, adhering to his body, filling in the distorted craters in Bedders's own body, becoming a part of him.

Bedders was healing himself, and it was killing his victim. Other interns grabbed their fellow and tried to pull him off. The victim screeched, then came apart.

The other young people fell away, spattered with gore. Most of the intern landed in pieces on the shiny floor. Bedders sat up, invigorated.

He grabbed another intern. The young Irish woman

had red hair and very pale skin, and she melted in front of them in the burning static energy. Bedders's wounds filled in, and his new skin was dappled with pale patches and freckles. The woman's tongue tore out of her throat and Bedders inhaled it, spitting out the old, torn-up tongue, allowing the new one to attach itself effortlessly where a tongue was supposed to go.

The young woman's body could no longer stand the catastrophic loss of tissue and energy. She collapsed violently in his hands, her body caving in upon itself.

She was used up. Bedders cast her aside.

A couple of medical interns didn't get Bedders very far. He felt improved, but not a hundred percent.

People were walking on top of one another to get out the door, but the mayor's man was in shock, unable to move. Bedders loped across the room on thudding feet and sent fleeing interns crashing to the floor. Then he snatched up the chief medical examiner of the County of Cook, State of Illinois, and sucked the life out of him as if he were sucking the pulp from an orange slice. Bedders's body was complete when he took the chief ME's jaw for himself.

"That feels better," he commented, moving the new jaw back and forth.

The mayor's liaison stared dumbly.

"Not that I couldn't use some more go juice," Bedders announced. "You know, some get-up-and-go."

He grabbed the mayor's man by the neck and didn't even dignify him with a look as he emptied his life. Bedders stared into the eyes of the aquarium director as the body in his hands fell apart. Vouzu couldn't tear himself from the spectacle.

"Refreshing," Bedders declared.

Vouzu swallowed.

"Where's my colleague, Detective Orson?"

"Not here," Vouzu stammered.

"Too bad. But here is my lady friend, the good Dr. Ordonez. I should be mad at her. She got me into this mess. Truth is, I feel great!"

"Get away from her." Vouzu couldn't bring himself to act.

"She's mine." Bedders bent low over the helpless woman on the autopsy table. Her eyes rolled helplessly onto Bedders, then to Vouzu.

"Oh, God, leave her alone!"

"She's here for me," Bedders said. "She's my super-duper battery pack."

"Don't touch her." Vouzu's repulsion finally motivated him to grab Bedders's arm, only to find himself flung across the room, slipping on blood and cracking his back against a countertop before collapsing.

"I need what's stored in her," Bedders explained coldly. "Keeping her alive keeps the go juice potent, see? So, if it weren't for me, she'd never get this second taste of life." He came so close his nose almost touched hers, and he showed his teeth. "You're welcome."

The marine scientist groaned in anguish, physical

and emotional, and Bedders clamped his hand over her face. The flicker of energy glowed from under his hand. Ordonez writhed.

"Stop this." Vouzu lunged at Bedders but felt a single blow crack across his face, and then he was hanging limp from Bedders's grip.

"Think of her as lobster. Ever boil a lobster?"

"She's a human being," Vouzu croaked.

"Not anymore." Bedders was done with Ordonez for good. He rolled his shoulders and blinked rapidly. "Don't know what was in that sweet lady, but it was extrafine. You ain't gonna be nearly as tasty."

Vouzu trembled.

"But I hate to pass up a free lunch."

Vouzu felt the fingers clamp around his face.

5

Mark Howard insisted on being at his desk, which was still crowded in the same office as Harold Smith's. The office was tight with the two of them in there, even more so when Sarah Slate was on hand to perform her duties. Still, it was the most efficient way for them to work. At the height of a crisis, Smith and Howard were like skilled basketball players covering the court and passing the ball without ever dropping it.

But very early that morning, they could only watch the sketchy intelligence emerge from Chicago and wait for their enforcement arm to arrive on the scene.

SOMETHING MAJOR WAS going on at the Chicago Aquarium—even bigger than the death of the Chicago Giant, and that was big enough.

The people were gathering, slavering reporters and interested onlookers. At eight-thirty in the morning, the school buses showed up.

"Closed," announced the police officer in front of the

bus drop-off loop, now blocked by a pair of Chicago patrol cars with blinking lights.

"Huh?" The bus driver didn't understand. "We're on the list. Gary, Indiana, Metropolitan School District field trip."

"The aquarium is closed."

"What's that supposed to mean?"

The cop sighed and boarded the school bus, standing over the bus driver as the line of buses behind him began honking and edging up belligerently. "What part of 'closed' do you not understand?"

"How can the whole building be closed?"

"That's a police matter."

"So where are we supposed to put these kids?"

"Take them back to school."

The driver curled his mouth. "That'll take an hour and a half, and there's nobody at the schools to hand them off to because it's field-trip day, and our break starts in twenty-one minutes. We're union."

"Look, buddy, do whatever you're supposed to do. The kids are not my responsibility."

"Then whose responsibility are they?" the bus driver demanded. "I'm union."

"Where's the chaperones?"

"We're taking them to the aquarium. They don't need chaperones at a museum-type place. It's the museum's job to take care of them. I just drop them off and pick them up."

"Then go to another museum or something."

The bus driver was exasperated. "Where?"

"Planetarium. It's a half mile down Lake Shore Drive. You can't miss it."

The bus driver looked at his watch, glanced out at the bumper-to-bumper traffic on Lake Shore Drive. He snatched the radio and relayed the message to the other drivers in line behind him.

"We'll never get through the traffic in eighteen minutes," another driver responded.

"Doesn't matter. I told him we're union. He gave us police orders, so whatever happens now is Chicago's fault."

Fifteen yellow-and-black buses roared around the end of the drive and pulled out onto Lake Shore Drive, then crawled through heavy traffic. The driver of the lead bus got on the intercom. "Okay, the cops say you all go to that planetarium instead of the aquarium. Shut up! We pick you up at the planetarium at three-thirty. Shut up!" His watch buzzed. "Time for you all to get out. *Now.*"

Fifteen school buses stopped dead in the middle of Lake Shore Drive. Hundreds of first- through twelfth-graders poured onto Chicago's famous LSD. The buses were beginning to roll before the last of them debarked. The students scattered in every direction. A few even headed for the planetarium—to do cannonballs off the rear walkway into Lake Michigan.

The city was a circus, but the cops stationed at all entrances to the aquarium kept at their posts. Nobody was getting in who wasn't authorized law enforcement or a city bigwig.

Or a Master of Sinanju. Remo Williams didn't need to pay the cops much attention as he slipped through one of the guarded doors, then stepped up and over the turnstile. The turnstile didn't register him as a visitor. He didn't pay admission price. Even the video monitoring systems in the halls caught little more than streaks of his image as he slipped through the corridors. It was as if Remo Williams were not really there. Like a ghost. A dead man.

And he was a dead man. Officially, Remo Williams died years ago. The old records, if anyone bothered to look them up, included his official progress reports and ward-of-the-state identification papers. A social security number. A military record and the legal affidavits necessary for a citizen's admission into police training. His short career as a police officer—and a thick sheaf of efficient legal documents detailing his arrest, incarceration, trial and capital punishment for the murder of the drug dealer.

The sham trial ended in a guilty verdict. Remo Williams received the ultimate punishment for the crime. He was executed. He died. He was buried. A headstone was erected on the grave of Remo Williams.

Every once in a while, he visited the grave. Sometimes it was unsettling. Sometimes it was amusing.

There was much that was grimly amusing about being officially dead, and especially about being officially dead in Remo's particular circumstances. The murder he was convicted of had not been committed by him. The purpose of the murder, however, was to enable him to commit many other murders. It made sense in a way.

CURE needed an enforcement arm—specifically an assassin—and Remo Williams's military successes made him an ideal candidate. Killing him off made him less traceable.

The electric chair was rigged to give Remo a nonfatal shock, and he woke up in Folcroft Sanitarium just in time to receive an offer to work for CURE. The pay was decent. Room and board included. His employer would cover all the training expenses. How could he refuse?

In fact, he could not refuse. CURE made it clear that Remo's only alternative was to be executed again, for real.

Remo accepted the job and was trained—oh, man, was he trained—and he began working for CURE. He still worked for CURE, but he no longer worried about how CURE would treat him if he wanted out. The training had made Remo more effective than anyone ever expected. Not Remo, not Harold Smith, not even Master Chiun, Remo's trainer, had expected Remo to take to his training as well as he did. Now Remo was a Master of the ancient martial art known as Sinanju. Moving undetected was just one of his many skills.

Five Chicago cops at the main entrance to the special-exhibits wing never saw him glide down the hall or pass within a few feet of where they stood beside the double doors. They never heard the slicing of the police tape on the double doors. They didn't hear the door edge open and close again.

Remo found himself inside the Squidarium, just him and the dead squid. The place was hushed and still, and Remo twisted his thick wrists nervously, searching the exhibit hall for signs of danger.

He wasn't sure what he had been expecting. This wasn't it.

Everything about the display hall was oversized, from the basketball-court-sized viewing floor to the heavy tank wall, a foot thick. The dead thing in the tank, lifeless in a few feet of murky water, was simply bigger than it ought to be, although it was in proportion to its surroundings.

The proportions felt wrong, Remo decided. Everything was too big. This could be the set for a movie about a geeky junior-high-school kid who collects weird sea creatures in his desktop fishbowl, only to be shrunken unexpectedly by Rick Moranis.

Remo willed himself to get closer to the glass, squinting through the scummy glass. The squid was a grotesque thing, a monstrosity. But it was dead. Even with a foot of tempered glass separating them, Remo could see the utter stillness of the carcass. He could smell the decay from its exposed flesh. He could sense the absence of metabolic activity. This was as it should be.

But it answered no questions. What had happened here?

Closer. There were few things on this planet that truly inspired fear in the breast of the Master of Sinanju, but this was one of the things.

This creature was a servant or slave of Sa Mangsang. That shouldn't mean anything now. Sa Mangsang was back on the ocean floor, his long-accumulated strength depleted again. Remo was the one who had put him back there.

Remo still didn't fully understand what Sa Mangsang was, but he knew that the Masters of Sinanju owed the thing some sort of fealty or allegiance. As the Reigning Master of Sinanju, Remo should have been the first to aid Sa Mangsang when it rose from the ocean depths in answer to an accidental summons.

Remo broke the pact. In fact, he turned traitor. He stabbed Sa Mangsang in the back, but Sa Mangsang was too weak to seek vengeance. It would be decades or centuries before the Dream Thing would again have vigor enough to exert its influence on the world above the waves.

So Remo Williams thought.

This colossal squid was acting on Sa Mangsang's orders when it was captured. That was prior to Sa Mangsang's defeat. What were those orders? What capabilities did this thing have? What was the meaning of the mayhem that had occurred in this room just hours ago?

He wasn't finding any answers, and with determination he reached for the glass, putting his fingers against it. It vibrated beneath his touch, contracting and expanding infinitesimally in the shifting of temperatures. The rumble of trucks a mile away could be felt in the glass, but Remo felt no answers to his questions. The glass was not agitating from the tank contents—another affirmation of the nonliving status of the squid.

But Remo's nostrils already *told* him that. The thing had been decaying for many hours. It was dead when the police diver went in; it had to be. So what killed the diver?

There were reports of electric shocks in the water and the movement of the squid. Had some current been accidentally applied to the water, stiffening the squid carcass and electrocuting the diver? What other explanation was there?

"I'm trying to find trouble where there isn't any," Remo told the dead squid.

The squid didn't argue the point, but the distant gunshots suggested that Remo was mistaken.

THE WIDE HALL HAD glass windows in the walls, displaying small marine specimens in five-hundred-gallon tanks, and there were benches and waist-high displays. Nothing big enough to obscure the view of the gun battle going on at the far end of the hall.

The five cops stationed at the special-exhibits entrance tried to make sense of the flying bodies of cops and the confused back-and-forth on the radio. Then there was a man coming down the hall toward them.

They could see dead cops. They saw one of them in a big pool of blood. The man who walked toward them was smiling.

"Hi."

"Jesus, Mary and Joseph. It's Bedders."

The shouting on the radio confirmed it. Oscar Bedders. Alive after all and on a rampage. Cops dead. No, he didn't have a gun.

"Stop right there, Oscar." All five Chicago cops trained their police revolvers on their colleague, Officer Oscar Bedders, who kept right on walking.

"I'll shoot," one of the cops warned.

"So shoot," Bedders said, grabbing a molded-concrete bench off the floor. He lifted it overhead and heaved it just as the cops started to shoot. Bedders staggered when the rounds smacked into his body. The concrete bench cracked on the floor and crushed two of the cops into the door.

The other three ran out of bullets, but Bedders was still coming. He seemed to sweep them into an embrace, then used them to batter the doors to the special-exhibits hall. The doors swung open, and Bedders tossed the cops aside.

On the far end of the hall was the Squidarium, where Remo could feel the *wrongness* even before he saw the perpetrator. The wrongness was transmitted to him by the patterns of air pressure waves coming from flying bodies. Bodies should not be thrown like that. Remo sensed the agile lifting and tossing of the immense slab of concrete, and felt the movement of the floor when it landed. His senses told him a man had made it happen, not a piece of machinery.

Remo knew one of his worst, vaguest fears was being realized before his eyes. Something extraordinarily wrong was coming to meet him, and somehow it had come from Sa Mangsang.

What strolled into the Squidarium looked like a man—or what was once a man. Now it was something like a figurine that was bashed to pieces and reassembled with mismatched hunks of clay. There were craters and chunks missing from his face and exposed arms and legs, but the wounds were sealed with fresh, discolored skin. His clothing was rags, but the embroidered tag on the remains of his dry suit looked official. Remo read it aloud from across the room.

"Bedders. You're the police diver."

"Who are you?" Bedders stalked to the steep stairs on the side of the tank, apparently uninterested in giving Remo the same treatment he'd given the cops. Remo hadn't tried to get in his way, yet.

"What are you doing here?" Remo asked.

Bedders ignored him and started up the ladder with a sprightly step, and Remo Williams had a premonition of disaster. He didn't know what was going on, and he didn't know what Bedders was trying to do, but he knew he could not let Bedders into the tank.

Remo skimmed up the ladder like a specter, and Bedders never heard him coming, never even knew he was being attacked until Remo snatched the police diver's foot and twisted it in a complete circle. The leg bones shattered at the knee joint. As Bedders's body swiveled, Remo thrust the heel of his palm into Bedders's abdomen, deep and hard into the soft tissues and under the rib cage. The diver arced off the ladder and landed hard.

The lower leg was still in Remo's hand. He dropped it and stepped down. The crooked twist of one of Bedders's arms meant the shoulder joint was ruined, and the flat chest told Remo that Bedders's ribs were broken. Still, Remo wasn't surprised when he saw movement within the body. Bedders was alive.

"I heard you were dead," Remo said. "I guess you get that a lot."

Bedders flopped onto his front and dragged his torso along the floor to pull the dangling arm into a more natural position, then he grimaced as the joint retracted into the socket. Bedders used the arm to roll himself onto his back.

The look he gave Remo was beyond hatred, but his eyes glazed as he expanded his crushed chest, yelped from the pain and held his breath deeply. When he exhaled, the chest remained expanded. The bones were knitting.

"Okay. *What* are you?" Remo asked.

Bedders breathed laboriously as he twisted and

stretched his body, working out the kinks. Remo heard a small and indefinite sound behind him, and even before he turned to look at it he knew what it was. Bedders's severed foot was wriggling on the floor, twisting, flopping, returning to Bedders.

Remo snatched it by the ankle, and it wiggled like a landed catfish.

"You tell me all about yourself and maybe I'll give you your leg back."

"Give me my leg back," Bedders said in a guttural monotone.

"We both have something the other wants, right?"

"Leg back." Bedders somehow careened onto all threes and scampered like a crippled spider, but his speed was tremendous, crossing the distance between them and swiping at Remo's own leg like a cat. Remo stepped high, sailing over Bedders and landing directly behind him.

"You ain't listening, Freakshow," Remo said.

But Bedders struck again, pivoting and lashing out. Remo should have been expecting it, but the reflexes required for the quick change far surpassed what most humans could manage.

Remo made a graceless dodge that would have earned him ridicule from certain picky instructors. He would have earned demerits, as well, for being unprepared for the attack. But how could any human being move like that?

He slipped to the far wall, putting plenty of distance

between him and it. Bedders laughed at him, a gargle in his throat.

"Come, leg."

The leg blew apart in Remo's hands, spattering bone and tissue on the floor below, and the parts seeped across the floor to Bedders, who absorbed the pieces.

"Enough of this festival of gore," Remo declared, and launched a pulverizing Sinanju kick at Bedders's chest. The diver rotated violently to dissipate the force, but it was too little, too late. The bones shattered to splinters and he flopped end over end, coming to a rest with his legs folded under his back.

It would have killed anybody or anything, but it didn't kill Bedders. Or maybe it did kill him and he just snapped out of it. His legs sprawled onto the floor. His muscles quivered to realign his body parts. The body parts knitted themselves back together. The drippings, sliming bits of broken leg, were sucked into the body and solidified more or less in the correct configuration. For the first time, Remo could make out the microscopic filaments of yellow energy dancing among the re-forming tissues, like self-guided sutures of static electricity.

They worked faster than before and Bedders got to his feet, his body continuing its process of healing and smoothing itself out, although it never seemed to get it quite right. Bedders was a walking ruin.

"That hurt," he announced to Remo Williams.

"Looked like it. Tell me what's going on, and I won't have to do it to you again."

"Rather show you than tell you."

Bedders charged, but by now Remo was prepared for his swiftness and removed himself shadowlike to somewhere a few paces away. Bedders snarled and charged again. Bedders made a bubbly, ugly growl.

"Forget you, Twinkletoes." Bedders turned his back on Remo and clambered up the ladder.

Remo slithered behind him and caught him near the peak, where Bedders snapped a kick at his head with the mostly re-formed foot—and he missed Remo entirely. Then Bedders flew into the wall. The police diver left a bloody splotch and flopped to the floor, more bones breaking. Actually, Remo thought, it was the same bones breaking all over again.

This time Remo wasn't going to sit around watching Bedders heal himself. He leaped and landed both of his expensive, handmade Italian shoes in the places where Bedders's shoulders were. The joints became mush. Bedders's eyes protruded from his skull as Remo snatched the arms off the torso, then leaped almost straight up, snatching one of the overhead support cables for the ceiling-hung display items. There were stuffed marine creatures, ship anchors and a genuine whale harpoon. Remo tightrope walked to the harpoon, skewering the wriggling arms on the dull point. They kept wriggling. Remo forced them past the barb, then bent the two ends of the harpoon into a ring.

It was a waste of time. Even as Remo alighted on the ground, the arms burst apart and rained down, only to wriggle their way back to Bedders. He absorbed them and used them to push onto his feet.

He opened and closed his fists.

"Stronger," Bedders announced with an unpleasant smile, and to prove his point he punched the floor. His hand sank as far as his wrist. The smashed pulp on the end of his wrist quickly re-formed into a human hand.

"Faster."

"I see that," Remo agreed from his tightrope.

"You're not convinced."

"I'm convinced."

Bedders charged, and it was like a bulldozer going suddenly into hyperspeed. Remo dropped and met the diver with pounding blows that broke the man again and again. Bedders rolled away and leaped to his feet, watching, enraptured, as the broken bones knitted and the muscles restored themselves.

"Yes," he breathed. "Always stronger." When he looked at Remo his eyes were gleaming. "Give me some more, Twinkletoes."

Remo responded like a slingshot, taking Bedders off guard with a swift slash. His long fingernail was stronger than steel, sharper than any sword. Bedders's neck opened wide. Blood sputtered from the arteries. Remo gripped the head in the crook of one arm and wrenched, but Bedders's hands wrapped around the head. Remo used his knees to pound Bedders's body. He could feel the bones shattering and vital organs squelching. Bedders was becoming mush, and yet he held on to his own head with strength Remo couldn't break.

Remo spun them both, decorating the exhibit hall with blood and gore, and still Bedders hung on. Remo exerted every ounce of pressure, crushing the arms, as well as the head, and even as he did he could feel the flesh re-forming—around his hand.

Remo had never felt anything quite like it when the neck muscles reattached themselves in a sheath on his fingers and tried to crush his grip. Remo twisted his hand, made his fingers into steel claws and pulled, extracting muscle and ligament and collarbone fragments, along with an artery that stretched like a garden hose— then snapped off.

Bedders became a berserk automaton, twirling ever more rapidly, then propelling himself into the floor. Remo stepped back. Bedders jerked in a spreading pool of blood.

Then he turned over and sat up. His neck wound mashed together and healed, and the fountain of blood halted. Bedders stared at Remo glassy-eyed and, grinning, allowed himself to fall face-first to the floor. The pool of blood drained into his mouth with a huge sucking sound.

Then he rocketed into Remo, moving faster than he had yet moved. Remo stepped aside, but Bedders moved faster still—faster than Remo. His hands locked on to Remo's unnaturally thick wrists, and Remo was lifted up. Their combined momentum hurtled them both into the tank, but Bedders turned them around mid-flight. Remo struggled and failed to change the direction of the momentum, and he knew what was coming next.

Remo Williams hit the glass. He should have at least been knocked out, but somehow he experienced all of it. The breaking of glass so strong it should never have broken. The hundreds of little tempered shards that penetrated his skin everywhere.

And then all was still. The pain was still there, yes, screaming in his mind, but there was also a funny kind of quiet. Remo Williams was motionless. He was confused. He was standing up, kind of.

Oh. The glass. He was impaled on all the tiny tempered crystal knives and he could feel the blood draining out of him from head to toe.

Funny, thought Remo Williams. Him and the squid, on display together.

Two dead freaks for the price of one.

6

That was that. Good riddance. Now he could finally get what he'd come for. Bedders pulled a nylon sound-dampening drapery fragment off the wall and started up the stairs with it. He hoisted himself from the stairs into the tank and fell down to the bottom. He sank knee-deep in the pulpous squid, then stepped carefully into the gravel.

Reaching gingerly into the rocks, he pulled away the stones and lifted out a translucent orb. A surge of very pleasant energy emanated into his hand. Inside he could see the mass, the embryo, churning impatiently. He placed it deep into the folds of the nylon and searched again.

He moved rocks for five minutes and had twenty-three of the sticky, baseball-sized spheres in his make-shift sack. He dipped the sack in the water to soak it thoroughly before wading to the stairs.

There was pain. The surge of energy from the eggs inside his sack was not like before, not a happy sensa-tion. It was horrid. It was awful. Punishment. Bedders never felt so agonized and, strangely, so sad and ashamed.

It took him two valuable minutes to find another egg, buried in gravel. He placed it in the sack with the others, then backed away slowly, watching the rocks. There was no more pain when he mounted the ladder. He had all the eggs. Twenty-four of the offspring of the dead thing in the tank.

Shouts came from a megaphone far down the hall, ordering Bedders to surrender. He couldn't go out the way he'd come in. There would be gunfire. The eggs might take a hit.

"Now what do I do?" he asked the dead man in the glass.

The dead man said nothing, and Bedders saw he was not dead. He was breathing.

Bedders experienced a new wave of worry. He didn't know how this man could be so strong and fast, and he hadn't cared before—just as he hadn't cared to know how he himself had become so strong and able to do strange things. The *why* just didn't matter.

But this enemy, after taking all that Bedders dished out, was still alive. Another realization occurred to him only now: this man had known what Bedders was coming to do and had come to stop him. That made Bedders even more worried and scared—for the eggs. He slipped to the doorway and dragged a dead cop into the Squidarium, ignoring the long-range gunfire coming from the far end of the special-exhibits hall. In seconds he had donned the cop's clothing,

The enemy pushed himself away from the glass like an uncanny insect dragging itself off a pin in a display case. The crater that he left in the glass was scarlet. Bedders didn't have time for this. He had to rid himself of this egg-threat once and for all.

"What's in the bag, Freakshow?" gasped the enemy. "I'm guessing they ain't sea monkey eggs. Squidlings, maybe?"

"You must never touch them," Bedders hissed.

"You think I'm going to let you hatch a bunch of little Sa Mangsangs?"

Remo's threats had an effect. Bedders looked scared. He lowered the sack and came at Remo fast. "I'll finish you now."

Remo chose to ignore the weakness of blood loss, to think past the pain, putting his mind in the place where he was simply a Master of Sinanju. Even wounded, he should be capable of reacting faster than any man alive. But Bedders was something different.

As Bedders closed in; Remo slashed his flat hand across the bridge of Bedders's nose, his long, sharp nail cutting into flesh, bone, cartilage and brain. Remo felt the skull plates shatter and expose the viscous fluid of Bedders's eyes. The eyeballs came away in his hands. Remo clamped his hands together. The droplets of smashed eyeballs flew a hundred feet.

Bedders fell against the corpse of the police officer,

and leaned his face low over the wide, dead eyes of the cop.

For a strange moment, Remo thought he was going to kiss the corpse, but what came next was stranger still. The ruined tissue of Bedders's skull seemed to sluice out, and then the eyes distended from the dead cop as if pulled by a suction. They popped out and dangled on their nerves and veins, then snapped free and sank into Bedders's head.

When Bedders got to his feet he had eyes again, and the bridge of his nose was re-forming. He snarled, took two great strides and slammed Remo back where he had come from—into the glass crater. Remo felt the shock of cold crystal entering his flesh yet again. He was too weak to be unaffected. He was too slow to fight off his assailant. Bedders pounded Remo's chest hard with both fists.

Remo felt the breath forced out of him.

Sinanju was all about breath. The breath was his strength. The breath was his life. Remo could not breathe and his senses told him only this: the blow that disabled him had weakened the glass too much. It was losing integrity all around him. It was coming down.

BEDDERS FACED AWAY from the crash until the glass stopped flying, and when it was done he heard the cops moving into their positions in the adjoining corridor. Special-tactics officers were prancing around the roof and soon they'd smash the upper windows and rappel inside.

Bedders had zero concern for his own safety, but the eggs had to be protected.

He climbed the ladder to the top deck of the tank and found the access ladder to the ceiling-mounted crane. He held the wet sack in his teeth while swinging hand-over-hand on a flexible electric power cable. There was a service trapdoor to the roof, which he pushed open with the top of his head while clinging to a steelwork platform.

Four SWAT team members busied themselves with rappel lines at the roof edge. Bedders slipped out of the trapdoor and closed it silently. They never knew he was there.

He crept along the roof of the aquarium buildings until he was a quarter mile away from special exhibits and all the hubbub, then found a fire escape ladder to the ground, and a police car with the engine running.

He drove away.

7

When Andrews answered the door he sucked his teeth. "Oscar, they said you were dead."

Oscar Bedders pushed past Andrews into the house, examining the living room. He didn't see what he was looking for, so he headed for the basement with his dripping sack.

"Oscar, what's going on? Are you in trouble?"

Downstairs Bedders ignored the people gathered around the television in the recreation room, all making sounds of astonishment. He headed for the lighted aquarium at the far end of Andrews's basement. He snatched off the plastic lighted cover and began removing the eggs from the sack. He had to reach all the way up to his shoulder to nestle them into the pebbly bottom of the aquarium. Andrews's collection of saddleback clownfish darted into the corners nervously.

Bedders's anxiety was intense. The eggs felt so dry. Could they survive being so dry? When they were all at last inside the precious salt water again, he examined them through the glass for signs of life.

"Oscar, hey, you in there?" It was Andrews. "You want to tell me what's going on?"

Bedders noticed the others in the room. His friends were gathered around the wide-screen television. Bedders remembered now that they were all supposed to get together today to watch Australian women's beach volleyball. But that had been in another part of his life. For Oscar Bedders, there was everything that came prior to today and there was today. The friends he had in his previous life meant nothing.

Still, he was grimly amused. "I see the party went on even though you thought I was dead."

"But you're not dead!" said Reid, a stout construction worker. "Why'd they say you was dead, Oscar?"

"Beats me," Bedders said. "You could have at least kept the TV off as a sign of respect."

"Wait a second, Oscar," Andrews said, waving at his aquarium. The tank was overflowing with the addition of the twenty-four large eggs. "What the hell did you put in my tank? You got water all over my floor."

"Those are eggs." Bedders turned back to the aquarium, feeling his anxiety again. He saw movement inside some of the eggs. Some had survived. But the eyes he was using now were sharp enough to pierce the cloudy water and determine that two or three of the eggs looked darkened and still.

"What kind of eggs?" Andrews demanded.

"Squid."

That brought silence to the rec room except for the

shrill of a potato chip commercial. Reid and Tony K. and Alan all knew that he'd gone that morning to dive into the tank of the colossal squid in the Chicago Aquarium.

This just kept getting weirder and weirder, thought Andrews. Then Bedders sucker punched him right in the snout.

8

E.R. was in a state of havoc already when the small Asian gentlemen appeared to usher in utter chaos.

"Where is my son?" he demanded of the admitting nurse.

The nurse looked perplexed. She was certain no Asian boys or men were admitted to the E.R. on her shift. "Can you provide me with his name?"

The old man waved her away with a wrinkled hand and glided to the secure doors, pushing through them as if they were not locked. The admitting nurse wasn't sure how he accomplished that. Fragments of the electronic dead bolts clattered to the floor. She snatched for the phone and dialed the security guards, who were already alerted by the door alarm.

MASTER CHIUN KNEW hospitals and despised them. He was assaulted with the stench of medical chemicals and the chill, unhealthy air common to these places. He listened in on the conversations happening all around him and found it easy enough to zero in on a babble of excited voices down the hall. He followed the babble to a room filled with medical personnel surrounding the bloodied body of his son.

Chiun heard the concern in the tone of their voices and he slipped amid them to the side of the slab on which they administered to Remo Williams.

Remo's body was a curious sight even to Chiun, who had seen much of death and wounding. Chiun had even seen Remo wounded and near death before. Still, it was unsettling to view him battered and bruised, as if he had endured violence on every inch of his exposed body. He was pillowed underneath by gauze that was soaked with blood, like a formfitting nest of bandages.

"The IV's in a wound," snapped a gray-haired man in a mask. "There's no splint on him. What paramedics made this mess?"

"I ordered the IV placement," said another doctor impatiently. "They had trouble with getting the IV needle into the skin—must be some sort of heavy callusing."

"Doesn't look callused."

"We tried getting a standard IV ourselves with no luck. There are no broken bones, so there was no need for limb splints—just the spine."

Chiun snatched the needle out of the bandaged wound in Remo's forearm and ran his fingers like spiders over his son's body.

"Who are you?" It was the younger doctor.

"Touch him no further. He is in my care now." Chiun was relieved by what his examination revealed. There was none of the sponginess below the skin to indicate great damage to the tissues, but there were bruises upon bruises about the front of his body and evidence of many punctures on the back side.

"Get your hands off him!" bellowed the older doctor, and made to grab Chiun's bony arms. The gray-haired doctor was in his sixties, but big and powerful still, while Chiun looked frail with advanced age.

In fact, Chiun was fantastically old, with flesh that appeared as if it would tear easily, like ancient, damp parchment. His muscles seemed but threads linking his old bones. The authoritarian doctor should have been careful, manhandling a senior citizen like that.

But he never touched Chiun. Chiun's arm wasn't there when he tried to take it. The elderly doctor went stiff, his arms straight at his sides, his hands spread wide, his feet angled up. He was standing on his heels and he couldn't move and he couldn't stay balanced like that.

It was a long, long fall. There was the little old Asian man slipping around the room. He took the mask off the patient, dismantled the wires and sensors and returned to capture the falling doctor before he hit the tile floor. Good thing, too. That kind of a crash would have caused serious head injury.

Then he was being scooted out of the room on his stomach. He slid to a halt and found himself staring up at the ankles belonging to a pair of security guards.

"In there! Get him!"

The guards were stymied at the door when they were met by a stampede of medical staff coming out. Then, when they tried to enter, the swing doors opened again just fast enough to tap them each in the skull. They fell in a heap beside the elderly doctor, now showing creases in their foreheads.

The elderly doctor, director of Cook County Hospital, shouted for more security guards.

"I SHALL ASK the questions—you shall answer them."

The old Asian man spoke in a squeak, like a formal cartoon mouse. But a very persuasive mouse. After what he had just seen, young Dr. Lyons was all for giving the man the benefit of the doubt.

"What has been done to this man?" Chiun demanded. "Start at the beginning."

Lyons wasn't sure what was meant by the beginning. "He was involved in some violence at the Chicago Aquarium."

"This I know. What was his condition when he was found?"

"Oh. The paramedics pulled him from under the glass of the tank. The integrity of the glass saved him from being crushed, but he had more puncture wounds on his back than the paramedics could count. They bandaged the bleeding as best they could, dumped in plasma, treated him for shock."

"He had no shock!"

"The trauma was immense. He was going to get shocky."

"You inserted drugs that pollute his body and keep him in a state of lethargy," Chiun accused.

The doctor looked at the old Asian curiously. "I ordered that, yes. What are you doing to him?"

Chiun was touching Remo with his gentle fingers, pressing into the flesh.

"Do you not think it wise to find if he has crushed organs? Ligaments that no longer attach to his bones? Do you not see the value in knowing if the blood flows uncontrollably inside his body?"

"You can't determine that by feel," Dr. Lyons said.

"I have determined it." Chiun put both his slender hands around the neck of the patient and pried off the neck brace, snapping the plastic rivets, then he massaged the base of the spine. "Awaken, lazy delinquent!"

"He's pumped full of anesthetic," Dr. Lyons pointed out. "He'll be unconscious for hours."

Remo's eyes fluttered and his pupils dilated under the glare of the bright white light.

"Chiun."

"It is midday and I find you napping," Chiun said, although his voice was gentle. "Dressed immodestly, I might add."

"How did you do that?" Dr. Lyons demanded.

Remo sat up, tearing gauze from his back and glaring at his midsection. His chinos were cut to ribbons.

When the medical staff scissored away the pant legs they left only a few rags draped loosely over his crotch.

"Those were new pants," he complained.

"This matters to you?" Chiun asked. "You dispose of them after a single wearing."

"Yeah. Keep your hands off," Remo half slurred to Dr. Lyons, who was trying to examine the wounds on Remo's back. All but the deepest punctures had been patched with emergency adhesive tape in the field. A dozen fresh seepages of blood appeared.

"Please lie down. You could start serious bleeding again. You don't know how much plasma you took to get stabilized."

"No, thanks. Gotta go."

"What?"

"Give me your pants."

Lyons stared at him.

"The pants. Give them. And the T-shirt."

"You can't mean it."

"I mean it," Remo said. "And all this arguing is not making me feel any better. Give me the clothes or else." Remo nodded significantly at Chiun. Remo didn't know what Chiun had been up to prior to his coming to, but he was sure it left an impression on the doctor. Lyons nodded eagerly and slipped out of his slacks. He dropped the hospital robe and took off his shirts. Remo declined the $150 custom-made Oxford broadcloth shirt and took the T-shirt that was underneath—Fruit of the Loom, eight bucks from Penney's.

Lyons seemed somewhat dismayed, standing there in his fleur-de-lys boxers and black support stockings.

"Do not despair, misguided practitioner of quackery," Chiun said, face brightening into a smile. "Your ignorant efforts to minister to my careless son shall be rewarded with a gift of high fashion."

Remo was fighting against the cocktail of chemicals in his bloodstream. "Chiun, what are you talking about?"

With a flourish, Chiun removed a slim, flat package from the sleeve of his robe and presented it to the befuddled E.R. physician. Dr. Lyons found himself holding a package of plastic. It had a label and a retail bar code.

Lyons looked at the young man.

"You got me," Remo said.

But the old Asian was eagerly expectant. Lyons tore the plastic and took out something folded and flat. It fell open in a cascade of cartoon-colored, shimmering silk.

"Is that some sort of a kimono?" Lyons asked.

"It is a Koh-Mo-No, a garment of exceedingly fine silk, styled in the most flattering lines," Chiun explained. "This is the latest fashion trend that is sweeping this nation. Soon, all who dwell in North America shall be wearing the Koh-Mo-No, or shall be envious of those who do."

"I'm way more doped up than I thought," Remo muttered.

"You," Chiun finished grandly to Lyons, "shall be one of the first setters of the new trend."

The doctor looked at the thing. It was fine silk, but the colors were big wide stripes of hunter-green, scarlet, sky-blue and lemon-yellow. He didn't dare refuse to put it on.

It went over his head like a simple shift and hung to just above his knees.

The old Asian was waiting for a response.

"It's a very colorful shirt."

"Ah, the colors are ideal for a man of your station," Chiun explained. "Do you see that they are the colors of the shirt you might wear to golf?"

"His dad, maybe," Remo said.

"But the Koh-Mo-No is more than a shirt and better, for no trousers are required. You are fully dressed for your day."

"Oh." Lyons felt as if he were wearing a negligee. "Thank you."

"You are most welcome for this valuable gift," Chiun said, then waved the man away.

Dr. Lyons didn't want to go out there dressed in a Koh-Mo-No. But he didn't want to go sliding out, either. He left.

REMO RUBBED HIS HEAD. "Chiun, what in blazes was that all about?"

"This is no time for idle chatter," Chiun said, in a hurry again. "We leave this place at once."

Remo slid from the table and gingerly dressed in the doctor's clothes. He could still feel blood oozing from many wounds on his back. What worried him were the little shrieks of pain that came from inside his muscles. Still, Chiun wouldn't let him go walking around if he were seriously hurt. Probably.

As they left the examining room, Remo stretched his limbs and tested his reflexes on the Chicago police officers who were just arriving. He slipped around them before they knew what they were up against, incapacitated them and sat them in the hallway with their backs against the wall.

"Kind of hurts when I move around," he said.

"It is fortunate for you that I arrived when I did," Chiun said. "Who knows what barbaric procedures would have been performed upon your body had I allowed the leech dispensers to have their way with you. They likely would have amputated your limbs were I fifteen minutes later in arriving."

"All I know," Remo replied, "is I'm laying there sleeping away, no cares in the world, after a hell of a bad morning, and now you've got me up walking around and bleeding all over the place like I just got off the front lines."

Chiun glanced over at Remo with a hint of compassion.

Remo said, "I had a bad morning, Chiun."

"We will speak of that shortly," Chiun said. He looked out through the double sliding doors of the emergency-room entrance, putting his hands in the sleeves of his robe. "For the time being we shall wait here in this waiting room."

"I thought we were in a hurry. No offence, Little Father, but I don't know if they want us waiting here."

"Then they should not be advertising this as a waiting room." Chiun stood watching through the door. His view included the parking lot and the underside of an ambulance that was lying on its side. Raw scratches on the asphalt showed that it had been shoved aside—after it was on its side.

"Chiun, please tell me there was nobody inside that ambulance when it fell over."

"Only the driver. He refused to move his vehicle as I arrived."

Considering the circumstances, the ambulance was the least of Remo's worries. Under the fearful eyes of the hospital staff, peeking from behind walls and desks, Remo sat on a waiting-room chair, closed his own eyes and reached inside himself.

BEING A MASTER OF Sinanju meant being a master of one's own body to an extent that exceeded the capabilities of all other human beings. Remo could adjust his body temperature to such an extent that he could walk in the hottest desert or in near arctic conditions without protection. He could control his use of oxygen so efficiently that he could stay under water for extreme lengths of time.

He could also optimize his body functions to heal

himself. Now, he sent blood and oxygen and enzymes and proteins directly to the wounded places in high concentration. This stimulated the healing faster than any medicine, bandage or therapy.

Still, he could feel the pain, and he could feel the damage to his muscles, and he knew it would be some time before he was completely healthy again.

It would be ideal to have a few days to recover before he needed to use his body again in any strenuous way. He was hoping he would not soon have to repeat his encounter with the man from the squid tank.

Somehow, though, Remo didn't think he'd be that lucky. This pessimistic thought stirred him from his moment of meditation. When he opened his eyes, Chiun was watching him, a shadow of concern on his brow.

"What exactly is it we're waiting for? "Remo asked.

"Our ride," Chiun responded.

Remo didn't bother getting more of an explanation. "Little Father, do you want me to tell you what happened?"

"Later," Chiun said tightly.

"It was strong," Remo said, knowing it was stupidly obvious to say so. Of course it was strong. It had to be something incredibly powerful to have bested the Reigning Master of Sinanju.

"Later. Keep this unspoken until we know more of its nature."

"I know what you're thinking," Remo said. "I'm thinking the same thing. It could be him."

"Yes, it could be, and so we must keep it unspoken."

"And if we run into it again, Chiun? You don't want to know what happened, just in case?"

Chiun asked, "If we encounter it again, is there something you have learned that will aid us in the battle? Did you discover its weakness?"

Remo made a wry face. "Not exactly. But I discovered it's a daddy."

9

Andrews couldn't believe this was happening. This couldn't be real. This was a wacky nightmare.

What started as a get-together with the guys for a few beers had become a scene from a cheap horror movie. Andrews was lashed tight in his easy chair. Extension cords were wrapped around his arms, legs, body and throat. Any attempt to struggle made the noose tighten. He struggled anyway, and now the cord around his neck was cutting off most of his air supply. The gag made breathing even harder. They were all gagged.

All the guys were there. Reid was lashed in a folding chair with yellow plastic rope. He was strong and short, a bulldog of a man, and it took a lot of rope to make him helpless—but Bedders had done it. The other two were on the couch, their ankles tied with strands of Christmas lights that went around the couch, crossed and looped on each other's neck. When one of them struggled, he strangled the other one.

Some ironic corner of Andrews's brain briefly considered that Bedders hadn't even had the courtesy to leave them with the TV on. Instead, he had moved the recliner with Andrews, and the three other prisoners, too, and placed them around the aquarium. The aquarium was crowded with the eggs of the squid—if that's what they really were. None of this made any sense to Andrews. All he knew was that his clownfish hardly had any room to swim. The lid was off the aquarium, and the water was to the very top. One of the clownfish went exploring. There was nothing to stop it. The fish flopped in the middle of the four prisoners and gasped for a long time before it was finally still.

Andrews became very afraid. He struggled some more. His throat was constricted further. He gasped for air just like the clownfish, and the others were watching him in stark horror.

Andrew froze. He wasn't going to die like the damned clownfish! He forced himself to breathe. There was some air getting through. Not much, but he could live on it.

He put his mind to work on the problem. Andrews was a smart guy, a sanitary engineer. He should be able to figure this out—but nothing made sense. There was no rational way of linking the events of that morning.

Why was Bedders reported dead? Why'd he show up alive? Why'd he take squid eggs from the aquarium? How'd he take them, for that matter? Why did he turn violent, knocking all his best friends senseless and tying them up in front of the squid eggs?

It was ridiculous. It was crazy. That was the answer

to some of the questions, anyway—Bedders was crazy. Had to have been hurt in the head and it affected his brain.

But they had to be looking for him, now. The cops would come to Andrews's house eventually and free the victims of the crazy man. Until then, they had to wait.

The waiting was the worst part.

Finally, after a couple of hours, something did start to happen. Andrews realized then that the waiting had not been the worst part at all.

OSCAR BEDDERS HAD planned to relax for the morning in the home of his buddy, Andrews. He did a good and thorough job trussing up his former friends. He could not allow any of the men to get away. They were of great importance. Bedders would just hang out with the guys while the eggs went through the hatching process, which was about to happen any minute. The hatchlings would come out hungry. They'd need food. Bedders had provided food.

But there was another danger that was almost as high on his priority list—it was a grave danger, indeed, to pull him away from the youngsters.

While he was tying up the guys, the TV was blaring away in the background and Bedders wasn't paying a lick of attention. It was only by chance that he caught the news bulletin scrolling along the bottom of the screen. Shootout at the Chicago Aquarium, where just hours ago two unexplained deaths occurred.

And then mere seconds of news footage. A body being rolled out of the aquarium into an ambulance. He couldn't see the face but he saw the hair and the IV. He recognized the dark hair. The IV meant he wasn't seeing a corpse.

Son of a bitch. His enemy was alive. Last Bedders saw of the guy he was getting a few hundred tons of glass piled up on him. Nobody could live through it— but Bedders's enemy, the enemy of the unborn squid youngsters, had lived through it.

Bedders couldn't allow the enemy to keep living. The man was exceedingly dangerous. Bedders had to strike him soon, now, while he was still weak. The Chicago news channel ran more complete coverage and told Bedders that the survivor was taken to Cook County Hospital.

"Mind if I borrow your wheels?" Bedders asked his old buddy, Andrews. Andrews tried to answer, but even that little movement caused the slip knot on his throat to tighten.

10

Police cars were parked with their lights on at the entrance to the emergency-room lot, still trying to get a read on the situation inside. A Jeep Grand Cherokee swerved in from the street, sideswiped one of the patrol cars and stopped quickly. It dropped into Reverse, slammed the front end of the second squad car, climbed the hood and crushed the engine, then it kept backing up until it crushed the passenger compartment.

Remo didn't see what happened to the cops inside, but he could guess.

"Hope that's not our ride," he remarked to Chiun.

"It is not."

As the SUV rolled off the squad car, the sunlight reflecting on the windshield vanished long enough for him to get a look at the driver. A hundred yards away, it was a face Remo recognized.

"Crap. Chiun, it's him."

"Him?" Chiun asked incredulously. "The human in the Spurt Futility Vehicle?"

"Him. The one you said I wasn't supposed to speak about? I'm speaking now and I'm telling you that's him."

THE SUV HEADED for the emergency unloading zone, where an ambulance lay on its side. Bedders was wondering about that, but he didn't wonder long. He entered the sliding glass doors, which were not designed for a Jeep Grand Cherokee. When he jumped out he heard nothing.

There was but one person in sight. A patient, as old as Moses's toes, was forgotten in the corner, helpless in his wheelchair.

Bedders found this amusing, but he couldn't take the time to truly enjoy it. "Where'd they all go, Gramps?"

The old man looked up at him with eyes that were clear and bright, but his every movement was a shaking and trembling of nerves past their prime.

"They ran away. Where is my daughter? She left me here."

He was some sort of Chink, dressed all pretty but shrunken and feeble with his great age.

"I want the man from the aquarium. Where is he? You hear about where he is?"

"Oh, yes." The old man nodded, and his nodding became repetitious, his concentration drifting, fading away.

"Hey, Gramps, focus, would ya! Where's the guy from the aquarium?"

The old man was puzzled. "Aren't you my nephew Tyrone?"

"Listen, old man, I want the guy they brought in from the aquarium! You know something, or don't you?"

Bedders loomed over the feeble, bent little creature, who was forced to crane his neck painfully to peer up at him.

"They took him away," croaked the feeble old man.

Then the feeble old man smiled.

And he straightened his posture, bringing a look to his face that said suddenly that he was not what he had seemed to be.

Bedders knew at once that this was something new and yet familiar. This was one like the man from the aquarium.

"And you are a fool," squeaked the old man in the wheelchair. "Nothing but a fool and the tool of a dying god!"

Bedders trembled for half a heartbeat with self-recrimination and humiliation. The old man had tricked him, fooled him, and he would show the old man how much he disliked being made to look a fool.

But the old man struck first, and fast. Bedders felt the sudden crushing blows that came up from the hands of the old man as they connected like sledgehammers below his rib cage and plowed through the ribs, breaking up and up and up like the rungs of a ladders collapsing one after another. Bedders flailed out, sweeping the old man away, but he was too slow.

Chiun sprang from his chair and landed atop the shoulders of his attacker. Before Bedders could react, Chiun brought his flat hands together on the sides of Bedders's head, crushing the skull, exploding the eardrums. Chiun slipped away as the bigger man went into a frenzy, balling his fists and slamming them like clubs into walls and chairs, zeroing in on the old Master of Sinanju.

Chiun let the man come, and when the weapons swung at him, Chiun simply moved aside, allowing the powerful clubs to whistle over his head. But something went terribly wrong—something unforeseen and unnatural. Bedders moved too fast. His forearms collided with the top of Chiun's head, and the old man sprawled on the floor.

Then Bedders snapped a kick at the old Master, so fast Chiun was again caught off guard, and he knew the blow could incapacitate him. He flattened against the floor. The blow missed connecting with his body. Chiun sprang to his feet under the kick and carried the foot with him, propelling it high into the air and thus carrying the already damaged skull of Oscar Bedders into the floor.

Bedders got up. With a shattered rib cage and burst eardrums and massive damage to his head, he got up.

Chiun knew from his brief experience with this foe that anything less than a killing blow would be wasted. He deposited a killing blow with the bottom of his sandal, but the foe reacted in a most peculiar manner—he leaped backward and away, bending his body double, in an ingenious way of absorbing a catastrophic kick to the abdomen. Chiun felt his contact; it was far less severe than he had intended it to be. Already he was following up the move with something more powerful and less easy to dodge. His hand snapped against the fleshy open part of Bedders's throat before he had a chance to regain his balance. The strange man staggered away, gagging, and was unfit to defend himself against a slashing cut that opened his chest like a ceremonial dagger.

Bedders took the only the defensive posture open to him; he turned away from Chiun, but that exposed his spine to the master assassin. Chiun, whose hands possessed five long fingernails, as sharp as a sword edge and just as strong, sliced through the living vertebrae of Oscar Bedders. The creature in the body of a man bent backward in a way that proved his spine no longer supported his body.

The collapsing thing never stopped struggling.

Everything Chiun knew about human beings told him the man had to be dead, but his eyes assured him otherwise. Chiun leaped on the top half of the body as it attempted to fold itself forward in a correct alignment.

What shocked Chiun most of all was that, even folded in two, spine severed, throat collapsed, his enemy could still move with unnatural speed. Bedders clutched Chiun's ankle hard, and Chiun experienced firsthand the energy that stoked the engine of this creature. Yellow strikes of energy shot from the hand of the creature into his leg, and Chiun felt as if the very spark of his life were channeled away into the thing on the floor.

Chiun jerked his leg free and stepped from it. "Incubus!" he shrieked. "What a great coward is a vampire. You are not man but leech."

To Chiun's wonder, his foe was folding his spine back into position and locking it in place. The creature rose to its feet, holding its throat wound closed with its hands.

"Whatever you got in you, old man, it's invigorating. I want some more."

"The leech, at least, has some purpose on this earth. What is your purpose, creature?"

"Right now, old man, I got one goal. I'm gonna suck you up. I'm gonna drain you dry. Take all that battery juice you got stored away."

Bedders struck, fast, hard, but Chiun glided away and kicked him from behind, crushing him into the wall. Parts of him cracked, and when he found Chiun again the old man was far across the room.

"You can't run forever."

"Many men greater than you have underestimated the Masters of Sinanju."

The creature made no response. It was as if he didn't recognize the name. Perhaps it was that he was suddenly distracted, but what distracted him Chiun couldn't say. There was no telling sound, nor was there any new vibration among the sea of movement and pressure of which Chiun was always aware. Bedders looked as alert as a rodent-sniffing cat.

That this creature could sense something Chiun could not infuriated the old Master all the more. Bedders bolted for the outside.

He was standing outside staring at nothing, alert to everything. Still, he didn't notice Chiun. Chiun glided alongside Bedders and snicked away four fingers from his adversary's left hand with a silent, shadowlike flash of the Knives of Eternity. Chiun snatched the fingers out of the air before they hit the pavement and flipped them away over the tops of the cars. Bedders bellowed and lunged, but Chiun slipped closer and took more fingers, then destroyed Bedders's hip bones with two quick blows.

Bedders collapsed. Chiun took the leg off with a twist and a slash and sent the leg flying away, high, end-over-end, until it landed in a backyard swimming pool a thousand yards from the scene of the battle.

Chiun fell back when Bedders rose, but instead of attacking him, Bedders galloped on one leg and the stub of his hands. In no time he reached the mob of onlookers at the corner of the hospital.

They were standing at what they thought was a safe distance from the violence—and now they knew the distance wasn't safe at all. Bedders snatched two men in the crook of either arm. Before Chiun could intervene the victims were screaming, their bodies torn by the claws of the yellow lightning. Bedders tossed the remains at Chiun.

The left body was missing a leg. The other victim was missing fingers.

Bedders, on the other hand, was whole again. He made a happy face at Chiun—happy for Bedders, not for Chiun.

"Your friend," Bedders said. "He's close. I can feel it."

Bedders ran back to the building and Chiun hissed, angry with himself. He had not tempted the creature away from the building quickly enough—and now Remo was in danger. The creature named Bedders scaled the building with inhuman ease and speed, punching into windows for handholds and ignoring the quick-healing wounds.

REMO SAT cross-legged in the sun and closed his eyes.

He was the Reigning Master of Sinanju, and according to the prophetic tradition he might even be the greatest of all Masters. Remo didn't know if he bought into all that malarkey, and he sure had a hard time, despite his training, buying entirely into the Sinanju tradition of Buddhist-like detachment. He should be down there, right now, helping Chiun. He knew that Bedders was some sort of force beyond human. Look what he had done to Remo. What damage would he perpetrate on Chiun? Chiun was a powerhouse in his own right, but certainly not as strong as Remo.

But Chiun was smarter. More devious, for sure. Maybe he could hold his own against Bedders for the time being. One thing was sure: Remo wasn't up for another fight. Not yet.

The blood put into his body had a strange effect on him. It replaced some of his own lost blood, and restored some of his strength. Still, it was like living poison. On top of being wounded, Remo was struggling to filter his system and clean it of a hundred different toxins from the blood of at least four different donors.

God, he could *taste* the poisons. Mercury and lactose, influenza and caffeine, others he couldn't identify by name. He was weakened and reinvigorated at the same time, and Remo felt his body shaking.

The sun warmed his flesh, and he forced himself to perspire, excreting poison as fast as he could. He felt stronger and more clearheaded in minutes. But how strong?

He listened to the battle below, and heard Chiun baiting Bedders away from the hospital. Remo should be down there—he should help Chiun. But he couldn't help.

Then he heard Bedders coming back. The onlookers were screaming and retreating again. How many dead down there? Remo didn't want to think about it.

He rose to his feet smoothly, testing his body with each step he took to the edge.

HE CAUGHT THE ENEMY. The enemy was trying to get away. But on the roof, the enemy had run out of places to run.

"What are you, Freakshow?" his enemy asked, panting and tired.

"Just the caretaker of the offspring."

"You have supersquid powers? Like climbing buildings, stealing body parts. All the things a squid can do, right?"

"Don't know. Don't care."

"Squid can't fly. Or can they?"

"It's gonna be a relief to shut you up," Bedders said, sneering.

Bedders came. Remo responded, as quick as lightning, and Bedders knew he'd been taken in as the kick was delivered to his chest and his body shattered. His rib cage collapsed; his spine snapped apart. His internal organs were pierced and smashed. But this was all secondary to the real problem—he was airborne, kicked so powerfully he was still ascending as his body shut down, and then he seemed to hang in the air for a long moment, listening to silence as the air movement stopped. Bedders began to fall.

Son of a bitch, he thought. Evil, sneaky-ass son of a bitch hadn't just tricked him, kicked him, killed him. The enemy had kicked him just right. Bedders knew it as he fell down at the perfect angle for his broken body to crash against the edge of the roof and break it even more.

Bedders could feel that his body was as solid and strong as the hot glop he used to eat for breakfast. It was only going to get worse when he came down. Bedders almost laughed as the flagstones loomed up at him. Even he was gonna be surprised to live through this little adventure.

But if he did, that son of a bitch in the fancy shoes was gonna pay big-time.

Bedders felt—actually felt—himself go splat.

"LET ME THROUGH. " It was a paramedic from an arriving ambulance. The paramedic had just transported in a patient with a half-severed thumb. That was nothing compared to the catastrophe on the hospital grounds. He was trying to find someone to keep alive.

"Forget it," announced a cop standing over the body.

"Let me check him out."

"No need."

"I've seen jumpers live through falls that high," the paramedic insisted. "Let me check him, at least."

The cop stepped to one side and the paramedic took a look at the jumper.

"Uck." The paramedic had never seen a body so—*ruined*. "What happened here?"

"I got no clue. But he did it." The cop nodded at the deflated corpse of Oscar Bedders.

The paramedic took a step away. Others gagged and gasped. The cop didn't understand the problem until he felt something wet touch his leg.

It was the jumper, reaching for him with a bone-less hand.

He was a Chicago cop with twenty years under his belt, and no murder victim or suicide he had ever witnessed was more repulsive than this thing that was still alive—but absolutely shouldn't be alive. He felt his stomach heave. Flesh was ripped off his shin. He gagged and screamed at the same time. How was this even *happening?*

Then there was a balloon of pressure expanding in the cop's chest, like his heart being filled with compressed gas, and in seconds it was too much.

One of Chicago's finest blew apart.

THE PANIC EBBED and flowed on the hospital grounds. Remo was always amazed that human beings were so damned curious all the time and had to come look at the mayhem even before they were sure the mayhem was all finished. Today, the mayhem at the Cook County Hospital kept restarting itself and you'd think the civilians would get the idea to get out of there—instead, they kept hanging around, convinced that every time the violence stopped it was stopped for good. Every time they were wrong.

The screaming was happening again when he hooked up with Chiun outside. People were running away in different directions from the dense mob.

"I knew it," Remo said. "He's in there."

The mob parted enough to show them Oscar Bedders, who looked like the scraps on the floor of a butcher shop, but with one limp hand extended. The hand was the source of a dancing trio of lightning bolts, their light sickly and curiously devoid of brilliance in the afternoon sun. The yellow bolts were latched on to a frozen Chicago police office.

The cop blew open. The lightning dimmed. The cop collapsed. The dismembered pieces of him were absorbed into Oscar Bedders, who became thicker, as if he were being pumped full of air.

"Jeez-us." Remo felt like spitting. He felt a hand on his arm.

"Hold."

"What for, Chiun?"

Bedders made more lightning.

THE POLICE OFFICER WAS jolted back to consciousness. Conscious? How? Why not dead? His heart had exploded.

He was on the ground and the smashed jumper was an arm's length away from him. The jumper looked less smashed, and the cop noticed that the jumper had stolen his wedding ring.

The cop glanced at his hand, where the wedding ring had been. There was only a stump.

The jumper had more than his wedding ring. He had the cop's entire hand. He was using it, raising it, making it work for him. This was a nightmare—but a nightmare with real pain. Now that he was conscious again, the cop felt it. The pain. The blood flowing from his body. He was seeing bright lights, but they were jaundice, yellow lights and they were holding him like iron hands. The pressure built up inside the cop again. He screamed.

"Now," Chiun snapped as the cop's body burst open for a second time and the lightning dissipated in the moment. Remo bolted into the mess of blood and body. It was Bedders's most vulnerable moment. Remo used it, bringing his foot down on his head.

Bedders turned his head away.

It happened too fast. Remo was too slow. He might have ended the thing then and there. He could have turned off its brain, and surely it wouldn't function without a brain. But Remo was too slow.

Remo cursed and plowed the palm of his hand down

into Bedders's face but failed to crush it. Bedders barked a laugh and snatched Remo with his freshly acquired hands. Remo felt the beginning of the pain, and when he pulled away Bedders held on, then iron clamps lifted Remo away from the dancing lightning.

The lightning transferred to the only human, alive or dead, within range of its energy. Remo witnessed the resurrection of the unfortunate victim yet again. The cop made a foghorn sound of horror. Why couldn't he just die?

The cop had nothing left for Bedders to use—he was just a place for Bedders to dissipate his energy. The cop exploded into more pieces and was still.

"This is sick," Remo said.

"At the very least," Chiun agreed, and his eyes traveled skyward as the sound of a helicopter grew and a Chicago PD chopper swung into view. It was outfitted for fighting terrorists, with a machine gun mounted on the open deck behind the pilots.

"Chicago Police Department," the bullhorn announced. "Stay where you are."

"Think he'll obey the nice policeman?" Remo asked.

"No."

Bedders was walking away on his fists faster than most men could run. He tried his new legs. They buckled, then he jogged on them.

"Stop or you will be shot."

Bedders sneered, not at the cops, but at Remo and Chiun, and he leaped at them. Remo felt the cascade of pressure waves homing in on him. He slipped away from a rain of bullets, but Bedders crumbled. The chopper homed in. Bedders pulled his legs beneath him, and pushed off. He ascended twenty feet like a swimmer coming up from the bottom of the deep end of the pool. He cracked against the roof inside the helicopter cabin and landed in an inelegant heap alongside the machine gunner.

"Oh shit," said Remo Williams.

"Do not," Chiun warned, placing a gentle hand on Remo's biceps. "It is already too late."

And it was. The helicopter ascended unsteadily, then the interior flickered with sickly yellow illumination, followed by a burst. Then came the rain of human flesh.

The helicopter began to rotate and it slid steeply into a construction lot. Remo watched a figure leap out just before the chopper hit the earth and burst into flame.

11

"Then we ran away."

"A wise move," said the sour, dry voice on the telephone.

Remo didn't agree. "He got away. Bedders."

"I'm glad he did."

"Why?"

"It has the eggs."

Remo considered it, and at that moment Chiun did something unpleasant with the filthy bandages that still clung in an ugly mass to Remo's back and buttocks. He felt many wounds become cold as they were exposed to the open air. Remo was not a man who was easily affected by pain. He knew a hundred ways to handle pain, channel pain, subvert the distractions of pain. But now, he hissed.

"What was that?" Mark Howard demanded. "Remo, was that you?"

"Air brakes," Remo said.

"You don't have air brakes on the camper," Smith pointed out. "Not to mention you are parked."

Remo said nothing as Chiun gingerly placed the ugly mass of bandage into the waste bin. Remo swallowed. He felt—sick. Infection was already setting in. Chiun would take care of it.

"What's happening? Is there a problem, Remo?" Mark Howard asked suspiciously. "How are you?"

"Marvelous, Junior, how're you? Glad to hear you're back at work. How's the girlfriend? Nice weather in New England this time of year. Enjoying the seasons?"

Chiun lifted the phone out of his hands. "I am attending to his infirmities, Emperor Smith. You're hireling shall be fit for his duties in short order."

"I don't feel fit," Remo complained loudly. "I feel like I just had the crap kicked out of me. Which I did."

"Remo the Complainer exaggerates," Chiun added, then cupped a hand on the phone. "Do not allow the Emperor to know you are sickly! Why would he care to pay for the services of an unfit assassin?"

"What's he gonna do? Fire me?"

Chiun took his hand off the phone. "Remo suffers from a large number of wounds. The poisons administered to him by the foolish physicians are hampering his ability to heal. Moreover, he was provided with a transfusion of impure blood from unknown donors."

"What was wrong with the blood?" Mark Howard asked.

"Nothing," Remo called.

"If the blood supply is tainted, we must act before other patients receive it."

"It's not tainted."

"It is the blood of meat-eaters," Chiun explained. "The poisons of the flesh of cow and pig were in the blood, and now they are in Remo. The smell is atrocious, if I may be blunt, Emperor." He added generously, "Remo is not entirely to blame."

"I'm not at all to blame."

"Although," Chiun continued, "I believe he enjoys the vicarious pleasures of meat poisons inside his body, since he has mostly sworn off consuming cow and pig flesh."

"There's no mostly about it. I haven't had a burger or a ham sandwich in years."

"I see," Mark Howard said.

"Do I *look* like I'm enjoying myself?" Remo demanded, glaring at Chiun over his shoulder and stretching his fresh scabs in the process. "Huh?"

"I do not answer to 'huh.'"

"Master Chiun," Smith began.

"You think I get pleasure from any of this?"

"Hush," Chiun chided.

"I'm a big boy now," Remo grumbled. "I don't answer to 'hush.'"

"He is uncomfortable and irritable," Chiun explained into the phone as he dribbled distilled water onto the wounds from a sea sponge. "His many complaints are not serious individually, but there are numerous insults. His recuperation will be gradual."

Smith replied, "There's no time for gradual recovery. Oscar Bedders is still out there. We need to track him down and track down the eggs he took from the aquarium. I think we can all see the need for that."

"Yeah," Remo breathed. The water felt good. It lifted the dirt and the infection-carrying fluids and took them away from his body. He helped his body, in ways even he did not understand consciously, directing the cleansing of the foreign blood that now mixed with his own blood. The worst of the contaminants were isolated first and taken to his pores and to the wounds for excretion. He could heal very fast, compared to the average man.

But he was nothing like an Oscar Bedders.

Something occurred to him, and he took the phone from Chiun. "Smitty, do you know something you're not telling us?"

"Not at all, Remo," Smith said. "That's precious little, to be blunt. But I know we can't let those squid eggs do whatever it is they're meant to do."

"Yeah," Remo agreed. "Picking up anything on the psychic radar, Junior?"

"No," Mark said. "We're trying to track him. Those eggs need seawater just to stay viable."

"Like, how much?"

"A few hundred gallons, at most, judging from the mass of eggs you saw him carrying."

"He could put that much water in some buckets in the back of any truck or van. Hell, Smitty, the holding tanks in Chiun's Airstream are that big."

Remo lowered the phone. "Little Father, you don't have squid eggs in the holding tanks. Right?"

"Do not even jest about such a thing. Besides, this vehicle has no holding tanks."

"Huh?"

"'Huh' means you disbelieve me? There is no holding tank. You think I would travel with a large container of human waste in my home?"

"We took them out during the latest restoration of the Airstream, at Master Chiun's request," Mark explained.

"Oh." Remo looked around the interior for the first time since arriving. It was the same Airstream, but it looked entirely different. Remo forced himself to observe the details, to keep himself distracted from Chiun's ministrations.

THE FIFTY-YEAR-OLD, thirty-foot Airstream Sovereign of the Road had been rotting away peacefully in a southwestern junkyard for recreational vehicles. Then Chiun spotted it. The Master of Sinanju Emeritus had recently come to the decision to leave their small condo and look for new housing. A recreational vehicle, Chiun claimed, would be a home they could take with them whenever they traveled.

Remo knew it wouldn't work out that way, but Chiun ignored his advice and commissioned the Airstream's refurbishment—and created a monster. The terrifically expensive reconstruction of the Airstream included its being grafted onto the rear end of an innocent new SUV.

The handiwork was good, and the mutant vehicle that emerged was a fine piece of deviant engineering that halted onlookers in their tracks like a two-headed calf at the state fair.

Then Remo and Chiun were involved in an unfortunate, highly publicized incident while traveling in their Castle Sinanju on Wheels. Across the country people saw the curious RV-SUV hybrid on the television news.

CURE called for the Airstream's immediate assassination. The hybrid vehicle could not continue existing without severely compromising CURE anonymity.

Chiun's custom Airstream Sovereign of the Road went through an extreme makeover, restoration, re-destruction and reconstruction. It was transported and given new legal identities at each step. It was face-lifted more in the past year than Remo had been in all his life—and that was many times.

It would have been far easier and cheaper to simply destroy the Airstream and buy a different one, but Chiun was determined to keep the camper he had chosen. Harold W. Smith was just as determined to shake off any tigers that might be clinging to its tail.

Still, a clandestine CIA subagency managed to keep tabs on the mysterious vehicle through its various identity changes, until Remo was sent to stage its theft as a part of a fake interstate hijacking spree. The CIA subagency was finally shaken—Smith and Mark Howard went to great lengths to insure this before they began yet another restoration on the Airstream. In the end, there was virtually nothing left of the original camper Chiun had found in the junkyard anyway.

She was beautiful by antique RV standards, but she now looked pretty much like hundreds of other restored Airstreams on the roads of America. Chiun didn't seem to mind. Even he had not seemed perfectly happy with the original hybrid vehicle. Besides, CURE, not Chiun, paid for all the work.

The off-gassing of all the new interior fixtures was almost as toxic as the poisons in Remo's blood. And to think, he had once loved New Car Smell.

One nonstandard fixture in the camper was the wooden tub with shallow sides. Remo was sitting in it, stripped to the skin, and the water that flowed off him was channeled to a spout and into a pail.

"Remo?" Smith asked in his ear.

He was so tired his concentration had actually drifted away. "I need a nap."

"No time," Smith replied. "We've got a line on Bedders and the squid eggs."

"When did this happen?"

"Fifteen seconds ago. Get dressed. You'll be there soon. It's not far from you. We're alerting your driver."

Remo heard the engine. The Airstream was now towed behind a conventional-looking, late-model SUV. They began moving, leaving their far-south-Chicago trailer park.

"Driver?" Remo asked. He had smelled all sorts of unsavory human beings in the vicinity, but he hadn't realized one of them was actually a part of the team. "Is it Sarah up there?"

"Of course it is not," Chiun chided.

"Well, I know Smitty and Mark are back at CURE Global HQ, so who else could it be? Mrs. Mikulka?"

"Pardon me? No!" Smith was only half paying attention to Remo's ramblings. The idea of Mrs. Mikulka, Smith's elderly secretary, behind the wheel of an SUV and hauling the big camper was ludicrous.

"We haven't put somebody else on the payroll?" Remo asked.

"He's hired help. Strictly temporary," Smith explained distractedly. "Don't concern yourself about him."

"'Huh.'" Remo said.

"'Huh' means 'what,' in this instance?" Chiun asked.

"'Huh' means, 'I get it.' Disposable humans. Somebody so mean and nasty he can be terminated when he's outlived his usefulness."

Chiun flitted his hand in the air. "Yes. Such as him are of no consequence to the world, even by your standards. Fear not that your sensibilities will be offended when this type meets his fate."

"Oh, sure, but who's got to off him when the time comes? Me, right?" Remo sighed. "So what did our driver do that makes him such a bad guy?"

12

Roy Candace never turned down easy money, but even he knew better than to take his current lucrative employment at face value. There had to be some illegal angle to it that he hadn't yet figured out.

It wasn't the first time he took crooked work. You name it, he'd done it. In fact the weirdest job he'd ever had, by his standards, was his only legit job—managing a car wash in Alabama. It took him about three days to realize he wasn't management material, and to figure out how to make some real money in that situation.

The franchise owner, a guy named Ernest, came by every Monday in the early-morning hours to pick up receipts, empty change machines, do the books, all that crap. Roy thought Earnest didn't deserve to have all the money he took in just from selling car washes to jerks.

Roy used his key to get back in on Monday about four in the morning, as Ernest was doing the books. They went to the bank together when it opened. Ernest dropped off his usual bags of quarters from the machines, but he also made a large withdrawal. It all happened at the drive-up. Roy kept the pistol in Ernest's gut the whole time. The withdrawal, plus the cash receipts from a weekend of operation at five franchise locations, came to near twenty grand. Roy never had so much money at once in his whole life.

Of course, he had to off Ernest. Ernest went into the drainage ditch behind one of his car washes. Black neighborhood. Lots of crime. Roy didn't even use the gun—he bashed Ernest all over with a tire iron. Some black kids saw him and called the cops. He thought black kids hated cops. Roy ran, but the cops took the black kids' word and started looking for a white guy matching Roy's description. What were the cops listening to some black kids for? Shouldn't the black kids be the suspects, you know, automatically?

Anyway, Roy learned a lesson that day. Never trust anybody to do what you expect them to do. In fact, never trust anybody. Always assume the truth is not what it looks like.

Especially when dealing with *them*.

Them might be black. Or Mexican. Women were *them*. *Them* might be cops. *Them* might be managers or bosses or any authority-type people.

Dress-wearing old Orientals were definitely *them*.

And this one was as suspicious as they came. Weird talking, weird acting and superior as hell. The fact that the old Asian was paying so much for the simple job of driving him around in his fancy antique motor home made him even weirder.

In fact, the old Oriental was too good to even talk to Roy. He issued all his orders to Nancy, his personal assistant, and Nancy relayed the orders to Roy. It was insulting. But Nancy was sure a lot more interesting than the old Oriental anyway. She sounded hot.

Roy was going to find out just exactly what the old man was up to, and if luck was with him, he'd get to meet sweet little Nancy face-to-face. Get to know her a little better, too.

Now the situation was even weirder. The old Oriental left in a big hurry when they were driving through Michigan. Nancy had Roy drop the old fart at a tiny farm-town airport. Roy's orders were to keep driving, get a spot at a little trailer park way down on the South Side of Chicago.

He was there no more than fifteen minutes before, what do you know, it's the little old Oriental guy showing up with a friend.

The younger guy looked strange, too, but in ways that weren't so easy to put your finger on. The younger one looked thin, but not wiry, and he still looked strong. He carried himself like he knew how to throw a punch. But he was beat-up, as if he'd just been worked over. His clothes didn't fit right, and they were torn and stained with blood. All this Roy got in one look as he was running back to the trailer park with a breakfast sandwich and a cup of coffee.

One more thing he noticed before the old man helped the younger guy inside the camper—the younger guy had the thickest wrists ever, but they didn't seem swollen. They seemed muscular.

Weird. Definitely another one of *them.*

Roy was going to bide his time and do what he was told and he was going to listen real good. Find out what was going on around here. See where there might be some money to be made, one way or another. He knew there was money here, lots of it. He could taste it in the air. This setup, with the classic old camper and the high-end SUV and the highest-tech built-in audio system ever, it had to have cost a mint. It smelled like something secret, but not government secret. No government agency would have ever hired Roy Candace for anything.

Roy figured the old Oriental man was rich, and all these toys were for his personal convenience. And maybe Roy could figure out how to get his hands on that money. It would be enough to set him up for the rest of his life. There was nothing he wouldn't do to get what he wanted.

He wheeled the SUV into a suburb just outside the Chicago city limits. This was no high-class neighborhood. It was Berwyn, where they stacked up junkyard cars on metal poles and called it art. The houses were dingy old bungalows.

"Park here, please, Roy," ordered the voice from the speakers on the dashboard.

"Anything for you, sweet cheeks."

"The name is Nancy. Stay in the vehicle and keep the engine running."

"Got it."

Another thing that was kind of queer about this job was the way they communicated with him. That voice. Nancy was polite, almost friendly, and sexy as hell. And just a little creepy.

He parked and waited. No noise from the camper. Another creepy thing was how quiet the damned camper was all the time. He should have been able to feel the shifting of the vehicle when the old man moved around back there, but he never felt a thing. Not one creak, not a single vibration. He pictured the old man lying down in a bunk and just staying there, hour after hour. How else could there be no sign of movement? Creepy.

He wasn't feeling anything now, either. The old Oriental and the younger man were still in there. He'd have felt the whole SUV shift around if that younger guy had left. But there wasn't any sign of movement now, either.

"Hey, sweetie? I'm due for a five-minute piss break."

"Stay in the driver's seat and be prepared to leave at any moment."

"Okay. Shit." He folded his arms and slumped in his seat. Creepy, weird, but mostly, this job was boring as hell.

ANDREWS WAS in hell. He decided it wasn't a nightmare because of the pain. There was so much pain and it never ceased. He had to be in hell.

Funny thing, that hell looked like the rec room in the basement of his Berwyn bungalow. Andrews supposed

that was some sort of ironic twist. He didn't understand
the point of this irony, but he'd have all eternity to think
it over, right?

Strangely enough, he hadn't known he was in hell at
first. He thought he had simply been tied up by his
crazy friend Oscar Bedders. Oscar tied up Andrews's
other friends, too—Reid and Tony K. and Alan. Everybody had come over to watch the TV and have a few
beers. But Bedders didn't even have the courtesy to tie
them up facing the TV. He put them in front of the
damned aquarium, with the squid eggs inside.

Soon enough the eggs hatched.

They filled the aquarium with slimy tentacles, so
many of them it looked like a fishbowl full of worms.
The things churned in the tank, devoured Andrews's
clownfish, then they began to probe outside the water.

Andrews's revulsion and horror grew when he saw
the tentacles stretch all the way to poor Tony K., who
was trying to wriggle away. The tentacles threw lightning bolts at him.

It was like somebody hacking at Tony K. with a
cleaver. His arms came off. Big chunks of his beer gut
came off. The tentacles snatched them up. Somehow the
wounds were fried closed by the electricity, but a lot of
good it did Tony K. He hung limp and motionless in his
chair, dead and gone by the looks of it.

More tentacles reached out and shocked Reid. They
took his legs and his hands and big chunks of his chest.

Then they came for Andrews.

Andrews screamed when the lightning hit him. It wasn't like any electric shock he'd ever felt; it was way worse. Then his body began coming apart. The pain was unbearable. But blackness ended the pain.

For a while.

He couldn't believe it when he came to. His bowels were half missing. His skull had been gouged over and over. How come he wasn't dead?

Reid and Tony K. were conscious again, too. The sunlight through the basement windows made Andrews vaguely aware that some time had passed. The tentacles reached out of the tank again. Taking more pieces off of Tony K. and Reid. Drawing the pieces into the tank, rolling them around. Oh, God, the squid were eating them alive, and keeping them alive to stay fresh.

No. Uh-uh. You couldn't stay alive with so much of you missing. This was something different. This was truly hell.

They took more parts off Andrews, and he was in agony until the blackness came again. If I wake up again, he thought, then I'll know I'm really dead. I really am suffering eternal damnation.

The next thing he knew, he was conscious and watching Reid being attacked by the tentacles yet again. Guess that proves it, Andrews thought. Soon the tentacles began to rip into his body for the third time.

"How's LIFE treatin' ya?" Oscar Bedders asked. At least, it looked pretty much like Oscar Bedders.

Andrews was now collapsed on the floor. Most of his lower face was removed, but his eyes were left to him. He cranked his head around and saw Reid and Tony K. lying nearby. They were still moving, although they had been delimbed and their torsos were trimmed of flesh. Their clothing was long gone. Their decimated bodies had slid from the bindings Bedders had put them in. They were nothing but naked fragments of their former selves.

"Thanks for brunch," Bedders said as hoisted the aquarium, stand and all, and staggered with it up the stairs. Some part of Andrews's mind told him such a thing was impossible. A three-hundred-gallon tank had to be too much for a man to carry. A door banged. There were sloshing noises and a crashing of glass. Bedders came back downstairs in a hurry and snatched up the three human beings, tucking them under one arm.

Andrews was confused. If this was hell, what was happening? Something to make it even more hellish?

Sure enough. Bedders had taken the three of them to the carport, where the back of Andrews's Jeep stood open. The squid had been transferred into three extra-large plastic camping coolers. The coolers were big, but the squid were still crowded. The squid had grown substantially since hatching.

Andrews knew what was coming next. He tried to protest, but he had no vocal cords or mouth or jaw. All he managed to do was make the air whistle from his gaping windpipe.

"You don't really want to keep living, do you?" Bedders asked rhetorically.

Keep living? He was still alive? Impossible! But Andrews felt something new. Even if he was an armless, legless, dickless, mouthless shell of his former self, he *did* want to keep living! He did not want to die!

He tried to communicate this through movement, and the only movement he was capable of was to shake his remains of a head frantically. Reid was doing the same thing. They knocked heads.

"Well, tough," Bedders said. He tossed Tony K. first. Plop! The living remains went into the cooler just behind the driver's seat. The water began to churn and boil, and arcs of yellow electricity danced on the surface.

Plop! went Reid in the center cooler. More splish-splash of water, more *zzts!* of energy. Reid made hearty bubbles.

Andrews felt himself get tossed, then he felt the water suck him in. He felt tentacles slithering against his bare skin. He felt the energy bolts tearing into his body yet again. He bubbled and bubbled.

The water became red with his blood, and a moment later an electric bolt ripped his eyes out of his head. His breath was gone. And still he went on.

Was he ever going to die? Or was this truly going to last forever?

Actually, he survived for one full minute, but it seemed like an eternity.

13

Remo went in the front door, raced through the upper story and down into the basement via the stairs at the rear of the house.

Chiun made his own entrance. He slipped alongside the house to the short, wide window into the basement. Chiun stepped off the ground and came down again at a sharp angle, his body as stiff as a plank, and he burst through the glass with great precision. The fragments flew away from him, never even snagging the fine silk of his kimono.

There was water spilled in the back of the room, and discarded bindings. These were not needed to tell Chiun—and Remo, who was just now making an appearance—what had happened here. Both Masters of Sinanju knew all too well the stench of the great squid.

Roy sat up when he saw somebody waving at him from a bungalow up the street. It was the young one—the thick-wrist weirdo—standing on the front porch of a house and giving him the thumbs-down. Roy nodded and the man went back inside. Now how the devil did

that guy get out of the RV without Roy even knowing it?

"Hey, sweetie?" Roy said. "The one guy just waved
to me from the house and gave me a thumbs-down.
That supposed to mean anything?"

"Yes, Roy, thank you," Nancy responded. She sounded a tad disappointed.

"Hey, ya know what?" Roy said, "I think I saw a car
leaving that house just before you had me pull over."

"Truly, Roy?"

"Yeah, I think so. Too far away to see plates or anything. Just a big brown Grand Cherokee."

There was a moment of silence. "Roy, pursue the vehicle at once, please."

"You kiddin'? With this load I'm haulin'?"

"Detach the trailer."

"Sure thing, sweetie pie."

Roy Candace hit the disconnection button, and the
Airstream immediately deployed its pneumatic autolevelers as the tow hitch released the grip pins on the ball
joint. As soon as it was free, Roy stomped on the accel-
erator, leaving rubber on the asphalt.

"WHAT DID you just do?" Mark Howard demanded.

"I sent him after Bedders," Sarah Slate explained
from the old leather couch. "Can't hurt."

"He's probably lying," Howard said.

"He might not be," Harold W. Smith added from behind his own desk. "We have nothing to lose." He was

snapping out commands on his keyboard and a ringing telephone came from the speakers in his desk. It was the phone in a house in Berwyn, Illinois.

"The party you are calling is now chum. Please leave a message."

"Remo, your driver said he spotted a vehicle departing the house just prior to your arrival. He's gone in pursuit."

Remo sighed. "That explains why Chiun just buggered outta here. Okay. We're on it."

"Hold on," Smith said.

But he only heard the phone bouncing on the carpet.

REMO JOGGED up the sunny, tree-lined streets, catching up to a dismayed Chiun, who stood gaping at the Airstream.

"The cretin has stolen my tow vehicle!" Chiun raged, stamping his small, sandaled foot on the pavement so powerfully it shook the pavement and forced the auto-levelers on the camper to make minor adjustments.

"No. He reported seeing a car leaving the house when we were pulling up. Sarah sent him after it."

Chiun's eyes became wide. "She sent a mindless criminal to perform the work of a Master of Sinanju?"

"I think he's just there to keep an eye on the car until we get there. Hey, you hear that?"

They heard it before they saw it—the familiar tonal quality of their own vehicle was as recognizable to Remo and Chiun as a particular human voice. It was coming closer on the next block. First an unfamiliar SUV tore down the street, glimpsed briefly between the houses, and then Chiun's SUV came a few hundred feet behind it.

"Bring it!" Chiun snapped, waving at the Airstream.

"No way."

"You would leave behind my Castle Sinanju on Wheels?" Chiun squeaked.

"We'll come back and get it later."

"You will bring my precious home!" Chiun said hotly. "Waste no more time protesting." Then the old Master was gone in a flash of silk robes.

Remo found himself being regarded by a frumpy, elderly woman in a plastic hair bonnet, standing crookedly on a nearby front porch.

"And I'm supposed to be the frigging Reigning Master," Remo snapped at her, making the old woman wince.

"You get out of here. I'm calling the police."

"See? See? Even old ladies from Berwyn go around telling me what to do." Remo grabbed the hitch of the Airstream and dragged it along behind him. The autolevelers struggled. The autobrakes screeched and crumbled, and soon Remo was jogging along at forty-five miles per hour.

He reached an intersection, where he stopped at a red light and searched up and down the through street. No Chiun. No familiar SUVs. Him standing there hauling a camper like a buffoon.

"Forget it!" he announced, and dropped the hitch. The Airstream's autolevelers were now dangling and useless, and the RV fell onto the hitch with a clang.

Remo stepped atop the nearest lamppost and found himself forty feet up. From here he could see farther in all directions, but if the pursuit had crossed into the next neighborhood, he'd never spot them among the green, budding trees.

There was a flash of color far to the north on the through street. Chiun's robe. Remo stepped onto the roof of a three-story building. It was a long step and Remo landed hard, and felt a menagerie of agonies along his back and butt and the back of his legs.

That made him aware suddenly what Chiun was up to.

MASTER CHIUN WAS ancient and tiny and weighed no more than a child, and yet he was a force of nature. Like a hurricane. Like an earthquake. Like an avalanche.

He spirited among the pedestrians, then became airborne, landing atop the Grand Cherokee like a collapsing mountain. The roof caved in under his weight, and at that moment Oscar Bedders slammed his foot on the gas. He swerved around traffic and tore through a red light. He heard the wail of car horns melding with screaming tires, and he tapped the brakes just right. One of the skidding cars sideswiped his own rear end with a jolt, then Bedders sped up again.

Whoever had crashed onto his vehicle had to be throw off by now.

Chiun's balance was never compromised, even when the other vehicle jolted the car. He kneeled above the driver's seat and punctured the roof with a stiff, flat hand, then grasped the head of the driver and twisted it powerfully. The driver's neck was twisted apart and the connective tissues in his neck were severed.

The car swerved off the road, but Chiun didn't leap from the roof. He twisted harder. He had to see this thing utterly destroyed—then claws of iron sank into his own forearm. Chiun withdrew his arm, dragging the driver's head along with him. The pain of the piercing fingers were as nothing to his need to end this monster's existence.

The front of the SUV jumped a curb and slammed down again, much slowed, then crunched to a halt against the concrete base of a signpost. As the claws sought to rend his arm to pieces, Chiun yanked the skull of the creature into the roof, damaging his own hand but crushing the head, too. He would worry them both until the head was turned to pulp or his own hand was ruined.

There was a sound like moving slime. Chiun knew the sound, and his eyes beheld the tentacles that stretched from the broken side windows of the Jeep. They sought *him.*

Chiun snapped at the tentacles with his sandals, turning them to pulp, but more tentacles were coming. More and more. Chiun beat them off with his feet and attempted to free his hand from the roof of the SUV, but the driver hauled him back in, up to the shoulder.

Chiun twisted his body through a somersault that left him on his knees, facing the tentacles, then slashed at them with his bare hands. His fingers were tipped with fingernails as sharp as steel scalpels and twice as strong. He tore into the tentacles as his other hand sliced and mangled any flesh it could come into contact with inside the vehicle.

The tentacles dropped off until the remaining ones withdrew, and hissing complaints came from inside. The struggles of the driver grew slack, and Chiun jabbed his hand down into the driver's body, blindly trying to pierce its vital anatomy.

Then Chiun became stiff and unmoving, except for his widening eyes and his gaping mouth. There was pain, such pain as he could hardly remember, and the dancing bolts of yellow fire penetrated his arm like white-hot nails being forced through to his old bones.

14

"It's the old Chink! He jumped on top of the Jeep! Oh, shit! How'd he do that! He's staying up there! He's punching a hole in the damned roof! They're crashing!" Roy Candace was not providing CURE with the most efficient field report. "Jumpin' Jesus!"

"What is happening, Roy?" Sarah prodded him firmly. She was pacing among the desks with a hand on her headset as Mark Howard and Harold Smith multitasked on their computers.

The video cameras on the SUV were mostly on the interior. The 360-degree roof-mounted video pickup was meant to monitor the driver's comings and goings, and Smith was getting only confusing, blurry images when he tried to focus on the battle. Howard was calling in police from Berwyn and every surrounding jurisdiction, even summoning Illinois State Police from their speed traps on the nearest tollway.

"That's right—secure the area," Howard was telling someone. "Keep everyone away from the vehicles. Yes, even police!"

"Roy, describe what is happening, right now," Sarah asked gently into her headset.

"Sweetie, you ain't gonna fucking believe it."

"Roy—"

"Snakes! Snakes are getting the old man! He's trapped! Wait a sec—he's cuttin' the snakes' heads off. Oh, God, them ain't snakes at all. What the holy hell on earth and Mary Mother of my sainted aunt—"

"Roy, snap out of it!"

"Sorry, sweetie. Oh, God, the old man is fryin'!"

Sarah Slate looked up. Smith was hearing all of it, but was engrossed in multiple activities. Mark Howard could only afford her the briefest glimpse, but there was some comfort in it. He knew she loved the old man. Then he, too, was back at work, and she had nothing to rest her eyes on except the pounding waters of Long Island Sound and the bleak interior of the office.

"Roy?" she asked gently.

"Aw, hell, he's just fryin'!"

15

Remo stepped off the top of a shoe store and just fell. He didn't try to make his landing soft. He didn't try to be any freaking bird. He just fell, and he landed hard. His body weight pushed the front of the Jeep down until the fenders crunched on the ground.

The impact was enough to put a stop to the energy discharge. Chiun went limp on the roof.

The driver's head was flopped over on its side, but it twisted around and straightened, the vertebrae knitting together, the ghastly face growing a grin at the sight of Remo.

Remo hit the face. He used his fist and everything else in his body, smashing through the window and into the face and through the seat and through the plastic wall of the big cooler behind it. Remo felt chill water and slimy invertebrate flesh. He sank his fingers into squid flesh and yanked it through the opening he'd made. The squid was dragged through the middle of the face. The squid grabbed at his wrist; Remo flicked it away. The squid landed with a soggy sound on a sidewalk.

The driver was flapping his hands mindlessly behind the wheel and no longer had a lock on Chiun's forearm. Remo extracted himself from the Jeep and jumped to Chiun, pulling him free. He leaped with the old man, as limp and light as a toy doll in his arms.

SARAH SLATE HEARD the car door open, then close.

"Roy? You still with me?"

"Uh."

"Roy, what is happening now?" she asked urgently.

"Tell her, Roy," Remo snapped.

"The guy and…the old guy are here," Roy stammered.

"What's their condition?"

"Uh."

She heard Chiun then, but he sounded feeble and a hundred miles away. "Where have you left my RV?"

"That's good enough for me," Remo declared.

"Wait," Chiun pleaded in a near whisper, but the door was opened and closed again.

Sarah heard Chiun say nothing more.

BEDDERS'S SUV CLUNKED into reverse, and it lurched away from the concrete base of the signpost. The scrambled eggs of Oscar Bedders's face somehow grew an eyeball that focused on Remo, then swiveled to the squid hatchling on the ground. Remo raced to the hatchling and stomped on its gelatinous head.

Bedders's face dropped open. It didn't look much

like a mouth, but out of the opening came an ugly howl that spoke of his displeasure. Bedders yanked the SUV into gear and raced onto the street, swerved through the mayhem of police cars and stopped traffic and was gone.

Remo couldn't have caught it. He knew better than to even try. At this point, he could barely stand.

16

Roy Candace was in some weird, dangerous place, where he never thought he would be.

Whatever these two guys were in his backseat, they weren't something he'd ever even *heard* of before. He wanted to get out of there and just start running away. Part of him was afraid that they would kill him on the spot. He was sure they could do it. Part of him was too intrigued—he just had to know what was going on.

So he did what he was told. He drove. He kept his mouth shut and he kept his ears open.

"We need the specimen," said the voice of a sour man over the SUV speakers. "Dispatch it at once."

"After nap time," the younger man responded glumly. That was the one who had jumped off a building. Roy kept picturing it. Jumped off a fucking building. On purpose and could still kick some ass after he did it.

"We must analyze the hatchling," intoned the sour man.

"Hey, Smitty, maybe you haven't been paying attention," the younger man said angrily. "We just got spindled and mutilated. I've got more bleeding scabs than a kid with chicken pox, and Chiun just stuck his tongue in a wall socket."

"He lies, Emperor. It was my arm that received the shocking attack, and it was not from being inserted into a wall socket."

Huh? Roy thought. Smitty? Emperor?

"You will ship the specimen at once," intoned the man who sounded as if he sucked on lemons.

"Roy!" the younger man bellowed. It was a hair-raising, bone-jarring sound like rocks sliding through the interior of the SUV. "Go there! Now!"

Roy was hardly holding on to his bodily functions, but somehow he managed to steer the SUV into the strip mall and park at a No Parking sign in front of the E-Z-Ship-It.

"Remo," said the sour voice with great weariness, "you cannot be seen in public as you are. Send in your driver."

Roy happened to glance in the rearview mirror as the younger one, called Remo, gave the finger to the ceiling light.

"I saw that," said the sour man.

But Remo was already leaving.

THE E-Z-SHIP-IT CLERK WAS alarmed by the slim, dark-haired, dark-eyed man. He was in tattered pants and a shredded shirt, which was soaked with blood spreading from many wounds. What was truly attention grabbing, however, was the mass of slime in his left hand.

It was as big as a beach ball and the dangling slimy parts were tentacles—yes, tentacles, with suckers and everything. It was oozing gore and had clearly been through as much violence as the man.

Holly Nott stared at the thing, then at the man, then back at the thing.

"Maybe you have a garbage bag or something?" the man said.

She hurriedly found a clear plastic bag and offered it gingerly.

"Thanks," he said, then glanced at her lapel name tag. "Holly," he added.

For some reason, it thrilled her when he said her name.

"We can't ship this," she said.

"Yeah, you can."

"I'd really like to help you, really. But there's restrictions against shipping, well, dead things."

"Call it calamari. Put it on dry ice."

"Foodstuffs must be *frozen* before you ship them."

"How's this different from a lobster in a box that they advertise on TV? This is all in your computer, anyway."

To her amazement, Holly found it was in her computer. Special privilege granted to her, Holly Nott, for the shipment of fresh biological specimen via special courier.

"This is very out of the ordinary," she said. "But I'm thrilled to be able to help you, Mr....?"

"I'm thrilled, too."

"I need your name as the sender."

"Remo. Remo Bumpass."

"And where are you shipping the calamari?"

"Hell if I know. It's in there. Right?"

In fact, it was in the computer. The shipping address, the shipper's address, the name of the special courier company that would pick it up. The funds to be transferred to Holly Nott's E-Z-Ship-It franchise were already paid—and were substantial.

"I guess the only thing that needs taking care of now is you, Mr. Bumpass," Holly said.

"Yeah. Thanks."

"You need some tender loving care."

"Okay, then."

"I'm bursting with TLC, Remo." Holly Nott straightened her back, throwing back her curly tumble of lustrous brown hair. Her smile was wide. Her shirt buttons strained.

"Thanks anyway."

Her face fell.

"Rain check, Holly? I'll look you up again, next time I'm in Berwyn. I swear."

Her smile came back on again and her mysterious customer left, dripping blood and leaving Holly alone with her bagged-and-boxed biological specimen.

She hoped it didn't infect her with anything.

Now Remo Bumpass was another story—she'd swap germs with that bad boy any day of the week.

17

Harold W. Smith had always been a step ahead of the current technology. To keep CURE at the forefront of intelligence-gathering, it was a necessity. Still, it became more difficult with every passing year.

A couple of decades ago, the state of the art was set by the Pentagon and the CIA. Then came a small community of university scientists who got the idea to share information over telephone lines. They began moving files of information from one computer to another. It sped up data processing, which reduced delays in research. Harold W. Smith was quick to see the potential of these file-transfer protocols. He became one of the world's first Internet users.

Soon the world's intelligence agencies were using similar systems to connect and share data. Some genius even got the idea of putting electronic padlocks on their data, restricting access only to parties with special clearance.

Harold W. Smith was making use of these files, and needed to continue making use of these files, regardless of the fact that he didn't have legal clearance to use them. So he found ways to bypass the electronic padlocks. He became one of the world's first hackers.

The number of systems grew, and in those days he was just one man, assembling electronic data, as well as data from many field agents—none of whom knew they actually worked for CURE. Smith needed a way to identify data. He created a program to collect key words from field reports and remote files and sort them, store them, make them available when he needed to find them. He created some of the first Internet search engines.

As the Internet grew, he appropriated as much technology as he invented, and soon he was running vast pattern-analysis routines, which devoured top secret international intelligence briefings and small-town police reports with equal voracity.

But instead of a small community of researchers, Smith was now racing to stay ahead of thousands of Internet development firms. In this, Mark Howard was a godsend. Mark had grown up with home computers and was more attuned to the twenty-first-century digital age than Smith could ever hope to be. Mark Howard had put in self-evolving systems to let the CURE computers do their own programming to meet their own needs at any given microsecond. A lot of oversight was still needed.

But then there were the times when human intervention was almost beside the point.

Right now, CURE was in wait-and-see mode. Smith could scan the reams of data flowing across his many windows, but there was nothing for him to actually do.

Mark Howard was resting. He would take the overnight watch for Smith if no progress was made before then. Somewhere, in a north-central Illinois campground, Remo and Chiun were resting in Chiun's Airstream camper. They each claimed to be only slightly injured. Smith knew better than to take their reassurances at face value.

Their driver, the unexpectedly useful Roy Candace, was sleeping, too, stretched out in the rear of the SUV.

Sarah Slate was wide awake, wearing her headphones, but relaxed on Smith's battered old sofa and reading a magazine.

Who would have thought Roy Candace or Sarah Slate would turn out to be truly useful? Not that there was any similarity between the two of them.

Sarah yawned, then held up her magazine and looked at him questioningly.

"Cosmo?"

"No. Thank you. You might as well call it a night. Mr. Candace seems settled in."

She said good-night and left with a smile.

Useful, yes, but she was just too *nice.*

IN FACT, THAT BABE WAS so nice it was irritating. Roy Candace couldn't decide half the time if he wanted to nail that girlie or if he wanted to backhand her precious face.

Nancy always knew exactly where he was and the radio was wired somehow so she could give her orders over the SUV's sound system. If he was playing the radio it would just go silent all of a sudden and there she would be.

"Good morning, Roy," she said that morning, just as he woke up in a campground a few hours west of Chicago. He always slept on an air mattress in the rear of the SUV, as per orders. He was sure they had hidden cameras spying on him. In fact, they'd come right out and told him from the start that he would be under constant surveillance. This was right after they made it clear to him that he was to follow his instructions exactly if he expected to be paid.

"That means you'll be living in the vehicle all day, every day," Nancy told him when she recruited him, over the phone at his Buffalo, New York, apartment. "You will be allowed to leave the vehicle for only minutes at a time, for visits to the men's room. Is that understood?"

"For the money you're paying me, I'd stay inside all the time and pee in a cup, honey bunch."

"My name is Nancy, Roy."

"Sure thing, sugar."

Man, it was harder than he ever thought, though, being stuck inside the SUV all the time. His ass was chafed from sitting and his legs were cramped constantly. He looked forward to just getting out and pacing alongside the SUV for five minutes an hour.

"You must stay close by at all times, so as to be prepared to react instantly to the needs of your passenger,
Roy," Nancy had explained.

The campground was quiet. Not many guests this
early in the season.

"This would sure be a lot less a chore if I had company," Roy suggested as he stretched.

"Absolutely not, Roy. You remember the bargain.
You cannot tell anyone about your employment."

"What about you, sugarloaf? I guarantee you a real
good time. It'll be a lot of laughs."

"Roy," Nancy chided him, "you don't know anything about me. What if you found out I was old enough
to be your mother?"

Roy chortled. "Nancine, my sweet, I bet you ain't
thirty years old. I can tell, just from how you talk. And I
bet you're cute to boot. So why not come on and keep
me company? Then you can tell me what to do in person."

"Hmm."

"You're tempted, I can tell."

HAROLD W. SMITH SAID nothing. Sarah Slate smiled and
cut the connection on her headset.

"Are you leading him on?" Smith asked.

"It's his proposition. I'm just not dissuading him,"
she explained. She had been strolling around the office
as she communicated with the driver, and now she
leaned on the wall near the glass picture window that

looked out at Long Island Sound. "A little flirting keeps him going."

The tiny tilt Smith gave his head was as good as a shrug. He couldn't argue with the young woman's results. Roy Candace had been in the job for almost a week—twice as long as any of Master Chiun's previous drivers.

CURE HAD AGREED to hire Chiun's drivers when he made known his intentions of embarking on a road trip. Smith disapproved. In fact, he wanted the RV gone.

But he knew better than to fight it. Chiun had been denied his Airstream for months. Any suggestion that he would be better off without it was simply ignored. Chiun wanted his RV. Smith knew he ought to be satisfied that the Master had agreed to restoring the peculiar hybrid to a less-conspicuous condition.

So when Chiun decided to go traveling, and without Remo, Smith had no choice but to become involved. He couldn't have Chiun driving it himself. Putting the Master of Sinanju Emeritus behind the wheel of any vehicle was a prescription for trouble. Driving the overpowered SUV and towing the Airstream would be guaranteed disaster.

Hiring a driver was problematic in itself, in that it was a guaranteed death sentence. Master Chiun was not the easiest man to work with.

Therefore, CURE chose hired drivers who wouldn't be missed. The sad truth was, there was no shortage of

Get FREE BOOKS and a FREE GIFT when you play the...

LAS VEGAS GAME

7

Just scratch off the gold box with a coin. Then check below to see the gifts you get! →

YES! I have scratched off the gold box. Please send me my **2 FREE BOOKS** and **gift for which I qualify**. I understand that I am under no obligation to purchase any books as explained on the back of this card.

366 ADL D749

166 ADL D747
(MB-05R)

FIRST NAME   LAST NAME

ADDRESS

APT.#   CITY

STATE/PROV.   ZIP/POSTAL CODE

| 7 | 7 | 7 | Worth TWO FREE BOOKS plus a BONUS Mystery Gift! |

Worth TWO FREE BOOKS!

TRY AGAIN!

Offer limited to one per household and not valid to current Gold Eagle® subscribers. All orders subject to approval.

NO POSTAGE
NECESSARY
IF MAILED
IN THE
UNITED STATES

BUSINESS REPLY MAIL
FIRST-CLASS MAIL   PERMIT NO. 717-003   BUFFALO, NY

POSTAGE WILL BE PAID BY ADDRESSEE

GOLD EAGLE READER SERVICE
3010 WALDEN AVE
PO BOX 1867
BUFFALO NY 14240-9952

men on the streets of America who deserved to serve in the employ of the old Master.

Sal Hiberus was the first driver. He took delivery of the RV and drove Chiun to his first stop at Schenectady, NY. What possessed Chiun to visit such a place was beyond Smith's ability to reason. All Smith knew was that Sal Hiberus met his maker in Schenectady. From what Chiun said, Sal entered and exited the SUV in a manner that was inconsiderate.

"I cannot be expected to be at peace in a dwelling that is being bounced about every minute," Chiun pointed out reasonably.

"He was just getting out to stretch his legs," Mark Howard said.

"I must disagree, young prince. He was a dullard who was overawed by the Master of Sinanju. This elicited the petty wickedness in the man. He deliberately and maliciously jostled my Castle Sinanju on Wheels."

"I honestly don't think he did it deliberately"

"Deliberately, and maliciously, jostled," Chiun stated, and then he severed the connection.

Sal Hiberus was—had been—a petty crook with a few sick tendencies. He liked to organize bands of drug addicts to commit armed robbery. He'd provide lots of free crack, get them wasted and send them wired to rob liquor stores, convenience stories and even a few banks. If they got killed or caught, then all he'd lost was some cheap drugs. If they came back, he'd call for a celebration that usually ended up in a lethal overdose for everyone involved—except Sal. Sal never touched the stuff.

A few of his partners had actually succeeded in their robbery attempts, then tried to flee the scene without giving Sal his share. Sal always found them in the end. Hard-core addicts were creatures of habit, never straying far from their supply sources. They always paid for their backstabbing. Always.

Sal hardly ever paid. He spent a couple of years in prison once, but charges didn't stick to him too often. Lack of evidence. Improper police procedure during the arrest. A couple thousand bucks for the judge.

CURE knew all about Sal Hiberus, which was why he was chosen for the job. He could serve a purpose, then be removed from the planet forever.

Sal met his match in the ancient Korean gentlemen. An annoyed Chiun stepped from the Airstream and approached the driver's-side window. Sal rolled it down. The old Korean gentleman stuck a finger deep into Sal's brain and withdrew it so quickly his finger didn't even need to be wiped clean.

Pete Brock was next. Like Sal, he was the kind of man who would take on an unusual job without knowing his employers—just as long as the money was up front. He found the Airstream camper right where it was supposed to be, in the KAC Campground just outside Middleburg. He found the SUV keys in the ignition. The floor was littered with food wrappers. The back was stuffed with canned goods and coolers full of food. It smelled bad, but Pete Brock saw no sign of the driver he was replacing.

That was because there was no sign to see. Not a droplet of blood had spilled from the wound that terminated Sal Hiberus. Sal's mortal remains had been neatly compacted and bagged and placed in the large trash bin. Sal, and all the rest of the trash, had already been landfilled.

Other changes took place before Pete's arrival. An engineering team arrived at the campground to outfit the Airstream with an electric tow disconnection device, which worked in tandem with the electric self-leveling gear. None of it was even dreamed-of technology when the Airstream first rolled off the assembly line, fifty years before.

Pete Brock drove to the next destination and parked the camper in a woodsy little campground a half hour west of Syracuse. With the push of a button, the Airstream disconnected itself from the SUV. Pete wasn't allowed to actually drive away in it, but he could at least get in and out of the SUV without jostling the Airstream.

Pete Brock lived for a full forty-six hours as the driver for the Master of Sinanju. His passenger ignored him utterly. When a cab came to get the man the next morning, he didn't even glance in Brock's direction, nor did he when he returned a few hours later. The old geezer might be blind.

"Keep your television down," intoned the sour, unpleasant man who issued Brock his orders. It was after eight in the evening and Brock was about to pull his hair out from boredom.

"Sure thing." Brock turned the TV down not at all. He could barely hear it himself. And what else was he supposed to do all day if he couldn't watch TV?

An hour later, Brock heard, "You will turn your television to a lower volume." It was the sourpuss who gave the orders.

"Look, there is no way in hell nobody can hear my TV," Pete protested. "Even I can hardly hear it."

"Your passenger can hear it."

"Fine!" Brock turned the volume down, waited a few minutes and then turned it back up. Just enough so he could actually hear the jokes. Why watch a sitcom if you couldn't hear the jokes? Ray Romano lost a bet and had to attend a neighborhood block party in drag. His wife thought he was at a friend's house and she was at the party, too. She would surely know it was Ray under the wig and false eyelashes if she encountered him. Could he keep away from his wife throughout the party? Could he pass himself off as a woman to all the other guests? The comedic tension was as thick as pea soup.

Pete Brock never learned the fate of Ray Romano. Brock died before the canned laughter did, and by the time the closing credits finished rolling, he was stretched thin and slipped inside a section of concrete pipe that lay by the roadside for installation the next morning. The pipe was jettisoned out into the dark night, far out over Oneida Lake. The lake bottom mud sucked in the pipe and Pete Brock was never found.

Another petty killer-rapist-thug removed from society. Another one took his place behind the wheel of Chiun's SUV. And another.

"They'd live longer if they listened to directions," Mark Howard complained. Each of the hired thugs earned his assassination by violating the strict but simple rules set forth by CURE. "And we're making a point of hiring the *smart* ones."

"Let me be the liaison," Sarah Slate suggested, placing a hand on Mark's shoulder and leaning over to see the next name on his screen. "Roy Candace. I'll be his contact."

"Why?" Mark Howard asked.

"Because I can do better. You and Dr. Smith aren't having any success. All you have to offer them is money. I've got charm."

Mark couldn't argue with that.

18

Remo Williams woke feeling achy but better. A solid night's rest had done him wonders. It was good, too, to have semifresh air to breathe. The campground was wooded and removed from any big cities, and the air was less polluted than the air of their suite at Folcroft Sanitarium, which had become their de facto dwelling place, again, for the time being.

The camper wasn't terrible, but it sure wasn't home, either. Even Chiun would tire of it soon enough, Remo hoped.

He lay on his mat listening to the Master of Sinanju Emeritus snoring softly. Sometimes he didn't snore softly, but of late his raucous midnight snorts had toned down somewhat.

This worried Remo.

Why should he care about Chiun's snoring? Was it just one more sign that his mentor was getting old?

Remo almost laughed aloud. *Getting* old? Chiun was *always* old as far as Remo was concerned—Chiun was in his eighties at their first meeting many long years ago.

Sinanju Masters lived inordinately long lives. They could have set world records if the people who kept the records got wind of them. But the Masters didn't live forever.

And there were the signs. Some obvious, such as Chiun's surrendering of the title of Reigning Master in recent years. Others were subtle. Like quieter snoring.

How much longer did Chiun have?

Remo mentally shook the thought away. It was point-less to consider. Chiun was still strong, clearheaded, sharp-eyed. He could star as Grandpa in *The Incredibles II*. They could cast him as the despicable geezer supervillain in a Spider-Man movie and they'd save millions on special effects.

Remo wandered outside. The campground had just opened for the season and it was too early and too cold for the families. The Airstream had the entire section of sites to itself. Remo stretched carefully, testing his injuries, and gradually increased the difficulty of his contortions. He rested in a lotus position, but balanced on the toes of one foot.

A teenager in a Bogey Bear outfit wandered by, looking for kids to entertain. The campground was named after Bellystone Park in Bogey Bear cartoons. Never mind that the cartoons were as old as Remo and kids these days had no clue who Bogey Bear was.

"Come one step closer and I will assassinate you," Remo told the costumed kid, who hastily veered off in the other direction. The look in Remo's eyes told the kid he just might not be bluffing.

"Fah!" said a voice from inside the Airstream. "Is there no peace for the old man, whose body is near dead from exhaustion?" Chiun appeared in the door of the Airstream, glowering. "First you shake the house like a drunken mule, then you stand outside the poor old man's domicile shouting at passersby."

"I tiptoed out quietly and I didn't raise my voice to the bear kid, and you're the healthiest AARP-card-carrier that ever lived."

"This gives you an excuse to wake me from my peaceful slumber?"

"If I woke you, it's because you have us sleeping in a tin rattletrap." For emphasis, Remo nudged the Airstream with one finger. Its stabilizers not yet repaired, the camper rocked on its wheels to a cacophony of creaks and groans.

Chiun sighed. "As long as we are awake, we shall make use of our time."

"Breakfast?" Remo asked.

"Later."

REMO NEVERTHELESS ATTEMPTED to prepare breakfast as the driver hauled them to their next, unknown destination.

"There's lots of rice, but no water," Remo said.

"Yes," Chiun agreed.

"Why no water?"

"The taste is foul when the water resides in a tank."

"Oh." Remo returned to the pantry as Chiun sat cross-legged on his mat in the rear bunk area, where the mattress was removed. Chiun was meditating amid a swirl of light through the multifaceted windows.

Remo opened more cabinets and found them empty. The fridge was ice cold and completely empty.

"Why didn't you buy bottled water?" he asked from the doorway of the bunkroom.

"I did."

"Where is it?"

"Used up."

"I'll just have our driver stop at a convenience store."

"Our destination is a store. At this store there will be water, and you may buy some."

"What kind of a store?"

"You ask too many questions. Soon enough you will learn what kind of a store."

19

"A *French* store?" Remo said.

"It is faux French."

"Even worse. Why are we here?"

"So that you may buy water," Chiun reminded him.

"I don't want French water."

"Then wait in the vehicle."

Remo had no intention of staying in the Airstream, and he followed Chiun outside.

"You shall be tagging along?" Chiun demanded. "I supposed I have no choice in this? You may serve a purpose, at least."

Chiun opened a storage hatch that was built into the belly of the Airstream. The hatch was tightly packed with narrow cardboard boxes, a yard long.

"What's this?" Remo asked.

"Your burden." Chiun flipped a box at Remo, who palmed the narrow edge. It weighed little, and the label was printed in pink characters. There was some English printing, as well: Proudly Manufactured By Koh-Mo-No Enterprises, Ltd.

"Are these those kimonos you were telling the doctor about?"

Chiun said nothing as he walked across the acres of retail parking lot.

"Is this Japanese?" Remo said, trying to make out the Asian characters.

"None of your business," Chiun said, without turning.

"What in the world are you up to, Little Father?"

The only answer he got was the back of Chiun's head as they strolled into the front entrance of the Tarjé (Paris) Discount Superstore.

Tarjé (Paris) was a rising star in the mass-merchandising arena. Tarjé was convinced that consumers were tired of buying the cheapest-possible merchandise, as sold by other discount chains. Tarjé offered the illusion of an upscale alternative.

"Looks like the same bottom-of-the-barrel crap to me," Remo said. "What makes it French?"

"This," Chiun said, waving at the cobblestone-print floor tile. "And this." He waved next at the plastic grapevines adhered to sales signs.

"You hate places like this," Remo pointed out. "Why are we here?"

"We have been over this and over this," Chiun said, thrusting a single finger at a pyramid of bottled water. "Purchase your water."

Chiun relieved Remo of the cardboard box, then scampered off. Remo grumbled as he snatched up several gallons of Oui Oui Water and headed for the checkout.

AT THE FRONT of the store was a parklike bench, where Chiun found Remo waiting, cross-legged. A tower of five-gallon bottles of water was balanced on each knee, and bridging the top of the tower was a plastic bag filled with clothing. The water bottles seemed to defy gravity.

The clerks at nearby cash registers were keeping a worried eye on the strange display. A janitor waited nearby with a mop and bucket.

"Tsk. You have nothing better to do than make a spectacle of yourself?"

"Matter of fact, I was doing research," Remo said. "Checking out the kinds of clothes the kids these days are buying."

"Ah." A high-pitched lilt revealed Chiun's interest.

Remo stepped to his feet. The towers of water bottles were momentarily airborne, with daylight showing between them. The bag of clothes toppled from its perch on top of the bottles. Clerks and customers gasped and the janitor covered his eyes with his arm.

Remo tucked the shopping bag under one arm and balanced the water bottles, still stacked, on either palm as they headed for the exit.

Chiun said, "And what have you concluded? Are there any new trends in fashion that might persuade you to update your own uniform of cheap underwear and overpriced shoes?"

"Naw," Remo said. "They're still wearing low-rise jeans and eighties retro. Some fashion pioneers appeared to be buying Asian silk robes, of all things. And leg warmers are back, too, I guess."

"How many were purchased?" Chiun asked.

"Maybe six, eight pairs. Never saw the point in them myself. Who gets cold calves, anyway?"

"Not the warm-leggers! The Asian robes you spoke of. How many?"

"Two buyers."

Chiun frowned. "How many each did they purchase?"

"Just one Koh-Mo-No each."

"I see." Chiun was disappointed.

"So what's the deal, anyway, Chiun? Why are you in the kimono-selling business now? It's not like you. Are we broke?"

"I am not broke, although you could use repairs."

"You know what I mean. Are we low on cash?" The idea seemed ludicrous to Remo. From what he understood, the wealth of the House of Sinanju was Bill Gates-ian in its immensity.

"It is not for money. Think you that a Master of Sinanju would stoop to trading cheap wares for profit?"

No answer was forthcoming. In the camper, Remo opened a bottle of Oui Oui Water and sniffed it, finding it reasonably free of taint. He poured it into a pot on the stove and lit the burner.

"Use the rice maker," Chiun scolded. "It is perfected with electronics to sense the doneness of the rice."

"Where?"

Chiun indicated a sleek gizmo bolted to the counter-top.

"I thought that was a computer."

"It is computerized, but the electronics are dedicated to the one purpose of making rice."

Remo examined the appliance and prodded the likely hidden panels. It beeped angrily at him and stayed shut.

"I'll use the stove," Remo said. "So you're a sweat-shop entrepreneur now, eh?"

Chiun didn't respond.

"I'm confused, Chiun. I can't think of *any* reason you'd want to be a wholesaler for cheap bathrobes. You want the whole country looking like bad Sinanju knock-offs?"

Remo turned away from the water pot and looked squarely at Chiun. "Huh."

"*Huh* in this context means that the rice is done?"

"*Huh* means *oh*. I get it. I understand what you're try-ing to do," Remo said.

"It is unlikely you understand much."

"You want to create a kimono fashion trend. You want lots of people wearing Asian robes so you don't stand out."

"Is the rice done or is it not?"

"I know Smitty's been coming down on you pretty hard about the robes," Remo said sympathetically.

"It is unreasonable to expect a Master of Sinanju, steeped in tradition, to perform his duties in the garments of a Westerner," Chiun conceded. Harold Smith had lately started hinting that Chiun was a bad security risk because of his manner of dress. Few people walked around America in Asian robes; fewer still were elderly men. Chiun couldn't keep himself invisible to the public all the time and he was bound to attract attention.

"So that's why?"

Chiun regarded him. "I will tell you of Master Hyun Huk. Huk who was wise, and yet he is known as Huk the Inconsolable."

"Always wondered about that," Remo said.

"Ah. It means he was incurably mournful."

"I know what *inconsolable* means. But what made him that way? The scrolls don't say."

Chiun pondered this. "You're guessing. You have forgotten Huk, but you seek to hide your ignorance by feigning knowledge."

"Am not."

"The scrolls in fact do not say. The story, though, is well-known to all Sinanju Masters."

"All two of us? Not me."

"Huk lived in a time when there was little strife between the kingdoms known to Sinanju, meaning that there was a scarcity of need for our skills. A most unfortunate time."

"Peace sure sucks."

"Don't scoff. But there is little enough of such times in all of history. Like the rare alignment of many heavenly spheres, periods of true harmony are rare in the cycles of time. At such times, when wars are few and even the intrigues that benefit from the assassin's touch are infrequent, Sinanju Masters are forced to strive more ambitiously to earn their gold."

"Most foul," Remo said. "Glad I live in an age of nonstop strife and horrendousness."

"Your sarcasm falls on deaf ears, but you should indeed be happy in this regard. In one aspect of your training are you grievously undereducated, Remo Williams—self-promotion. You have never been forced to seek out employment. Many Sinanju Masters live all their lives traveling from place to place, always in search of gainful employment. You do not know what a blessing it is to have steady employment that pays good gold. Sadly, it is a lesson I cannot teach. Only need can instill motivation to make oneself known and needed."

"I could take a marketing class at Rye Community College."

"Hush. I was speaking of Huk the Inconsolable. He who was forced to seek employment in the least desirable kingdoms. He went to the Keltoi, who were crude tin mongers and nothing more, and who dressed in scraped hides and poor woolens. Fierce they were in battle, and ruthless in their wiles, and they used all means to take their riches. Tribe after tribe fought against each other, then banded to battle the Romans, defeated them and fell upon one another again. Here, Huk found many tasks that paid good gold, but he was forced to hide who he was—Sinanju, Korean and man of dignity. So rife with spies and traitors were these dismal Galatian courts, and so mean and uncivilized in their ways, that he could not appear as a Master of Sinanju."

Remo was staring at the rice pot. Without thinking about it, he was sensing the amount of steam and heat seeping from under the lid. It would tell him exactly when was the best moment to serve the rice.

"Was he, you know, slow?"

"There is no such thing as a slow Master of Sinanju. What are you implying?" Chiun demanded.

"Why couldn't he just stay out of sight, then?" Remo asked. "Nobody had to know he was around."

Chiun shook his head. "You again show your ignorance of the daily existence of the Masters of Old. You who never needed to be present in one warlord's court after another, year after year. You have just one employer who insists on secrecy to a ludicrous degree. You are most lucky."

"Huh."

"Would you like to stay removed from all human beings for year after year, meeting with only those you are to kill and those who pay the gold to do it? Even barbarians are company, Remo. So Huk had to choose either self-imposed isolation or adopting the hideous garb of the Celtic tribes."

Chiun shook his head sadly.

"Tough choice," Remo commented.

"He did what he must do. Huk felt as if he had surrendered his identity and his dignity, but such was the sacrifice needed in those years when the Celts dominated the tin mines and held sway over all other with their trade in bronze. And a bruised dignity was a small price to pay to save the starving babies of Sinanju.

"Uh-huh," Remo said without much true sincerity. He didn't think there were babies starving in Sinanju in the time of Master Huk.

In truth, there was a time when Sinanju was a miserable place with little food and no money. What do you expect when you put a fishing village on the most barren stretch of shoreline in Korea? But it wasn't the babies' fault, though it was the babies who suffered the consequences. In the ancient past, when starvation took its miserable grip on the tiny Korean village of Sinanju, the people had "sent the babies home to the sea," which was a euphemism for infanticide.

The men of the village, skilled in the art of assassination, had gone out into the world to make their living as hired killers for any warlord, king or pharaoh who would pay them.

Sinanju prospered, at times. Even when there were many skilled Sinanju assassins plying their trade, there would always be periods of great want in the village. There was also much infighting among the Sinanju killers, as they strove among one another for control of the village.

Then came Wang, the greatest of all the Sinanju

Masters up to this time and the one who was gifted by the gods with the exemplary skills of the Sinanju Master. Wang was not just a great assassin; he was the most powerful man the earth had known until that time.

Wang slew the warring assassins of Sinanju. With his new abilities, it was like a man swatting bothersome fleas from his arm. When he completed the task, there was only one Sinanju assassin still alive, and it was Master Wang.

From that day forward, there would always be but one Reigning Master, but his skills were so great he could demand immense sums of gold for what he did, and the village of Sinanju enjoyed increasing prosperity as the Masters of Sinanju became renowned.

Remo suspected it had been ages since any Sinanju babies were sent home to the sea. In fact, the wealth of the House of Sinanju—Remo's wealth, technically— was by now so vast that the interest alone could probably sustain a never-ending buffet for the whole village for all eternity.

But the Masters of Sinanju continued to ply their trade. Remo knew the reason: unstoppable avarice. Chiun claimed it was the way of the Masters, the tradition, the culture, which should not be lost.

"A tradition of greed," Remo had decided. Still, he was one of them and he kept at it. He was a traditionalist, he guessed.

"Violating our tradition is a difficulty when one is removed from his home for year after year. Another dilemma you have never faced, my son. Forced to give up all vestiges of your home, too, makes this much harder."

Remo nodded and spooned rice into wooden bowls, then he descended onto his reed mat to eat, and Remo realized with some surprise that Chiun had stopped talking.

"That's all? What about Huk?"

"He did what he must do. This troubled him greatly. Time after time did he return to the East in search of employment with the kingdoms where he need not hide who he was, and inevitably he was forced to return to the mud pits of the Celtic realms. It robbed him of his identity and dignity until he retired to the blissful seclusion of Sinanju."

"Huh."

"And this means?" Chiun sounded not so much haughty as weary.

"You're not like Huk, Chiun," Remo said. "You're a champion of Sinanju tradition. You don't need to feel so bad just because you have to cut back on the kimonos."

"But I am different from Huk, too, in another manner. I am old—in fact, well past the age of Huk when he retired. And an old man feels the sting of traditions denied more sharply than a younger man."

"You're a young kind of old, though," Remo said. "How many supersenior citizens are into worldwide Internet stuff? You know more about computers than I do."

"I am a traditionalist at heart," Chiun said.

"So that's why the crazy Koh-Mo-No scheme."

"I admit it is a self-imposed humiliation, and yet, it shall serve its purpose," Chiun said. "Once the Koh-Mo-No becomes the fashion of the day, the Emperor will see that I do not stand out among the rabble in cheap silks. None of the peoples in the country know the difference between a fine robe and a machine-fabricated rag. It is beneath my dignity, and yet it is a better choice than to be forced to terminate our contract with the Emperor on the grounds of the incompatibility."

"That's in our contract? I must have missed it." Remo was thoughtful. "Think it'll work?"

"My plan will succeed, for my target customer is the average American white, who is unsophisticated, mundane and prone to suggestion."

"Maybe Mr. and Mrs. America have better taste than you think."

"Nonsense."

"Koh-Mo-Nos are not exactly flying off the shelves."

"They do not need to fly from the shelves or even jump from them. Simply dropping off the shelves on occasion into the wire carts of the gullible public will be sufficient. I have been offering my consultation to the merchants to enable them to better market the Koh-Mo-No."

"You haven't killed any?" Remo asked.

Chiun sniffed. "As I said, I am providing consultation."

Remo looked at the ceiling. "I guess what's really important is that people be seen wearing them."

"Obviously."

"If you want to sell them, you have to make people want them, and that means people have to be comfortable in them. They're not going to buy something unless they think it's going to be cool."

"True," Chiun agreed. "Even trendsetters of American style are merely proactive conformists."

Remo nodded. "Yeah. That's what I said. So what do other style-setters do to get attention? They promote themselves in certain ways to reach the kids these days."

Chiun frowned. "What are kids these days?"

"You know. They always talk about them. Kids these days buy more stuff than all the other people put together. Kids these days buy all the movie tickets. Kids these days buy all the clothes, set all the trends."

"And how are they different from kids before these days?"

"Huh. They're not. Kids these days are pretty much like all other kids ever were. What's important is that kids these days are the ones who are the kids right now, so they're the ones who're making all the style and trends happen. Except they're not, really. They're still doing what the corporations tell them to do."

"You spout contradictions," Chiun said. "And yet, I see in what direction you wander. You feel Koh-Mo-No Enterprises, Ltd., must capitalize on the same kind of promotional efforts as would the makers of two-hundred-dollar basketball shoes."

Remo considered that. "Who in their right mind would pay two hundred dollars for basketball shoes? Besides, I was talking about TV ads."

"Koh-Mo-No Enterprises has already retained an advertising agency. They have performed acceptably. Perhaps the executive in charge of the Koh-Mo-No account will have suggestions for reaching this audience you describe."

REMO WAS CLEANING the bowls when there was a knock on the door. Chiun did not seem surprised, which was surprising.

"Good morning, Mr. Chiun," said the sickly, skinny young woman with honey-maple hair. "Oh, hello, Remo. Good to see you again."

"Hi." Remo struggled with the face. "Sunny Johns?"

She beamed. "I'm flattered that you remember. We met at the Governor Bryant commutation ceremony last year."

"Oh, yeah." Remo nodded. "How's the guv'ner these days?"

"Still assassinated," she said brightly. "He was shot during the ceremony, remember? Never got around to delivering all those commutations. It was just as well. I sleep better."

"Ms. Johns was the maestro who orchestrated Governor Bryant's magnificent scheme," Chiun explained proudly. "Truly a masterstroke of public manipulation, regardless of how it turned out."

"Real work of art," Remo said.

"Why, thank you!" She beamed. "Do you have anything to drink?"

Remo recalled Ms. Johns from the sky box at a Chicago university arena. She was the PR account executive who dreamed up a publicity stunt to divert attention from Governor Bryant's long list of pending corruption charges. In the name of justice, he had been prepared to commute the sentences of forty killers and rapists on the theory that new technology might someday be developed to prove their innocence. Following this theory, Remo recalled, anyone and everyone convicted of a crime would be eligible for release on the grounds that new methods of evidentiary analysis could someday, maybe, prove them innocent.

What it really proved was how far the bleeding hearts could be pushed off the deep end. Bryant had intended to leave office as a worldwide human-rights hero, then get rich from speaking fees for years to come. He never got around to cashing in, as his head was blown off minutes before he could perpetrate the fiasco. Still, Chiun had been impressed by the young woman who got the public to swallow the story. In fact, he took her card when they met that day.

Remo poured Ms. Johns a tall glass of Oui Oui Water. She protected it like her firstborn as she labored to get in a sitting position on the floor. When she sipped from the glass she almost gagged and rolled her eyes at Remo.

"Strongest stuff we have in the place," he said. Ms. Johns, he remembered, enjoyed her liquids in a much more high-proof state. She struggled to swallow the plain water, then placed the glass on the counter above her head.

"We were discussing methods of reaching the kids these days," Chiun said. "White American juveniles are impressionable and dull witted, but flush with cash, making them the logical market for the Koh-Mo-No."

Remo hadn't said that, exactly. He didn't think any American kid in his or her right mind was going to get conned into wearing cheesy, generically Asian kimonos. He kept the thought to himself.

"We've been working on the young-people demographic," Sunny said. "All our television ads are targeting teens and twentysomethings."

Chiun smiled. "You see, Remo, Ms. Johns is a professional in her field."

"We're getting a good return on our budget," Ms. Johns said. "Of course, we can't afford advertising on *The OC* or anything."

"My son believes we must try other promotional activities."

"We talked about product giveaways," Ms. Johns said. "Also, I thought we might get Mr. Chiun on some radio shows."

"That might cause problems," Remo said quickly.

"What of placing signs in concert arenas?" Chiun posed, recalling Sunny's successful turnout at the university auditorium. "I have heard of firms that sponsor traveling musical acts."

"Well, that's doable, sure, but it takes hundreds of thousands of dollars to promote a concert tour by a major act," Sunny said. "It would take months to put together a deal."

"I have not months, but days," Chiun said. "What other sorts of young-people gatherings could serve Koh-Mo-No Enterprises?"

Sunny moved her mouth around thoughtfully, and Remo decided she would be attractive if her eyeballs and pores weren't oozing poison.

"Spring break," Remo suggested. "It's going on now."

Chiun was deadly serious. "Tell me of this break."

"You know, college kids letting off steam during their week off from school," Remo said. "They go to Cancun or Florida and get drunk and then the guys yell at the girls to take their shirts off."

Chiun's brow was wrinkled in thought. "I see."

"Lots of advertising," Remo added.

"You attended a gathering such as this?"

"Naw," Remo said.

"Sure," Sunny mumbled. They looked at her expectantly. She seemed to become aware she had spoken. "Back in college. My sorority had a big trip every year."

"And you engaged in these sports? Intoxication and garment-shedding?"

Sunny colored red. "Well, sure, I mean, I partied, you know." She looked everywhere except at the two men. "In some ways it would be an ideal venue for the Koh-Mo-No promotion."

"It is settled, then," Chiun stated.

"Well, there's some problems, too. It's just like sponsoring a rock concert. You have to set up deals. You can't just go to Cancun—you need prime placement where the kids are flocking."

"I thought the kids flocked all over the place—can't you just set up a booth on the beach?" Remo said. "What about hiring some spokes-models to walk around in Koh-Mo-Nos with music blasting?"

"Why make the music blast?" Chiun asked.

"Kids these days like it blasting. They always have."

"But where would you stage your event?" Sunny protested. "Most of the prime beach space is spoken for."

"But not all?" Chiun demanded.

"Wait, wait, this is all beside the point," Sunny said. "It's too late. Spring break's over. The kids are all back home."

Remo scrunched up his face. "Really? What month is this?" Chiun shot him a venomous look. "January, February, April... Oh, crap, is it May already? And I haven't filed my taxes."

"Ignore my son, please," Chiun said, waving Remo away. Sunny Johns was trying hard to do just that, and the distraction of her sober state wasn't helping.

"Do the college students drink only during this brief spring hiatus?" Chiun asked.

Remo smirked. Sunny Johns swallowed a laugh. "They drink at other times, too. Parties."

"Toga parties," Remo suggested. "But with kimonos." He tried to picture Bluto Blutarsky stomping around in a Koh-Mo-No with a beer stein in one hand and a bouffant blonde in the other. "Naw."

"You know, there are versions of spring break that go on, sort of on a smaller scale. Lake parties. River parties."

"Kids these days attend these events?"

"Oh, sure. I went to them. It's mostly for the kids who don't get to go to spring break. And the ones who don't get enough partying at spring break and want more. I bet I could get you sponsorships at some of these."

Chiun stroked his threads of yellow beard. "How soon?"

"I'll have to see. We'll need to plan some sort of event, hire talent, ship in product. A couple of months?"

"This weekend," Chiun replied.

Sunny opened her mouth. Her stale booze breath was anything but sunny. "I don't think I could make it happen. We don't even have the entertainment lined up. Who will MC? What's going to be the theme? Are you going to give away Koh-Mo-Nos or sell them or what? We need time to plan."

"Are the parties not under way now?"

"Well, sure."

"Where?"

"Why are you asking where?" Remo was alarmed.

"Where?" Chiun repeated.

"Lake Havasu is always a scene," Sunny said.

"That's a thousand miles from here," Remo added helpfully.

"Key West. Outer Banks." Sunny was ticking them off on her fingers. "Bogunhurst Bayou Bash was always one of my favorites. Sheboygan Nights is coming up. That's maybe an eight-hour drive."

"We have places to go anyway," Remo said, trying to sound like he was concluding the conversation. "Sheboygan's the opposite direction."

"Festival in Festus is south of here."

"West Virginia?" Remo asked.

"East-central Iowa."

"Sorry."

"Pharaoh's Phest in Cairo."

Chiun looked expectant.

"Southern Illinois."

"Ah."

"Huh."

"Hush."

"In fact, there's a string of really wild river parties over the next few weeks."

"Chiun, we have commitments," Remo insisted. "Remember?"

"No. In fact, I would say we now have no plans whatsoever."

"But this could change without notice."

"Or not at all."

"The phone could ring this minute."

"Or not for weeks."

"Argh!" Remo grunted.

"Huh?" asked Sunny Johns.

20

"Smitty, I've never been this glad to hear from you. Where's the fire?"

"I've ordered your driver to head west," said Harold W. Smith. "There's been activity that might point to our Oscar Bedders. Suspicious crime scene outside of Galena, Illinois, in a seafood eatery overlooking the Mississippi River."

"That's not what I wanted to hear," Remo said.

"What did you want to hear, Remo?"

"I don't know. Guess I was hoping he'd show some-place more east."

"I see." Smith clearly did not see. "There are several employees missing, along with hundreds of pounds of fresh and frozen seafood. The crime-scene technicians gathered curious evidence suggesting squid fragments. They think the squid tissue comes from spilled seafood that was somehow mixed with the blood of victims."

"Those things aren't just hatched. They're attacking."

"It would appear so," Smith said.

"Yesterday they could barely move," Remo said. "The one I stomped couldn't lift its head off the sidewalk. He just laid there."

"The head is called a mantle, and we're having the specimen analyzed now," Smith said. "We think their growth may be accelerated."

"Obviously." Remo pictured the bucket of slime he had squashed just twenty-four hours ago, but grown up and strong enough to attack human beings out of water. He became aware of the scattering of minor aches and pains. Another good fight and they would stop feeling minor.

"We better find those things soon, Smitty. If they're really growing up that fast, we won't be able to deal with them. Let alone Bedders."

"You are healing?"

"Feeling great, thanks," Remo snapped. "But I'm not a hundred percent, and I won't be for a while. And I might remind you that my best wasn't good enough the last time I tried to off him."

"It is unlike you to complain about the strenuous nature of your work," Smith said, as sour as a bad stomach.

"It's unlike me to get my ass whupped at the fish museum. I'm not complaining, either. You want me to go face the squid wrangler, then I'll go. I just won't promise you his head on a platter."

21

The hostess gave them a plastic smile. "Two? Smoking or non?"

"Kind of coldhearted, isn't it, opening for business when your entire closing shift is missing, presumed murdered?"

The forced smile grew extratight. "I don't know what you're talking about, sir."

"We're here to see the kitchen," Remo said. "We'll show ourselves in."

The hostess tried hard to put herself quietly between Remo and the kitchen door. "I'm afraid our insurance regulations prohibit customers from entering the food-preparation area, sir."

"Lady, a customer I ain't—you can be sure of that." He picked her up by the waist and stood her up in the big decorative aquarium against the back wall. She managed to hold her smile in place as her blue-check-ered skirt floated around her waist and feathery koi tickled her ankles.

"Always you must play," Chiun said as he nudged

open the kitchen swing doors. "You waste your precious energies in frivolities."

Chiun didn't glance through the window in the swing doors, but he sensed the quick-striding restaurant manager, who pushed through in a fury. Chiun stamped his foot in the path of the doors, stopping them fast. The manager's shiny pate hit one, then the other, like a ball bouncing off angles at the minigolf range.

Remo found the kitchen partially sectioned off with crime-scene tape. A busy short-order crew was working around the cordoned section. They were deep-frying shrimp and piling it under a heat lamp in a stainless-steel pan.

"Who are you?" A local law-enforcement officer was stationed just outside the crime-scene tape. He could barely keep his eyes off the mound of golden-brown shrimp.

Remo thrust an ID card at the officer, then pulled it back, read the name and shoved it back in the man's face. "Remo Amberjack, Department of Agriculture. We understand there was a murder on the premises and the county board of health neglected to close the establishment."

The deputy didn't quite know how to respond, seeing as he wasn't technically asked a question, and it didn't matter anyway since now the pair of agents were ignoring him and examining the various evidence marks. They were finished before the deputy approached them with the manager, who nursed his bruised head.

"You people got no right being here," the manager said.

"You have no right advertising fresh fish," Chiun snapped. "What manner of restaurateur are you to claim any sort of freshness? All I smell is fish that are dead for days."

"Our fish *is* fresh!" the manager stammered.

"Take the clothespin off your nose," Remo said. "Show me one fish that doesn't have gray gills and I won't close the place down."

"You can't do that," the deputy said, sounding unsure of his facts. "On what basis?"

"This kitchen reeks of decaying fish, not to mention human flesh," Chiun said.

"Human flesh?" the manager stuttered.

"Freshest meat in the joint, although that's not saying much." Remo sniffed the smell to its source under another two-vat deep fryer. This one was cold and the vats were filled with thick, cloudy vegetable oil with black detritus floating among the heating elements at the bottom. The fryers weighed in at close to six hundred pounds, and over the years the steel feet had sunk a quarter-inch into the linoleum, so the manager and the county deputy were both surprised when the man from the USDA lifted the fryer out of its slot, then placed it down in the middle of the work space.

Underneath it was a human hand in a pool of black blood.

"Guess the crime-scene team didn't do such a great

job looking for signs of attack," Remo pointed out to the deputy. "What's that—the catch of the day?"

"It is probably the most appetizing flesh within these walls," Chiun added.

ROY CANDACE GOT the word from Nancy, his liaison, that it was time to move on.

"Already? They've only been in there ten minutes."

"Be prepared to depart at once, please," Nancy said.

Candace started the engine and maneuvered the Airstream from the rear parking to the front entrance. The doors were open and people were streaming from inside. None of them looked happy. It didn't take a genius to realize the place was being closed down.

"I wasn't finished with my crab legs," said a man in a plastic bib. "I got the all-you-can-eat crab legs, and I ain't ate all of them yet!"

"Sorry, fella." Candace was doubly surprised when he realized it was the guy from his Airstream, the younger one, who was propelling the customers through the door.

"I want my crab legs!"

"Don't push your luck, fella," Candace murmured.

"Yeah," Remo said to the irate diner. "Don't push your luck."

Candace found himself trembling. Had that guy heard him talking under his breath, twenty feet away, in all the hubbub?

"I'll sue your ass if I don't get my crab legs!"

Remo stared at the customer, and Roy Candace swore his eyes had some sort of unholy glow to them. "Okay," he said, vanished back inside and reappeared suddenly with a buffet pan full of iced crab legs. He spun the irate customer in a circle and yanked on the rear of his trousers, creating an unpleasant chasm. The tray was dumped inside, then the steel pan clattered on the ground. The diner stood there with his eyes getting rounder and rounder.

"Is that enough crab legs?"

The diner nodded.

"Anybody else?"

The place cleared out in seconds. The diner with the crab legs in his pants waddled carefully to his car, tears streaming down his face, and he didn't dare attempt to empty his pants until he was ready to jump in his vehicle.

By then, the old Chinaman and his younger, freaky friend were climbing into the Airstream. Candace pulled them out of the parking lot just as a small squad of county sheriff's cars came screaming in.

"Uh, Nancy, you seeing this?" Roy asked. Two of the wailing police cars spun gravel and pursued the Airstream. They were on Roy's rear bumper in seconds.

"It's taken care of, Roy," Nancy said without excitement.

"You want I should pull over?"

"Just keep driving."

Roy couldn't believe when the police cars broke off the pursuit a moment later and headed back the way they had come.

"Just as well," he said nervously.

"How's that, Roy?" Nancy asked, as cool as a black cat.

"Heh-heh. That place wasn't any good anyway for fresh fish."

"You know of a better place?"

"Sure, sweetie," Roy said. "There's Frederico's in Savannah. Maybe twenty minutes down the river from this joint. Best fresh fish in the northwest corner of the state. You know something, baby cakes, I'll take you there some day, how about that?"

Nancy seemed to be positively purring. "How about right now, Roy? And step on it."

THE PHONE CHIRPED and it was Mark Howard calling. "We have a new lead, Remo. Another seafood place down the river called Frederico's. Supposed to be the best fish place in the vicinity. Relatively famous in the Midwest, so maybe our friend Bedders would know about it, too."

"Can't be worse unless it's got a drive-through," Remo said. "Wouldn't it be faster in my car?"

"Not really," Mark Howard said.

"Unthinkable," Chiun added.

"Just a thought," Remo said. "I don't think I like being chauffeured around by some disposable scumbag," Remo complained.

"There is another option," Mark offered.

"Come on, Mark, you guys don't really want me driving this vee-hickle. We've gone that route and it didn't work out well for any of us."

"You've got a point," Mark Howard said. "Don't worry. Your current driver is doing fine. Sarah is keeping him in line."

"Sarah?"

"She's his liaison. She extraordinarily effective."

"You're letting your girlfriend get tight with that creep? What's she got that you haven't got?" Remo said. "Oh, yeah. Personality, charisma, appeal. Stupid question."

"And she's a woman."

"I've noticed."

"I've noticed you noticing," Mark said.

"How could I not?"

"You could try not to notice."

"Come on, Junior. When she goes romping in the hallways in a crop-top and short-shorts it'd take a eunuch to look the other way. I'm surprised the deepcoma patients aren't raising tents in their sheets."

"She doesn't romp in the halls!"

"When you normals walk, it sounds like romping. Especially in the quiet wing at Folcroft. I'm not saying I'm gonna touch her goodies or anything, Mark."

"What if I talked about your girlfriend like that?" Mark demanded.

"Cleansing breath. In through the mouth, fill the

lungs, out through the nose, long and slow. We were talking about our chauffeur, remember?"

"Yes. He's the one who let us in on the popularity of Frederico's, if you must know."

"Really. Maybe I misjudged the scumbag. Tell you what, to make amends I'll adopt the scumbag as my protégé?"

"What?" Mark Howard exploded.

"What?" Chiun bleated.

"Kidding," Remo said. "You people are touchy."

22

If there was one thing Remo knew well, it was how to judge fresh fish. It was just about all the protein he ate. As a Master of Sinanju, red meat was out. No beef, no pork. No hamburgers, no hot dogs, no Italian sausage. Just fish and the occasional duck. The problem was, Remo wasn't all that fond of duck. So that left fish.

After eating fish regularly and exclusively for years, he'd had his encounters with a number of unfresh fish. It was amazing what some people would try to pass off as the catch of the day. Combine that with the olfactory senses that would humble a bloodhound, and Remo could sniff out bad fish from a mile away.

The restaurant in Galena, Illinois, had announced itself like a bluegill that falls under the car seat after a fishing trip and remains undiscovered for a week.

Frederico's, in Savannah, Illinois, proved itself to be a better seafood restaurant before they even laid eyes on it—they couldn't smell it from down the street. They could hardly catch the aroma of fish when strolling to the entrance. That was a very good sign.

As they stepped through the twin front doors, Chiun's footsteps slowed and he gently drew in the fragrances of the place.

Remo could smell it, too. Lots of deep-frying going on. Lots of butter being melted for dipping steamed sections of shellfish cadavers. Pan-searing in oil, stewing, sautéing and breading. None of these cooking methods were agreeable to Chiun, and yet it was the least you could expect of any restaurant. What they still did not smell was the twinge of decay that spoke of rotting seafood.

"Excellent," Chiun said with a nod of his small head. "We shall dine."

"I think we're supposed to check out the scene," Remo said. "Stake the place out. Perform some clandestine reconnaissance. The whole undercover-secret-agent-commando routine."

"We shall order first," Chiun declared.

Chiun nodded politely and dumbly at the hostess as she walked them to a booth at one end of the restaurant, then he strolled to the table that best suited his needs, at the other side of the restaurant. It was in the least crowded and most delightfully decorated wing.

The hostess hurried after him and began to protest as the elderly Asian man took his seat, but Chiun adopted his pleasant, old-Korean-man smile, which told his listener he understood not one word of English.

Remo resignedly unfolded bills from the back pocket of his chinos and pressed them into the hostess's palm.

"He just arrived in America."

The hostess said nothing as she tried to come to terms with the number of bills in her hand.

"I see," she said. She added with a smile, "Welcome to our country."

They ordered dinner. Fresh fish. Unseasoned *wehani* rice.

"Don't even salt the water," Remo warned the waiter.

The waiter agreed, recorded his notes and seemed to genuinely understand what was required. This was rare enough. The place was rapidly turning into Remo's favorite restaurant in this state.

"Now, if we can only get through the meal without any unwelcome visitors, we'll be doing okay."

"You do not fear jinxing our luck with your careless remarks?" Chiun asked.

"Should I?"

"I do not know. Perhaps you should knock on wood." Chiun stared pointedly at Remo's forehead.

"I don't believe in that kind of superstitious stuff," Remo said. "You know that, Chiun."

"I know you believe in virtually nothing," Chiun said.

Remo sniffed the air. Chiun observed him and drew in the aromas of the place again, searching for something Remo sensed but he did not.

"There's squid on the raw bar, Little Father."

"No, thank you, Remo," Chiun said.

"I wasn't suggesting you have some. Just pointing it out."

"You are full of tension, my son." Chiun sounded un-characteristically concerned.

"You saw what it did to me and what it did to you. What's to stop that from happening again? What are we going to do the next time we run into that guy that will make it any different?"

Chiun regarded the reflection of the shell-encrusted table chandelier in the heavily varnished tabletop. He had no answer.

"Roy, PLEASE DESCRIBE your precise location."

Roy Candace just about jumped out of his skin. He would never get used to the constant companionship of the woman who called herself Nancy. His caretaker. Man, he was high-strung lately. Constant terror could kind of get to a guy.

"Uh, hi, sweetie. What's going on?"

"Roy, please describe your precise location."

"I thought you could see exactly where I was all the time with the satellite feed."

"Certainly we can determine where you are. We have GPS monitoring on your vehicle. I'm asking you to identify the terrain. I want to know how hidden you are."

"Hidden?" Roy's mind did leaps. "Hidden from who?"

Then his slow-moving mind realized what it was he should be hidden from. "Oh, shit. What're you saying, honey? What's gonna be happening?"

Nancy said, "How should I know what's going to

happen, Roy? Now please address the question. How well are you and the Airstream concealed?"

Roy twisted his head in every direction. He had only been half listening when he was instructed to park the Airstream in an out-of-the-way place, where Frederico's Seafood Restaurant patrons wouldn't notice him.

"I guess I'm hidden pretty good," Roy decided aloud. "Sweetie, you'd tell me, right, if something bad was about to happen?"

"My name is Nancy, Roy."

It was at that moment that the station wagon rolled through the intersection at the end of Roy's street. Roy Candace noticed it right away. It was an AMC Ambassador, just like the one he drove back in the early 1970s. The only car he had ever bought new off the lot. A V-8 engine, piss-yellow paint and enough sheet metal to make an Abrams tank. It sucked gasoline like a tank, too, and broke down every hundred miles after the first eighty thousand, but for some reason Roy Candace had loved that car, and he hadn't seen one in years.

This one looked pretty much like you'd expect a thirty-five-year-old station wagon would look. He was surprised the hunk of junk would even start up, but there it was chugging down the street with sparks trailing behind it. The muffler was dragging. That brought back memories, too.

But, actually, the muffler on this antique wasn't dangling so much as it was being ground off by the low rear end of the station wagon. The Ambassador's long snout was pointed up and the back was weighed way down, and the great big cargo area, with its fold-down vinyl seats, was full of heavy, square somethings. Roy Candace's reminiscing gave way to stark terror.

"Honey-honey-honey bunch?"

"Yes, Roy?"

THE WAITER LAID the plates in front of them hesitantly, sure the orders were wrong. They had to be wrong. Who would want to eat a plate full of plain, unsalted *wehani* rice and plain, unseasoned tilapia?

Remo examined his plate. Chiun frowned at his. For a moment there was silence.

"Can I get you anything else, sir?"

"In fact, this is just about perfect," Remo said.

"Really?"

"Mr. Williams," the intercom blared. "Mr. Williams, your other parties have arrived."

The waiter stared at the ceiling. "That's weird. We never make loudspeaker announcements."

"Special case," Remo said, sorry to leave his plate behind.

OSCAR BEDDERS SWUNG the rear hatch of the old beater station wagon and flipped the lids of the plastic coolers. The smell slapped him across the face. It was the smell of sickness.

The youngsters weren't doing well. Their water was

stagnant and stale. He needed to find a supply of clean marine water. And where the hell was he going to find that in this god-awful armpit of the god-awful Midwest?

He needed food first, and maybe he'd find enough water in this place, too. But he doubted there'd be enough clean marine water in the lobster holding tanks. Even coming to this place was a desperate gamble.

But Oscar Bedders was slave to the compulsion in his head. While his common sense told him to wait until after closing, the powerful instinct to take care of the ailing youngsters spurred him to come to this busy restaurant during its busiest part of the day.

He slipped through the rear doors, finding himself in a hectic restaurant kitchen. Bedders almost shouted for joy when he saw the large holding tanks for live seafood. Hundreds of gallons of clean, filtered salt water.

But how could he get it? He'd be lucky enough to get food for the youngsters without getting himself killed. There were people everywhere. The restaurant staff wasn't going to just stand there and let him do it.

Which meant he had to make sure that there was nobody left to stop him.

He should come back after closing. That was the smart thing to do. He felt as if he was arguing with himself—the smart part arguing with some other part that insisted he get what he came for and get it *now*. The youngsters were suffering.

There were cooks, wait staff and an annoying bustle of busboys. The busboys came through their own service door bearing trays of rattling, dirty dishes, presenting them to a pair of dishwashing staff stationed on either side of a conveyor heading into a dishwashing machine. The busboy who came through the door at that moment wasn't dressed like any busboy and he didn't move like one. The huge stack of soiled porcelain and food-encrusted cutlery in his tray didn't make a sound.

The busboy placed his tray on the conveyer in absolute silence and slipped behind Oscar Bedders, who was already alert to a strident alarm going off in his head. His attention was drawn to the figure who came through the doors used by the waiters. He came silently, gliding like some phantom.

Bedders's lips curled away from his teeth. "Back for more, old man?"

The old man simply inclined his head, almost politely. He didn't come closer. Bedders barked a laugh. "How's your friend feeling, old man?"

The old man now shook his head, almost sadly.

"He is not well," the old man admitted in a high-pitched but very dignified voice. "But, here, you may ask him yourself."

The old man stepped to one side and looked to a place beyond the door that Bedders couldn't see, then Bedders felt the alarm in his head grow in intensity. The enemy was almost upon him. The old man was just a distraction.

The enemy cut into Bedders from behind with a ringing, empty-handed blow that snapped Bedders's spine in two places.

Bedders felt himself fold in two as he tumbled across the kitchen, where he was intercepted by the old man, who once again used his fatal fingernails and whirled his arms like some sort of martial-arts maniac playing on the television at fast-forward speed. Every flick of his hands sliced through Bedders's flesh like the cleaving of butcher blades.

The attack was over in a heartbeat, and Bedders was tumbling toward the young one, who struck at his body with a series of bone-breaking kicks and hits that were over before Bedders could figure them out.

Then it was the old one's turn again, and Bedders knew that these two had his measure. Their attacks were vicious and damaging and instantaneous. Bedders fought to summon the energy, the only thing that could save him now—but even it could not save him. These two knew his weakness. Bedders couldn't lash out at them fast enough; their strikes were too quick. They volleyed Bedders back and forth across the kitchen floor, spiking him like a volleyball that had already been ripped to pieces.

Bedders reached out to snare one of the restaurant staff, to take energy and flesh, but the staff was fleeing.

Bedders used what energy he could summon, but it didn't get him far. He healed his spine, then it was snapped apart again. He healed his head, but the next

attack smashed it. The enemy and the old man were dec-
imating him faster than he could repair himself.

Bedders didn't care about himself any longer—only
the youngsters. But when Bedders was destroyed, the
youngsters would be destroyed, too.

Bedders screamed a warning, knowing the youngsters in the car would hear him and knowing, too, that
they were helpless. They had no way to escape.

REMO WILLIAMS FELT good. Oscar Bedders was being
overcome. Each and every strike against him whittled
him away. Bedders was trying to mend his broken bones
and his torn flesh, only to have Chiun or Remo drift in
and deliver another wound to his body. Slowly but
surely, Remo and Chiun were breaking Bedders down.
He was only a mass of rising and collapsing human
flesh, and soon enough he would be entirely dismantled.

Then Remo felt the pressure shift in the air and heard
the click and swing of the opening door behind him, and
he felt the stench envelop him. When he turned he saw
the tentacles reaching through the door, graceless and
swift.

Remo stomped the tentacles but many more slithered
past him, longer than he could believe. The things had
grown tremendously, and they were more powerful.
Squid arms twisted between his ankles and curled
around his feet.

Remo was still faster. He snatched up a handful of

tentacles and yanked a squid from its miserable container in the rear of the station wagon. The thing shrieked as it flew through the air, turned on Remo and constricted its two longest tentacles around his neck. Remo pulled it closer and plowed his fist into its torso. The squid shrieked and sputtered and spit a fountain of black liquid.

Remo could feel the elasticity of its body and knew he hadn't killed it. He leaped to the nearest bank of cookers, forcing the elongated wings of its head into the boiling water alongside a basket of rotini that was well past al dente. The thing tightened its grip around Remo's neck, trying to crawl up Remo or choke the life out of him.

Remo made his muscles like iron. His neck could withstand the tightening tentacles, and he ignored the other tentacles that beat and pummeled him from all sides, and quickly enough they weakened as the squid's head boiled. Remo shrugged the thing off him, tucking the enfeebled arms into the boiler, too.

Bedders was beyond helping himself, but the squid were retrieving him. Chiun was butchering squid arms. Remo leaped over the stretched arms and landed hard, crushing more tentacles.

Then the tentacles beneath his feet began to spark. They emitted their own energy, and the energy sought more energy from Remo Williams. Remo cursed himself for his foolishness.

Remo should have guessed. There was no reason the

squid offspring should not be able to heal themselves in the same way Oscar Bedders did. It was the power of Sa Mangsang. As this realization hit him, so did the bolts of static energy that ripped into his body, pierced his flesh and seemed to wriggle like fiery worms into his very bones. He felt the life being sucked from his body and through the tentacles, and he watched the damaged arms heal themselves. They dragged Oscar Bedders to within range of Remo's draining energy. Bedders's mutilated hands rose from the ruin of flesh and seemed to warm themselves, like at a campfire, on the energy coming from Remo.

He saw something flying above his head, flapping and colorful, and Chiun landed with both feet on the door as if he were landing on level ground. The door crunched against the tentacles. The bolts of energy flickered off abruptly.

Remo slumped to the floor, inhaled sharply and pushed up again as the door creaked open and Bedders was dragged through the opening on wounded squid arms. The arms tossed him up and over the car. He collapsed alongside the station wagon with a crunch. Then Oscar Bedders stood up and stretched, knitting the most ghastly wounds in his flesh and setting the most grievous breaks in his bones.

Remo went after him, and only managed to land against the doorjamb like a drunkard.

Bedders fumbled with the door of the station wagon and collapsed inside. Remo found himself unable to move. Chiun was holding him back, like a man holding back his friend from a bar fight.

"Chiun, let me go."

"Remo, let *him* go." Chiun wouldn't loosen his grip, and Remo hadn't the strength to break free.

Remo had no choice but to watch the station wagon speed away.

23

Oscar Bedders was crying like a baby. Last time he cried, he couldn't even remember. Yeah, he could. A dog had bitten him on the way home from kindergarten and his old man beat his bare ass with a belt for crying like a little baby.

Another jolt of energy from the back of the station wagon. They were giving him their energy, the youngsters, and it was weakening them. He was staying alive while they were dying. That was what filled him with the deep sorrow. Another youngster was dead in the restaurant behind them, and the survivors in the back of the car were fading fast.

The truth was, they had banded together to channel their energy into the few individuals who had attacked the enemy in the restaurant and saved Bedders. That hadn't been the gesture of power it appeared to be. It was a desperate gamble, like the adrenaline rush of strength of an accident victim pinned under a car in rising floodwaters. The adrenaline rush helped to get the car off him, so to speak, but he was still in the middle of the levy break and he wasn't sure he could escape the flood before it drowned him—and his entire family.

Bedders couldn't let the youngsters die, and he didn't know how to prevent it. All he knew was that they were helpless, and they were depending on him. He needed to get them food and fresh water and he needed it fast.

When the cops came it was like something out of a Spielberg friendly UFO movie—four cars came around the bend on Illinois Highway 3, side by side and all their lights blazing, while a pair of police cars emerged from hiding places on either side of the road behind him, more lights flashing in the darkness. They parked across the road with outcrops on either side. Nobody was getting past them.

Bedders swore. Cops. He hated cops. Even when he was a cop he hated them. It was satisfying to kill them.

But this was sure a lot of cops.

HAROLD W. SMITH SAID into the telephone, "I do not appreciate being hung up on, Governor."

"This is General Who?"

"General K. Kastle of the U.S. Joint Chiefs of Staff."

"I didn't hang up on you, General Kastle."

"Your staff did. After they ignored my requests. Now please listen to me very carefully or there will be grave consequences. There is a manhunt and police chase being conducted at this moment, including a roadblock in southwestern Illinois on Highway 3. It must be halted."

The governor exhaled. "General, maybe you haven't been paying attention to the news. We've had more murders in this state this week than I can keep count and it's all blamed on just two or three men. We've got at least one of them surrounded and we're about to take him into custody. We are not going to pull back."

"You will not take him into custody. He will kill anyone who gets near him. I'm ordering you to stand down your operation."

"With all due respect, General, you don't have the authority—"

"Department of Homeland Security Emergency Management Authority is granted and transmitted to all State of Illinois bodies. These authority certificates have been ignored."

The governor of the State of Illinois lowered the phone and shouted out of his office. "Have we received any DOHSEMAs recently?" The governor shook his head vigorously.

His executive assistant looked at the executive law-enforcement liaison. They had all gathered to monitor the police chase. "No," said his assistant loudly. "No, we have not."

"You heard him. We haven't received it," the governor told the unpleasant general from the Joint Chiefs.

"I believe you did."

"Our system is not that great. Do you know we're funding Homeland Security in this state off of cigarette taxes and riverboat-gambling fees? Maybe you federals should consider tossing us a few bucks to bring our systems up to date."

There was a short moment of silence. "If you do not obey this order, you will be in violation of Homeland Security authority—not to mention, you will be guilty for the deaths of many good state and local police in your state."

"I'd love to help you out, General," the governor said, until the line went dead.

"Asshole."

He stared at the phone for a long minute, and it rang again. Secure executive line. "Hello?"

"Hello, again, Governor," said General K. Kastle.

"Look, General, what's it gonna take—?"

"Bob, it's the President," said the voice of the President of the United States. "Have you guys really fumbled a DOHSEMA in your state? What in the hell is going on? I'd all like an explanation."

"Go ahead, Governor, give him an explanation," said General Kastle, who had to be the most sour bureaucrat it had ever been the governor's displeasure to meet up with.

"PULL BACK at once and that is an order," snapped the high-ranking dispatch trooper.

"He's right here," Trooper Bocarna argued. "We've got him pincered. You want us to let him go?"

"At once."

"Then the locals will get the arrest!"

"The locals are being ordered to fall back, as well."

Trooper Bocarna snorted. "Their locals. They'll ignore the order. You know that."

"This is now a DOHS matter. Anyone who violates this order is committing a federal felony."

"Shit!"

BEDDERS FORGOT all his troubles for a moment when the most curious thing happened. The roadblock broke up. Three of the four police cars slowed, did U-turns and headed away. One of the cars behind him slowed and was lost in the rearview mirror. Was it some kind of trick?

"I can't believe them yokels fell for it. It has to be some kind of trick," snapped the Cairo County Sheriff Bosky. His deputy was reading off the dashboard communications display.

"They think it's a legitimate DOHS emergency powers order. What if they got it right, Sheriff?"

The sheriff turned down the corners of his mouth. "All I know, if we leave now, it leaves just old Chief Gerhard to make the arrest. We'll never hear the end of it. And there ain't no way they're gonna charge us with violating orders if we bring a mass killer to jail."

The deputy was thrilled. He'd made his case. He was just following orders. The blame would fall on the sheriff if there was blame to be leveled. The glory would be shared by him when they arrested this wanted killer.

For the deputy it was a no-lose situation.

BEDDERS COASTED at forty miles per hour, and when he reached the one-car roadblock the police car burned rubber, aiming right at Bedders's front end. Crazy-ass move, but it was so crazy it usually worked to scare the car-chase perps into swerving hard, and that would have put Bedders right into the blasted rock on either side of the road. He was better than that. He compensated just right, turning around the squad car and slamming his heavy front end into the cop's rear, blowing the cop's tire.

Bedders stopped, then reversed until his tail collided with the front door of the cop car. A dazed sheriff was sitting behind the wheel. His partner was crawling out through a shattered window and bringing out his gun.

TOWN OF PENANCE Police Chief Gerhard saw the crash and hurried on up to the scene. Now he could make the arrest and Cairo County Sheriff Bosky would look like an idiot. Pretty nice piece of luck. He'd have to thank Bosky in private for setting this up so perfect.

Gerhard emerged from his squad car with his shotgun out in front of him, wondering why it was so quiet. Bosky was a dark, still shape in the front seat of his car. Maybe he was hurt. Maybe he was dead.

"Deputy? What's going on?"

The deputy was sitting on the windowsill of the crashed patrol car. His gun was in his hand, leveled at the station wagon. No sign of the perp.

The deputy's head rolled to face Chief Gerhard. In the flashing of patrol lights, Gerhard thought he saw little sparks of electricity dancing on his face.

"You okay?"

The deputy exploded. Fragments of flesh flew in every direction. The deputy's head bounced off the blasted rock and rolled into the highway, where it was pursued by a long slimy arm protruding from the rear of the station wagon.

Gerhard tried not to lose his steak dinner.

Tentacles were reaching through the police car and grasping at the chunks of flesh, while more tentacles were encircling Sheriff Bosky, and they were dancing with little bolts of energy. Bosky blew apart a second later, coating the inside of his broken windshield.

"Gaw!" Gerhard remembered the shotgun. He fired it at the tentacles that stretched between the cars.

There were shrieks. Not human shrieks. But he was too far away and the buckshot spread too far to do enough damage. Gerhard swallowed hard and pumped the action—then felt the gun lift out of his hands.

There was a man standing next to him, and that man should not have been alive. He was covered in wounds and bloody scabs and his joints were crooked. It had to be the killer. And the killer had Gerhard's weapon.

"Don't shoot me."

"I won't shoot you," the killer said, flinging the shotgun over his shoulder, then placing his fingers around

Gerhard's throat. He squeezed just enough to hurt—and then the yellow streaks of light began to dance before Gerhard's eyes.

24

The Action-Cam was mounted on a helicopter from a St. Louis television news channel. The live pictures were feeding across the country. They saw it in the offices in Rye, New York.

There were two lonely-looking police cars on the highway below. One was intact, lights blazing. One was crushed and silent. The road surface was littered with sparkling glass and unidentified stains, and a rifle or shotgun was laying there. There was no sign of movement or survivors.

THEY SAW the same news feed in the Oval Office, as the Action-Cam moved up the road a few miles to another scene in which the action was long over. A police car on the side of the road, lights dead, no evidence of survivors. An old, rusty station wagon, just sitting there.

"Illinois State Police are confirming that one police car and a police van are unaccounted for. The suspect was believed to have been driving the station wagon. The state police have now issued an alert for the police van."

The President squinted at the screen, trying to figure out if he could see any sign of bodies.

"We're going to descend to try and see inside the station wagon," the helicopter reporter announced. The helicopter descended, its harsh white spotlight beaming into the open rear hatch of the old station wagon.

A state trooper was looking out at them. He still had his hat. He didn't have anything below the chin. His head was propped inside the AMC so that he looked out at them with a grinning mouth and wide, horrified eyes.

"Oh, damn." The President rubbed his tired jowls. He dragged open a desk drawer and snatched the red phone inside. "I'm watching the news, Smith. What's going on with your guys? Where'd they screw up?"

Smith was deadpan as ever. "The hatchlings turned violent, Mr. President. They exhibited energy-discharge capabilities similar to those of Oscar Bedders. My operative took the brunt of one such attack."

"I see," the President said impatiently. "How is he?"

"Recovering. Depleted."

"Depleted? As in out of commission?"

"Unknown. It appears the hatchlings were transferred to a police paddy wagon—we're attempting to track it now. I'll report when I have any news of importance."

"Sure, you will," the President said sarcastically, but he was already on an empty phone line. He dropped the red phone back into the drawer with a clatter and nudged the drawer shut.

This was going to reflect on him. He just knew it. Everything bad that happened anywhere in America seemed to get blamed on him.

Never in all of history had there been a lame-duck President catching so much flak from so many sources. Sure, he made some bad choices during his years in office, and of course the opposition party tried to make him look like a bumbler during the 2004 election. But now, it was as if the ball were rolling and he was being scapegoated for every problem that reared up. Health-care costs going up and Mideast wars costing lives and an economy that would simply not get back on solid ground and he was the one responsible for all of it. Even his own party was out to get him.

Really, it was his vice president's fault. That man's political indiscretions made it impossible for him to get the nomination in 2008. That meant the reputation of the administration itself didn't have to be preserved. So even his own party was using the President as the scapegoat. They blamed him because the soldiers in the Mideast were digging in dumps for scrap metal to armor supply trucks. They blamed him because prescriptions cost three times in the U.S. what they did in Canada. Every time an Eskimo fell through the thinning arctic ice, they blamed the President. Every time a grammar-school class was hospitalized from breathing coal dust from a power plant, they blamed the President. Every time another hundred thousand old folks lost their pension in a corporate bankruptcy, they blamed the President.

Didn't they know the globe was warming *before* he ever came to office? Coal was being used before his first term. The economy had started going sour months before he was sworn in for the first time—why didn't anybody remember that? It was the President's 2004 opponent who single-handedly robbed the soldiers of their needed truck armor by voting down the needed appropriations—but they blamed the President anyway.

On the intercom, the testy Secret Service detail asked if they could now return to the Oval Office.

"Yeah," the President snapped, then glowered at them as they filed back in. The Secret Service glowered back. They weren't pleased when the President kicked them out, even for just a few minutes.

The President was tired of Secret Service agents and their attitude. They acted as if they could order him around. Well, nobody was supposed to order him around. He was the President. Why didn't anybody respect that? He knew they were muttering about him in the halls and the kitchens. Not nearly as fun to work for as that nice Mr. Bill. That asshole left office more popular than ever. Why, dammit, why?

These murders in the Midwest—somehow, it was gonna be another crime added to his record of crimes and misdemeanors. Somehow they'd end up blaming the President yet again.

25

"This is Simone Hottenville from Public National Radio, reporting from the scene of the latest killings by a mass murderer who appears to have started his work in Chicago a few days ago, and is now carrying his irrepressible violence into the Southern states. At least six state and local police were killed in the latest attacks. PNR has learned that the President himself was responsible for pulling the plug at the last minute on a coordinated roadblock that had already trapped the killer."

"What?" the President thundered.

"Only after the President ordered the state police away from the scene were three local police officers murdered. The killer then pursued the state police vehicles, destroying one, stealing the second and killing at least three more officers in the process."

"That's not what happened!" the President said. "And how the hell did I get tied to this fiasco anyway?"

The stony-faced Secret Service agents didn't answer. The President's assistant looked nervous.

"Somebody leaked," the President complained. "I

bet it was that pretty-boy governor in Illinois. What a punk."

"He has an exemplary security rating, sir," his assistant said, then immediately wished she hadn't.

"How can he? He's in the other party. Somebody breached security and I want his ass nailed. Who'd handle that?"

His assistant looked around wildly. "DOHS? It was their security directive."

"Get my chief ass-nailer on a plane to Chicago, now."

"He should probably go to Springfield, Mr. President. It's their capital."

"Whatever." Springfield. Real original name for a state capital. He didn't like that ugly blotch of a state—a stain on the map of electoral returns in every federal election.

"The President is believed to be 'observing' events from his vacation ranch in Texas," droned Hottenville from the radio.

"I'm in D.C., idiot."

"It is not known how or why he became involved in manipulating police officers who were working on what was strictly a state matter."

"To save their stinking lives," the President barked. This got the interest of the Secret Service agents, who showed microscopic flickers of facial movement, and brought the President's jittery assistant to a stop. Oops.

"What, sir?"

"I didn't say anything. Shut off the radio."

26

Bedders felt good. The youngsters were stronger, and Bedders himself was healed again, with a fresh set of internal organs extracted from a big weight-lifting state trooper who no longer needed them. A new left eye. A pair of new legs. Amazing how it all knitted together and adjusted itself to fit in with the whole body—but he didn't really care about that. All he cared was that he was perfectly fit and full of energy yet again. The only emergency still to be addressed was getting fresh water for the youngsters. The extra energy they'd absorbed from the cops would only keep them going for so long in a choking, waste-filled environment.

Bedders pulled the police van into the parking lot of the Wickliffe, Kentucky, Grand Central Shopping Center. It was after midnight and the place looked deserted. The six-foot PetStør sign was unlighted. Supplies, Birds, Reptiles, Fish the banner promised.

The alarm was active, but the cop in Bedders knew how to gain entrance. He rang the delivery bell. The late-night crew consisted of one young man in heavy glasses, with a bar-code scanner clipped to his belt and a box cutter in one hand.

"I can't sign for deliveries." He sucked on an asthma inhaler.

"I'm not delivering," Bedders said. "I'm picking up."

"THIS IS GETTING OLD," Remo Williams said. "I'm thirsty."

Chiun handed him a bone cup of Oui Oui Water. Remo sat up slowly on his mat. Sipping the water was made difficult by Chiun's hands roaming his flesh, seeking out new signs of damage.

"I'm fine. Nothing busted. Just drained."

"The energies of your body are still depleted by your healing," Chiun commented. "There was less to lose when the offspring took it from you. Yet you are awake and alert."

"So? I lost less energy than you thought."

"Or regained it more quickly," Chiun added. "I will admit to being surprised at your tenacity in the face of the offspring."

Remo nodded. "Yeah. I was a real tough guy. Seems to me I was saved by a fashionable senior citizen. I owe you, Little Father."

"More than you can possibly understand." Chiun nodded agreeably.

"You know what I mean. Thanks for saving me."

Chiun didn't respond to this. Remo got to his feet, testing his legs, willing his blood to circulate more vigorously. All systems checked out A-OK except for the familiar lethargy that was his companion since he woke up in the hospital in Chicago two days ago. Three days ago. Whenever it was.

"Where are we?" Remo asked, feeling the rattles and groans of the Airstream in motion. "Where we headed?"

"I know not. I have allowed the Emperor to set the course for now. He would have us in place to face this creature again, when it shows itself."

Remo groaned. "I think I have vacation time coming."

THE MANAGER of inventory replenishment, first name Gary, was draped across the stacking bars in a loading cart. Until very recently the cart held a stack of Amish Brand Large Breed Puppy Grub.

Gary didn't know why the Amish were supposed to make the world's best food for boxer puppies. The world had made a lot more sense back then, a half hour ago. Now the world was a crazy, miserable place.

Here he was, hanging over the bars like a rug. What kept him from falling off was the firm grip of a tentacle—yes, tentacle—that came from the creature in a plastic cooler that was also on the cart. There was an octopus in the cooler, along with some very foul-smelling water.

Then he saw the upper torso of the creature emerge briefly from the slime-green liquid. It wasn't an octopus, after all. It was a squid, with squid-wing things sticking out of its head. Not that it made much of a difference at this point. One was as weird as the next when painful suckers were holding you by the ankles and chest.

"I don't see the containers," said the man who was wheeling the cart. He seemed to be the caretaker of the squid.

"End of the aisle," Gary wheezed. He really needed to use his inhaler. The stench from the squid water was filling his lungs with gunk.

"Oh, yeah, these are good." The man was examining plastic feed-storage bins. Bigger and deeper than the coolers he was using now. Gary understood the squid needed bigger tanks.

"What's this?" the man demanded a moment later. "Where's the rest of your fish?"

Gary didn't understand the question.

"Most of these are freshwater," the man cried in alarm. "Where's the rest of your marine fish? I need a lot more water than this."

"That's all we have."

"That's all?" The man was suddenly on the verge of hysterics. "That's not enough. Tell me where the rest of your tanks are. Tell me now or I'll kill you!"

Gary was confused, but he was pretty sure he was going to be killed regardless. "I never said we had a lot of fish."

"Your sign says fish!"

"Not a lot of fish," Gary squealed. The suckers on his ankle were stinging bad.

"Do you have supply tanks in back?" the man demanded. "I need a lot of salt water. Tell me where it is."

Gary's self-preservation instinct kicked in. "I can get it for you. Enough to fill the whole feed bin."

"I need to fill four feed bins."

What? That meant there were more squid. Gary didn't allow himself to be distracted. "No problem. I'll tell you where to get enough water for all of them, but you have to let me go."

The man didn't bargain well. "Tell me where!" he shrieked, but it was a deep, insane shriek of a grown man, and it was accompanied by a horrible pain from the suckers, which seemed to be drilling barbs into his chest and legs. Gary yelped, but somehow managed to not give up his only bargaining chip. He just kept yelping. The man kept shrieking at him. The squid stingers kept hurting.

Then the stinging stopped.

"Okay, son of a bitch."

Gary found himself sprawling off the cart onto the floor, and he picked himself up slowly, then crept to the front of the store, never taking his eyes off the cart or the man with the blazing eyes or the reeking cooler with its distended tentacles.

At the end of the aisle the man snapped, "Far enough. Now tell me where to get the water for the tanks."

Gary sucked his inhaler and stood straighter. "You

can use plain tap water from the hose, then treat it with marine aquarium salts. Aisle two."

Gary bolted for the exit, ran between the silent checkout registers and almost slammed into the emergency exit. The orange lever was just out of the reach of his fingertips. He could read the white letters, which informed him that the door was for emergency use only, that an alarm would sound if he went through it. That was what he wanted.

But his head reeled and he collapsed two steps short of the door, and from the floor he saw the pet food cans falling all around him. Several had smashed into his head.

And now the man was wheeling the cart to him again. Gary tried to get up. Freedom was so close. But he never made it out. The stinging tentacles had him by the leg, and he was dragged behind the cart.

"I would have thought of this myself," the man said as he examined the plastic canisters of marine aquarium water treatments salts. "It's so obvious I'm surprised it didn't occur to me before. So I can't really give you credit for the information, understand? So that means I can't let you go."

Gary was in too much pain to speak and, anyway, at that moment, he started up with a really bad asthma attack.

27

Oscar Bedders was jubilant, then he was confused.

He was in a delivery truck with an enclosed rear and enough room and horsepower to transport the youngsters. The youngsters were feeling fine and happy now, in their big new containers and their fresh water. They were well fed. They were feeling frisky. What more could they ask for?

But Bedders's mind was playing games with him. There was this new urge he didn't understand. It wasn't right. It went against all the other instincts that drove him.

Oscar Bedders was always an impulsive guy who took crazy risks with his own life. When he worked in police forces on the Atlantic coast of Florida, they said he was the most dangerous police diver they had ever had. Nobody would work with him.

That was nonsense. He was still alive, so how could he be a danger? He never took risks that were so big he couldn't handle the situation. So, really, he wasn't taking risks at all.

That was all fine when it was his life on the line, but now it was the youngsters who were at risk. Now he was feeling downright paternal. He couldn't understand why he was putting the youngsters in danger.

They had already been fed, and they weren't starving at the moment. Bedders intended to search for a very secure place to take more feed—a place where they would go unnoticed. But fate conspired against him. As soon as he read the billboard for the Town Of Dupo Geniuses of the Sea exhibit, he knew he had to take the youngsters there.

He fought the urge, but the billboards came up again and again. They featured photos of Albert and Jamie, the two bottlenose dolphins who starred in the Dupo Marine Show.

The youngsters had never tasted dolphin.

"You can wait awhile," Bedders said over his shoulder.

The youngsters thrashed in their tanks.

Bottlenose dolphins were a lot more like the food the youngsters would eat in the wild. When they were big they ate whales, so Bedders guessed they probably ate littler marine mammals when they were youngsters. An adult bottlenose weighed as much as three or four people. Albert and Jamie would make a nice filling meal for the youngsters.

"Forget it," Bedders said. "It's too risky. You can eat all the dolphins you want when you're in the ocean."

The youngsters thrashed in their tanks. Were they agreeing with him or arguing with him?

"I said no!" Bedders snapped when the next billboard loomed along the road. Now they flaunted Einstein, the cartoon dolphin who jumped from cartoon waves wearing a graduation cap with tassels.

The youngsters splashed, agitated, and Bedders found himself shifting in his seat, which was irritating his patches of mismatched skin, and chewing his inner lip. Dupo came up ahead and a big billboard insisted he take the off-ramp.

Exit Now for the Dupo Marine Show.

"Fine!"

He swerved off the road.

This was nuts. It was late in the evening. The Dupo Marine Theater was dark and closed; it catered to families, and the last show cleared out at 9:00 p.m. There was no traffic to blend with. Anybody in the vicinity would notice a panel truck pulling into the theater this late.

"You want marine mammal for supper, I'm giving you marine mammal for supper," he announced belligerently.

The youngsters splashed in their troughs.

The drive ended before the Dupo Dolphinarium. There was a security guard inside, who watched him drive by.

"We should *not* be doing this."

He pulled around back, to the service entrance, lit by a single light, and back to the truck-size receiving door.

"Now what?" he asked angrily.

The youngsters sprayed water.

Bedders stepped out of the cab and jogged to the receiving entrance, which was a solid steel fire door with a burglar-proof steel knob. For the first time since he became the keeper of the youngsters he found himself wishing for a handgun. But he didn't need a handgun. He was strong. He could take out any doorknob you threw at him. Bedders wrapped both hands on the knob and turned it.

The doorknob didn't budge.

Bedders growled angrily and gripped it harder and grunted, putting all the force he could muster into the effort. The doorknob snapped.

"Stay back," warned a voice inside as the fire door swung open. "I got a gun."

The security guard was gumming his lips and standing sideways to the door, one hand on his belt. He was pretending to have his hand on the butt of a pistol.

"You're not even wearing a holster, old-timer," Bedders pointed out. "Open the big doors, will ya?"

"Ain't nothing here worth stealing."

"Ain't here to steal. Kids made me stop for dinner."

"What's that supposed to mean, son?"

"Forget it. Are you gonna open the doors for me?"

"Naw, I ain't gonna do that."

"Well, I am in no mood to argue," Bedders said, and he covered the distance separating them in five long strides. The old guard put up his hands to fend Bedders off, but he was socked right in the jaw and he collapsed.

Bedders poked buttons on the panel beside the door, only to get a red error light.

"What's wrong with it?"

"You need the code," the old man explained, pushing his upper body off the floor.

"What is the code?"

"Why would I know it, son?"

"I need to get the door open!"

The old man wheezed and coughed. "The Dupo Police Department has an emergency override code that'll do it. They'll be here any second."

Bedders cursed savagely.

"What did you think would happen, son?" The old guard seemed genuinely confused.

"Look, I didn't even want to make this stop. It's the goddamned kids. They can't be satisfied with what I give them for dinner!"

The old man shook his head. "You lost me," he said with a whistle in his breath.

Through the broken door came the flashing of police lights. The cop parked his car and strolled up without even bothering to remove his weapon—not that it would have made a difference to Oscar Bedders.

"Hey, there, Norm, you in here? You got trouble?"

Bedders grabbed the police officer by the arm when he was inside and pushed him into the wall alongside the truck door panel.

"Open it."

"Hey, now, why the rough treatment?"

"Enter the door code or I'll bash your head in."

"Don't know the code," the cop said, his speech slow and lazy.

"What?" Bedders yelped. "*He* said you could open the truck doors!" He waved at the sprawled guard.

"Well, I can open the door, but I don't know the code. See, I got this override key, same's the fire department."

"Well, why didn't you *say* that?" Bedders didn't know who was the bigger moron—the cop or himself for not realizing there would be a key to override the doors. There was even an emergency key slot in the panel, just like an elevator, and he had entirely overlooked it. Bedders made an angry noise and took a keychain from the cop's belt.

"Show me!"

The cop was in no hurry, but he sorted the keys until he found the right one. Bedders stabbed it into the panel and turned it, getting a light near the fireman icon. He opened the door.

"Now, you want to tell me just what in the world you think you're doing here?" the cop drawled.

"For the last time, it is not my idea," Bedders insisted. He pounded the cop's head into the panel with each word as he insisted, "Not my idea."

"Aw, no," the security guard said sadly when the cop flopped on his back. "Now, why'd you do that?"

Bedders yanked at the back of the panel truck. "Here we are. Come and get it."

The youngsters glared at him out of their tanks.

"Well, come on. This is what you wanted, right?"

The youngsters barely moved.

"Then why are we here?"

He knew then that something was very wrong. The youngsters hadn't wanted to come here. Something else wanted to come to this place, and it was telling him to wheel the youngsters to the dolphin tanks.

"Who are you talking to, mister?" demanded the security guard.

Bedders made an enraged sound, and he took the guard off the ground and pushed him into the rear of the truck. The guard tripped over the rim of a trough and splashed in with the youngsters. He began to thrash in earnest. The youngster consumed him without relish.

"Come on. Hurry it up. We gotta do this." Bedders wheeled a feed trough off the truck, onto the loading-bay lip. The plastic wheels on the trough weren't meant for that kind of abuse, and they began to buckle. Bedders shoved the trough around the corner of a wide corridor and the wheels collapsed. As strong as he was, it took tremendous effort to drag the trough into the Dupo Dolphinarium pavilion until it was within squid-arm's reach of the water.

"You get 'em," he panted to the half-dozen youngsters in the trough. "We'll take 'em back to the truck for everybody to share."

There was only room for three of the youngsters to crowd along the side of the square trough. Each gripped the sides with their eight short arms while reaching out with their two tentacles, which were twice as long as the arms. They probed into the water and reached to the distant floor of the tank.

Two faces emerged from the water and watched.

"There they are," Bedders said.

The squid reached across the tank. Albert and Jamie chattered.

"They're laughing at you," Bedders said.

The squid stretched their tentacles until they were taut. Albert, the larger of the Pacific bottlenose dolphins, skimmed fin-deep through the water and nipped the tip of a tentacle.

The squid thrashed and withdrew. Albert surfaced and giggled, waving his front fins at Bedders.

"They're making fun of you. What are you gonna do about it?"

The squid roiled in their trough.

"Are you fairies or what? Get in the tank. We don't have all night." He curled his fingers under the trough and lifted with his legs, dumping it into the Dolphinarium tank. The squid flowed out with the water, and Bedders could feel their eyes looking at him beseechingly. But the squid *had to do this*. It was their obligation or a responsibility or something.

Once in the water the youngsters warmed up to the hunt, and he watched them stiffen in the water, uncurling their tentacles to the bottom like a yawning cat uncurling its tail. The dolphins hovered just below the surface and the squid faced them upright like bobbing clothespins. Their tentacles began to wave and extend to the sides and vibrate like rattlesnake rattles.

They were doing some sort of instinctive hunting behavior. Any marine biologist would have given a right arm for the chance to be the first human being ever to witness the hunting techniques of the colossal squid— but Oscar Bedders was in a hurry.

"Just grab 'em and let's go!"

This was taking a lot of time, and more law might come any second. Hell, once the call went out they might send in the National Guard. It wasn't as if his trail was hard to follow. This was a stupid, stupid risk.

He slapped the water. "Hurry it up."

He could fight off an army of cops. The youngsters could hold their own pretty well. The real danger came from being halted before they could reach the Gulf of Mexico. If the cops disabled his truck, the youngsters would be poisoned to death by their own wastes within a half a day. What if the cops surrounded them and drove Bedders off the road and the tanks spilled? The youngsters would die within minutes. Every fiber of his being told him that taking the dolphins was a bad, bad idea.

The dolphins weren't distracted by the jittering tentacle tips. They darted away and circled the tank in opposite directions, keeping just out of reach of the squid school but nipping at the tentacles as they zipped by. All six squid youngsters tried to grab the dolphins at once.

Twelve tentacles tangled together and a few mantles collided, and in the moment of confusion the dolphins zipped in, snapped at the squid and zipped out again. There were billows of blood and an explosive cloud of black ink, and the squid recoiled in all directions.

"No, no, no, what are you *doing?*" Bedders lamented.

Two angry youngsters sped after the dolphins, who fled and crossed paths, and the squid kids knocked heads, then grappled with one another savagely. Two others sulked at the edge of the pool with messing wounds between their eyes.

The dolphins had some instincts of their own when it came to dealing with cephalopod predators. But the trick with the swimming in circles—that wasn't an instinct, Bedders realized. That was a sneaky ploy that took advantage of the squid's weakness. Because squid instincts didn't account for pack hunting, at least not in cramped quarters like this.

Bedders loved his kids, but he knew they weren't the smartest marine creatures in the tank.

The squid flickered with lethal static energy and they advanced on the dolphins with new wariness. The dolphins turned their heads from side to side. This was something new. Maybe they were frightened. Good, Bedders thought. He hoped the smart-ass ocean apes crapped their drawers. They saw now that they were dead meat, one way or the other.

The energy slashed from tentacle tips. The dolphins

shot away, dodging the bolts and crisscrossing far below the squid school. The youngsters dived to get them. The dolphin arced powerfully and shot straight for the surface, passing between squid tentacles and into the open air. Their leap was postcard-perfect, but when they penetrated the water the squid were following at magnificent speed. The dolphins leaped again—over a metal door. They splashed out of sight on the far side of it, and the steel reverberated with deflected energy bolts.

"Son of a bitch."

Energy ricocheted into the squid school, and the youngsters lashed out at one another viciously.

"Stop fighting," Bedders shouted. "What's the matter with you? Hey, I'm *talking* to you." He slapped the water surface angrily until the tussle ended and the wad of arms separated into six sullen youngsters.

The dolphins had their heads out of the small holding pool, watching curiously. Bedders spotted a circle of brushed aluminum on the wall with an embossed icon of a door with waves underneath it—he brought his fist down on it. A motor whined and the metal door rose. The dolphins chattered. Bedders gave them the finger.

The smaller dolphin, Jamie, slipped below the waves.

Squid jostled to be the first to squeeze through the widening gap.

Jamie zipped to a metallic disk in the wall several feet below the surface and touched it with his snout.

"Shit!" Bedders exclaimed. The door reversed direction. The squid retreated in a hurry—but not quickly enough. Two of them thrashed with their limbs trapped at the bottom, their boneless mass too flat to trigger the door's safety sensors. Bedders pounded the wall switch. The door moved an inch—then Jamie poked his button and it crushed down again. Bedders hit the switch. Jamie hit the switch.

"I ain't in the mood to play fucking games with a fucking fish!"

Then he saw blood in the dolphin tank, and Albert surfaced with writhing hunks of slime in his mouth. Squid arms! He swam to the side of the pool and deposited the arms in a filter uptake the size of a heater duct. Bedders hit the door switch again, and it moved just enough for the trapped squid to pull free—but only because most of the trapped arms were amputated. The youngsters bobbed to the surface, eyes wide in some kind of shock.

"Oh, Jesus, please no." Bedders almost wept. His children were hurt, in terrible pain, and he let it happen. They didn't even have the arms to reattach them. That bottlenose bastard threw 'em away! Bedders's fists balled and trembled.

"Go. Go cook 'em." He thrust a finger at the holding spool. The unmaimed youngsters returned, reached over the door and turned on the juice. The energy danced below the water in the holding cell. The dolphins were as good as gumbo.

Albert and Jamie left the water in a hurry, bellying up on a black rubber landing platform just above water level. Tails held high, they watched the water boil.

Bedders stomped around to them. "Get in before I kick your fucking heads in."

The youngsters ran out of power and the dolphins rolled their glistening bodies into the water before Bedders came close enough to deliver on his promise.

"Again," Bedders ordered.

The energy started. If Flipper and Fucker tried getting on their platform, Bedders was ready to stomp their blowholes. This time, the dolphins simply emerged onto the concrete lip of the pool on the opposite side. Bedders darted around the pool, but before he reached them the dolphins retreated to the water and the youngsters' kill juice gave out.

"More!"

The youngsters tried again. They were about used up. The dolphins emerged on the landing platform, then returned to the water as the energy dissipated. They glided to the door and sank their teeth into a buffet of dangling tentacles. The squid thrashed on the opposite side of the metal door. Both dolphins dragged off slimy mouthfuls of flesh and deposited them neatly in the filter uptake.

"Argh!" Bedders shouted.

The dolphins chattered above the surface, laughing at him, as plain as day.

"I'll kill you myself. I'll tear your hides right off." He crashed into the holding pool, berserk and power-

ful, only to feel his claws come up empty. His preter-
natural strength didn't give him the speed of an adult
dolphin in its natural element. Albert and Jamie leaped
effortlessly over the metal door. Bedders scrambled
over it to find the battered, depleted youngsters clump-
ing together and eyeing the dolphins with undisguised
terror.

"Pathetic," Bedders spit.

The dolphins emerged and nodded. They nodded!

"Shut your yaps. Only I get to say they're pathetic."
He did a breaststroke that beat all Olympic records, but
the dolphins slipped away. Now in the big tank, there
was plenty of room for them to stay out of his reach.
They lured him to one side, then glided into the huddle
of youngsters and nipped at them.

Oscar Bedders hadn't felt this way since he was beat
up in middle school by a bunch of eleven-year-olds
who no longer wanted to give him their lunch money.
They banded together, damned sissies, and thrashed
him on the playground. He remembered lying there
helpless as the little shits kicked him in the gut. The
teachers who watched recess took their sweet time res-
cuing him, and being rescued by the English teacher
was just as humiliating as being beat up in the first
place.

"How's it feel to take little of your own medicine,
Oscar?" the teacher asked loudly. Everybody heard it
and people were ha-haing and the worst thing was that
Oscar realized, even at moment of his worst disgrace,

that he couldn't go out and get revenge on those little shits. Now the little shits knew that they were stronger than he was.

When he got home, his dad switched him for being a pansy-ass who let himself be bested by the smart kids. "You ain't smart, so being strong is all you got. And now you got nothin'."

That was exactly how he felt now. He dragged himself out of the pool. The dolphins kept surfacing and chattering. As he hoisted the wounded youngsters from the tank, the dolphins harassed them with nips. Bedders dragged the trough back to the truck, and then he was forced to face the dolphins again to collect water. He scooped the water up in fish buckets and it took ten trips to the Dolphinarium, and every single time Albert and Jamie splashed him in the face.

On the last trip, he made them a solemn oath. "If I ever see a dolphin again, I promise you, I will tear its heart out with my bare hands. You understand me?"

The dolphins did the trick in which they emerged high out of the water on their powerful tails, then landed with big splashes. Bedders was drenched one more time. He stomped to the truck with the chattering of delighted dolphins humiliating him anew every step of the way.

28

The truck exceeded the posted height limit for the drive-through window. It didn't drive through so much as back up to the window with its reverse signal beeping.

"What is this?" Haff Dully said, leaning his body weight on the lever that opened the drive-through window. The truck driver was coming around the back.

"Just you tonight?"

"You can't park that truck there."

"I need food."

"We can't serve walk-ups. Insurance says so."

"But your doors are locked."

"Dining area is closed," Haff said. "Now you need to pull that truck out of here."

"What about my youngsters?" the driver demanded. "They're hurt and they are hungry." The driver pulled the back of the truck open.

"What are those?" Haff said when he saw the feeding troughs. Something shot out of the feeding troughs. Haff Dully took his weight off the lever and the windows closed, but slimy arms opened the window right back up again.

Haff tried to run, but he didn't get far.

BARRY ARMANDO WAS tired and hungry, and the only drive-through open in town after midnight was Pirate Perch. He didn't care for their food. It was all glopped in the same batter and it was all fried in the same grease, so even the Chicken Peg-Legs and Buccaneer Fries tasted like fish.

But it was late, he was tired, he'd had a bad day and all he wanted was to fill his stomach and fall in bed.

The Place Order Here sign was taped over with a hand-written note that said, "Speaker broke, order at window."

Barry pulled around to the window, which stood open. The lights were on, but nobody came.

Barry honked. "Can I order?" he called.

He heard the alarmingly close beeping of a truck in reverse. He hadn't noticed it parked nearby, but it was heading right for him. He depressed the brake, pulled the car into Drive—and was bashed before the transmission engaged. The back end of his old Hyundai was crushed between the truck and the outside of the Pirate Perch.

Armando leaped out and examined the damage.

"You better have insurance, mister," he called to the driver. He could see the man's arm on the windowsill. The guy was just in the cab, watching Armando in the side mirror.

"You're gonna buy me a new car!" Armando added. If the Hyundai was totaled and the driver was insured, this could be a windfall. He'd like a new car. Yeah, the wheels were twisted. Bent axle. Frame damaged. Totaled for sure.

Barry noticed that the back end of the truck was wide open, and water was dribbling out. Something slimy emerged and wrapped around his neck.

Barry's bad day became infinitely worse.

THE YOUNGSTERS WERE well fed, which helped them heal their wounds. Everybody felt much improved after digesting the meal from the Pirate Perch.

There would be no more risky detours, Bedders decided. From here on, it was a straight shot to the Gulf of Mexico.

But the urge started up again in Ripley. There was a Dance till Dawn at the Ripley Civic Center, and Oscar Bedders experienced the strange compulsion to drive his truck right up to the loading dock. Hundreds of people there. The youngsters would have a good time with them.

Too dangerous, Bedders realized, and forced himself to stay on the highway.

Next he spotted a lock-in revival for teenagers in Millington, with lots of cars in the parking lot. Bedders found himself pulling into the pavilion at the county fairgrounds before he knew what he was doing. The front entrance was all glass, and inside were lights and lots of people, and Bedders could drive right through the doors and into the revival and the youngsters would be able to feed and feed.

Why was he thinking these things? Stopping now was the last thing they should do. They were safe. They were healthy. Nobody knew what they were driving now. Bedders hoped to drive this truck all the way to the Gulf. They would need to make one or two fuel stops. Otherwise, they should be on the Gulf of Mexico shores tomorrow afternoon. Bedders could picture himself opening the rear panel doors and backing the truck down a boat launch into the water, and the glorious moment when the youngsters would swim free in the ocean.

There was a protest from the back—an angry thrashing in the water. Bedders was startled back to reality.

"Christ!"

He had just caught himself driving toward the three-story-atrium front of a banquet hall, where some sort of formal event was happening inside. The men and women in formal evening wear were gaping at the big truck that was accelerating straight at them, as if to crash through the glass.

Oscar Bedders swerved away, stomping the brakes, and managed to maneuver back to the road with his heart pounding in his head. He forced himself to take the interstate on-ramp, but the compulsion was growing stronger—and he didn't even understand it.

The youngsters didn't need to feed. There was no reason to take them to a public place with lots of people and let them kill and kill. It would serve only to attract attention, draw in all those people who were hunting for the mass murderer who began his spree in Chicago.

Oscar Bedders had an unpleasant moment of sudden recognition.

"Son of a bitch!" he shouted. "You want to attract attention? Is that it? You want to bring the cops down on us, huh?"

Bedders didn't even know whom he was shouting at. The voice in his head. It wasn't even a voice, just the commands that compelled his actions.

"Who are you?" Bedders demanded, looking up at the ceiling of the truck cab. "What are you?"

There was no answer. He twisted in his seat and peered through the small window into the cargo hold, where he could see the faint sloshing of the water in the containers. The force in his head didn't come from the youngsters, as he had assumed from the very start. Now he imagined he could feel the tenuous thread of the mind that dominated him.

"Where are you? Show yourself."

He turned his head to the front. Then the sides. He felt it, like a weak, night-colored filament that stretched from his head back to the source of the commands. It went north, back the way he had come.

"Mamma squid, is that you? I thought you were dead." He laughed harshly. "Are you a big squid-bitch ghost now?"

Oscar Bedders was closer to the truth than he would ever know, but he realized he was wrong about the direction. The direction from which the dominating thoughts came was not north, back to Chicago, but west.

"I get it. These orders ain't coming from your mamma at all, is it, young 'uns?" Bedders said aloud. "They're coming from your daddy, in the big dark sea."

The youngsters thrashed in their tanks.

"Daddy can go to hell," Bedders announced. "What kind of daddy is he anyway, putting his own babies in harm's way? No proper daddy."

The water splashed.

"He don't care about you. Not like me. I'm your daddy now. Hear me, youngsters?"

But Bedders's will was helpless against the compulsion of daddy squid. At every exit, Bedders felt the force compelling him to get off, find some sort of late-night public gathering and cause some mayhem.

"I don't understand," he choked out. "I thought you wanted to save the children. I thought that's what this was all about."

There was no answer.

"It's not about the children at all," Bedders decided. "They are just a tool. I'm just a tool. You made me love them and my love is just a tool, too."

The green sign ahead told Bedders that the city of Memphis was twenty miles ahead. The compulsion sprang to life anew. Bedders understood he wouldn't be able to resist it. Daddy squid's brain was stronger than his brain. It would be far safer to succumb to the compulsion now, on the outskirts of the city, than to do it in a big place like Memphis.

"Squid daddy's a rat bastard, youngsters," he called out. He heard the turmoil in the tanks. Ah, the youngsters knew it, too. On some level they understood as well as he did that their lives were forfeit for the father's selfish purposes. "I'll try to keep you safe, youngsters," Bedders said. "I'll do everything I can for you. I'll lay myself down for you, if need be."

Promise made, Oscar Bedders steered onto the off ramp, where a fifty-foot sign for the Budget Aristocrat Motel announced the Dutton High School Class Of 2000 Annual Reunion.

Bedders didn't know that the Class of 2000 was famous across southwestern Tennessee for being the biggest bunch of partiers ever to come out of Dutton High, which was why they had a class reunion every year. Another excuse to celebrate. All Bedders cared about was that the party was still going strong. He could see flashing lights and dancing in the convention area alongside the pool. Some of the attendees were in the pool, fully clothed. Some of the attendees were in the pool fully naked, not caring that the entire shindig was visible through the floor-to-ceiling pool atrium windows.

The kids from Dutton High Class of 2000 knew how to have a good time. In fact, that was about all they knew how to do, so what happened to them wasn't the great blow to society that the loss of any other group of young people might have been.

Oscar Bedders backed his panel truck into the glass floor-to-ceiling windows. The noise of the glass falling was big enough to cut through the alcohol haze.

Every male graduate of the Dutton High School, Class of 2000, dropped his jaw and exclaimed in unison, "Whoa!"

A few of the women screamed. A few fell over. A trio of dripping screwers scampered out of the steamy hot tub to see what was going on. Only the bartender was smart enough to get the hell out.

The truck driver jumped out, stepping over glass, and unlatched the rear of the truck. He was on the verge of tears.

"Dude, are you okay?" asked Steve "Stoner" Rossly.

"Please help me," the driver asked as he swung open the door.

"I'll help you, dude," Rossly said. "I'm class president. Come on and help the man, everybody."

It didn't take all forty of them to open the rear panels. In fact, most got in the way and a few of them were tripped and fell into the glass, getting bloody.

Stoner Rossly looked at the big containers inside the truck. "Now what?"

"Please hurry," the driver pleaded. "It's inside there."

Into the panel truck went the boys of the Class of 2000.

"THEY'RE SCREAMING. They're trying to get away. The bodies are flying out of the truck." The shell-shocked bartender was looking through the porthole of the service door window and trying to describe the scale of the destruction to the 911 operator.

"Is there gunfire?" the emergency operator asked.

"Just screaming and electric sparks and people are getting killed."

"We have police and emergency medical coming to the scene."

"Please hurry. There's Stoner—he's dead."

"Stoner?" The emergency operator repeated. "Stoner Rossly? Is the Class of 2000 having another damned reunion?" She sounded disapproving.

"Yes. Please hurry."

"Don't worry about that bunch, Carl. We'll get to them sooner or later."

29

Remo listened in silence to the report from Mark Howard about the attack at a class reunion in southern Tennessee.

"It's a strange one," Mark Howard admitted. "Many deaths, but none of the mutilation we've seen in all the previous attacks. We're still trying to figure it out."

Remo felt something unpleasant niggling in a corner of his brain. "I want to see this, Junior." He pushed the power button on the remote control on the countertop. The ceiling fan began to rotate. He pushed the channel-up button. The rice maker honked at him. "Chiun, turn on the TV. Please?"

Chiun didn't respond well to requests made in that particular tone of voice. Remo tried the mode button, the TV-DVD button and the communications button. A sunroof opened and the phone disconnected. The rice cooker smelled hot.

"I shall do it," Chiun said unhappily, relieving Remo of the remote control.

"What, do you run the whole camper off that one remote?" he asked.

"Yes."

"Really?" Remo hadn't believed such a thing was possible. When it came to electronics, he was all super-powered thumbs. "Why not just have an on-off switch and a channel knob so I can use the thing?" The TV came to life and the appliances powered down.

The phone rang and Mark Howard said, "It's me."

Remo watched the news feed from the disaster. The hotel was surrounded by emergency vehicles, and the news correspondent was forced to make his report from a hundred yards away from the scene.

"We don't know how many fatalities occurred, but there were no police casualties this time. The police response was described by a spokesman as measured and cautious."

"This doesn't tell me anything," Remo said as the long-distance video shots tried to pierce the activity at the motel. "What's the problem here, Mark?"

"The problem is, we don't know why the attack was made, Remo," Mark Howard said. "Every aggressive act prior to this had a purpose. Feed the hatchlings. Get water for the hatchlings. After he robbed the pet store in Kentucky, we thought Bedders had everything he needed."

"Yeah?"

"So the question remains, why strike here?"

Remo watched news footage of bodies being carried out in limp vinyl coroner bags. "I know why."

"Yes?" Mark Howard said.

"To get our attention," Remo said.

"That's what we think."

"Oh, God," Remo groaned. "Shit, Mark, that's why. That's the reason for all of this. Dammit to hell—it's all for me. I'm the one who pissed off Sa Mangsang. He's getting back at me. More to the point, he wants me dead."

Chiun was looking at Remo thoughtfully.

"What?" Remo demanded angrily. "You want to tell me I'm wrong?"

"I think you are correct."

"It's becoming clearer. Sa Mangsang's got almost no power right now. He'd have to rest up for a few centuries before he could start stirring up trouble on the large scale like he tried to do. But he had this ace in the hole. A big squid that still had instructions or telepathy-connection or whatever, so he could tell it what to do. He's still got a link with it, so he can make all this happen and he does it all just to pull me in and make me dead. I'm right, aren't I, Chiun?"

The old Master inclined his head. "I think so."

"We think this may be, essentially, what has occurred." Now Harold Smith was on the line, trying to add a voice of reasonableness to the conversation. Despite his assurances to Chiun, he had never bought into the concept of Sa Mangsang as ancient, sea-dwelling god. To him, the phenomenon that had occurred was called Sa Mangsang only because it matched the Sa Mangsang legend.

Remo was agitated. "It is what occurred, Smitty. You know it is. Ah, shit. Where is Bedders?"

Smith didn't answer. Mark Howard didn't answer.

"I want to know where he is, Smith," Remo said calmly.

"We don't know. You're in no shape to take him on. You need to recuperate."

"How many more people have died already just to get my frickin' attention?" Remo said. "How many more will die while I go on R & R? Tell me where he is."

"I don't know, Remo."

"Are you lying?" Remo looked at Chiun. "Is he lying?"

"He is not lying."

"I think he's lying."

"You are allowing your emotions to befuddle you. This is not how a Master of Sinanju behaves."

"Hey, that's me. Master out of the ordinary. I'm white, I'm American and I have a conscience."

"This is uncalled-for," Chiun remonstrated.

"Everything I do is uncalled-for." Remo tossed the phone into the air. It arced and vanished just as it was about to hit the countertop. "I'm gonna get some fresh air."

Remo stepped through the door. The air blustered inside, then Remo was gone and the door was shut.

Chiun pursed his ancient, dry mouth and extracted the phone from his robe sleeve. "Alert us when you have more information, wise Emperor," Chiun said, and clicked off the phone.

REMO GOT into the SUV alongside the driver, then grabbed the steering wheel as the driver swerved wildly from lane to lane.

"Get a grip, Mac," Remo said.

"Sorry. Just didn't expect anybody to be getting in with me, you know, when we're moving at seventy miles per hour."

"Life's full of surprises."

Roy Candace was trembling, but he calmed down eventually. The guy—named Remo, if Roy recalled right—was just sitting there, glaring at the road ahead, and twenty minutes passed in silence.

"How far to Dutton?"

Roy's eyes were flickering. "I never heard of it."

"You listen to the news this morning?"

"Yeah."

"Hear about the class reunion that got snuffed?"

"Yeah."

"That's Dutton."

"Oh." Roy was panicky. So what if there were some famous murders there—how was that supposed to help him tell the guy how far away they were?

"Hey, whoever, how far to Dutton?" Remo called.

"Seven miles," said the very feminine voice of Roy's handler. It was Sarah Slate, but she was putting a dose of cheesy Marilyn Monroe into her speech.

Remo smirked. "Laying it on a little thick, aren't you?"

The dashboard didn't try to defend itself.

Remo spotted Roy's atlas and examined the page for Tennessee, then turned to the map of Mississippi.

"Should I, uh, plan on exiting at Dutton?" Roy asked.

"No, Roy," said the dashboard voice of Sarah Slate.

"Yeah, take the exit," Remo said more loudly. The conflicting orders sent the driver into a panic. "Relax, Roy. You wet your pants when I'm in the car with you, that would really tick me off."

"I won't do that."

"I guess you don't need to stop at Dutton. He'd have cleared out of Dutton. Right, you?"

"I'm called Nancy, Remo," Sarah Slate said. "You're right. He would have moved on."

"But where to, *Nancy?*" Remo said. "He wants me to find him."

"Yes."

"But on his terms, right, *Nancy?*"

"Yes."

"So where?"

"We're trying to determine that ourselves," Sarah said.

Remo heard somebody else start to speak. It was just the inhalation of breath that comes before the *uh*. He knew the *uh* was Mark Howard.

"You leave me alone. I don't want to talk to you. Or your old man. Not unless you have something concrete to tell me."

In the ongoing silence, Remo could hear the driver's eyeballs working overtime. When he looked at the guy,

Roy was rolling his eyes wildly and meaningfully. At the road atlas, at the dome light with its hidden camera for monitoring the interior of the SUV and back at Remo.

"I have to take a leak," Remo shouted. "Hey, *Nancy,* we're gonna make a pit stop at the BP."

"I see," Sarah Slate replied slowly.

"Don't get your knickers in a knot," Remo said.

Which, unfortunately for Roy Candace, made him start thinking about Nancy in some old-fashioned British underwear, and that made it difficult to drive again.

30

Remo followed Roy Candace into the gas station store, to the hot-dog machine.

"The steel bars screw up long-range listening devices," Roy explained, waving his hand at a couple of wrinkled wieners that had been revolving on the heating elements for at least a full day. "I don't know how much you want those people overhearing stuff, you know."

Remo shrugged.

"Better safe than sorry, though, you know?"

"I guess. Sure. I appreciate your thoughtfulness. Now, what?"

"I think I might be able to help out some. Maybe, I'm saying. Mind if I get some lunch while we talk?"

"How could you maybe help?"

Roy was feeling more confident now, although still nervous as hell. He would never, ever forget seeing Remo, the skinny guy, step off a building and beat up a Ford Excursion. Roy lowered his voice. "I think I kind of have a clue what's going on. I mean, I don't *really* know, but I know you're chasing the guy with the octopus, right? And he's the one doing all these killings, right? And for whatever reason, it's none of my business, I guess it's a personal thing between you and the octopus man, huh? Am I right?"

Roy fished two stale buns from the bag on the counter and used the tongs to grab the raisinlike hot dogs. "Look," he continued, "I got friends in Jackson who owe me favors. I call them in. They send some of their people out onto the streets to watch for the octopus man, right?"

Remo's stomach turned when Roy spread vibrant green relish on the dog, followed by vibrant yellow mustard. "Don't see how that could help. We don't even know what he's driving, or if he'll go through Jackson."

"No, we ain't gonna be trying to spot him, so much as we're gonna be in position to get on his ass when he makes a move." Roy was very pleased with himself. "He'll do some other stunt, right, to attract your attention? We'll be closer than he thinks with our people to keep an eye on him. That'll give us a heads-up on him, right? Instead of you walking into his trap, way he wants it, he'll be falling into yours."

Remo considered it. "Your friends in Jackson. They're not cops, right? They're more like, what?"

"Business people," Roy said brightly.

"I see. Because cops would have to go in and try to nail the bastard. Your guys would have to keep their distance. Not get involved."

"That's what they do."

"How many guys are you talking about?"

"I can get you ten guys," Roy said, feeling better all the time. "I'd be happy to help out."

Remo was seeing the possibilities. It might help. It couldn't hurt. The worst that could happen was that a bunch of "business people" from Jackson, Mississippi, went to feed Bedders's squid. More than likely, they would be of no help whatsoever.

"Sure. Call your friends. I'd appreciate the assist," Remo said.

Roy Candace couldn't have been happier. "Great! Hot dog?"

"No, thanks. I have breakfast waiting in the camper."

"Uh, uh, uh," Roy said before Remo could leave the convenience store. "One other thing. I wanted to ask you. It's about her. You know. *Her.*"

"Nancy?"

"Yeah. Is she, you know?"

"As hot as she sounds?"

"Yeah."

"Oh, yeah."

"Yeah?"

"Oh, yeah."

"All right!" Roy went to the counter with his hot dogs, chortling. "All right!"

THE CANTON FISH MARKET was hit before daybreak. An estimated 1,500 pounds of fresh fish, trucked in overnight from the Gulf, were stolen and the only eyewitnesses to the theft were dead.

"Six staff worked the shift from 1:00 a.m. and through the morning sales rush," Smith explained. "They were struck prior to the market opening at 5:00 a.m. All the fish were stolen."

"All the fish?" Chiun piped up from his mat.

"I thought you were meditating," Remo said over his shoulder. "What do you mean, all the fish?"

"Every scrap of fish," Mark Howard explained. "Every anchovy. Every single Gulf shrimp. There isn't a single remaining bit of fish in the place."

"A cleanup job like that would take a lot of people," Remo said, "unless the cleanup crew had eight arms each."

"Ten arms. Squid have ten arms. The overnight staff were gutted and put on ice," Mark added.

"All that beautiful fresh fish," mourned Chiun, "chewed by the beaks of the filthy hatchlings."

"People were killed, too, Chiun."

"Yes, and an honest fishmonger is rare enough in this land of fries and burgers," Chiun agreed. "But they only sell the fish. It is the loss of the fish themselves that is truly sad."

"Chiun's all broken up over this," Remo reported into the phone. "Where's the next one?"

"We're just getting the reports of vandalism at a Captain Jack's Fish Planks restaurant in Yazoo City. Several hundred pounds of uncooked, packaged food was dumped in the parking lot. This occurred at daybreak."

"Any deaths?" Remo asked. "There's always some-body dead when Oscar Bedders is behind it."

"Homeless man, strangled and stuffed in the freezer in place of the food. Numerous circular skin punctures on his body."

"Okay, that's Bedders. He doesn't want us to get lost."

"He's changed course," Mark Howard pointed out. "Yazoo City is west of Canton. I'd say he's heading back to the Mississippi River. If he takes the direct route, he'll pass through Orcgonville and Fertile, both small towns."

"How far behind are we?" Remo wished he had a map. Their driver was already taking the off-ramp from the interstate, and in seconds they were headed for Yazoo City, Eight Miles.

"He's twenty minutes ahead of you. Maybe less."

"Get me a chopper, Smitty," Remo said. "I want to get a step ahead of this bastard for once."

"No." The answer came from Chiun. "You will not face this creature on your own. You will be defeated."

"You can come. Did I say you couldn't come?"

"We don't know yet where he is, Remo," Harold Smith said. "We can only guess. Even now, you're as close as we can put you with any precision."

"Bulldookey. You said he was heading for the river. So fly me to the river."

"Just as likely that he backtracked from Yazoo City, waiting for you to show up. He could be watching for you now," Smith said.

"He doesn't know we're in this retirement condo on

wheels," Remo said. "Last thing he'd expect is for his enemies to arrive in the Em Oh Ess Battle Camper. I get your point. Okay. I'll stay in the trailer, but I have to tell y'all, I'm getting awful squirrelly being cooped up in here."

Remo got in beside Roy and grabbed the wheel just seconds before they crashed.

"You're high-strung," Remo said when Roy got his wits back and took control of the steering again.

"Hard to get used to you coming in that way, Mr. Remo."

Remo was gone. Vanished. As if he went invisible. "What the—?"

"Down here. Somebody was staring at us," Roy spotted Remo on the floor of the front seat, now emerging as if from a hidden cave and peering out the window. "It was just a local kid. What's he staring at us so hard for?"

Roy cleared his throat. "Maybe he was, you know, interested in you walking around outside of the camper while we're driving."

Remo bit his lower lip thoughtfully, thinking he should have been more careful. "You may have a point. Guess I'm high-strung, too."

"Who could blame you, Mr. Remo?"

"Just Remo," said Remo, getting back into his seat. "You know where we're going?" he asked pointedly.

"Yeah. Sure, I do."

Remo was gone again. Roy Candace looked on the floor. No Remo. He checked in the rear. No Remo.

Remo emerged. He had been on the floor in front, after all. Now, how could he have hid *that good?*

"Just an old lady," Remo said. "Which is how I'm acting. Why's everybody so interested in us?"

Roy made a you-know-how-it-is face. "We're shiny."

"Shiny."

"Like new shiny," Roy said jovially.

"We have another incident to report," Sarah Slate broke in.

"Go ahead."

"Please return to the Airstream."

"Negative, HQ, that's too risky while we're in motion. Go ahead with the report ASAP, over."

"Another fish place in Yazoo City."

"Fresh or fast food?"

"It serves both."

"Hit when?"

"Unknown. Maybe this morning, with the others. Maybe within the last hour. Place named Lili's on the highway west of town. Three bodies."

"Three more bodies," Roy said. "This guys makes lots of dead people."

Remo Williams knew that Roy was talking about Oscar Bedders the squid keeper, but he might as well have been talking about Remo Williams.

Oscar was rolling his eyes again, at Roy, out the window. A small, grungy gas station was coming up.

"I need to take a whiz," Remo hollered.

"Again?" Sarah asked.

"Men's room coming up." Roy Candace maneuvered off the road. He parked in the rear of the grungy gas station, with the marshy woods cushioning the camper on one side.

"Why all this stopping and starting?" Chiun asked from within the Airstream. "I hope there is a purpose to disturbing a frail old man who simply wants the peace of meditation and reflection."

"Pit stop," Remo answered. "Mountain Dew?"

"No, thank you," Chiun said.

Roy was looking all around while trying to appear as if he wasn't. He couldn't hear Chiun's side of the conversation, only Remo talking into the empty air. The guy had to be wired.

"Okay, Roy, where's your friends from Jackson?" Remo asked when they ducked into the men's room on one side of the building.

"Let me make a call. They should be around here. They knew exactly what you're looking for and this guy's not exactly hiding his trail, is he?" Roy pulled out his cell phone and thumbed a number.

"Uncle Lawr, it's Candy."

Remo listened in to both sides of the conversation. Uncle Lawr was middle management with some sort of a crime organization in Jackson. Uncle Lawr mentioned some of his business partners, and the names lacked the ring of Italian family tradition. The good old days of Mafia Crime Families running the big cities were long gone. Whoever they were, they had to have owed

"Candy" some hefty favors. There were thirteen auto-mobiles in and around Yazoo City, all staking out both the restaurants where known hits had occurred.

"A new crime place was just on the police bands," Uncle Lawr reported. "Place called Lili's. We've got a car on the scene already, Candy. I think we're closing in on this fish crook."

"Sounds like you got the town locked up, Uncle Lawr."

"Shame to steal so much good, fresh fish. I need to be able to call you when we finally get this man in our sights. Can I call you directly, Candy?"

"Tell him okay," Remo said before Roy could relay the request. Roy got a chill. Remo could overhear the telephone. He should have expected as much. Lucky for him, Uncle Lawr hadn't said anything derogatory that Roy would have agreed with.

"Call me," Roy Candace said into the phone, and for the umpteenth time he wondered if he was possibly going to get out of this job without losing his life. The octopus-man, he was ruthless and a killer and a monster—but Candace's own bosses were truly terrifying.

31

The convenience store had a small display cooler filled with old ice and fresh Gulf snapper. This Chiun accepted graciously, after satisfying himself that it was indeed fresh, but lunch only stalled his complaining for several minutes.

"Why must we stay in this place?"

"Because Bedders might be here," Remo said. "It's the best lead we've got."

"This is not productive."

"You have a better idea?"

Chiun's face brightened and he hoisted the telephone, dialing an 800 number from memory. "I am in Yahoo City," he told the phone.

"Yazoo City."

"Yazoo City, in the state of Misserippi."

"Mississippi," Remo corrected him, as did the operator on the phone.

"As I said," Chiun continued, "I am in need of inexpensive, stylish clothing. Is one of your stores located here?"

Chiun smiled broadly when he got his answer.

THE AIRSTREAM PULLED into the Yazoo City Tarjé (Paris) Discount Superstore and came to a stop at the concrete posts that prevented runaway cars from plowing through the front entrance.

"We're on his freaking tail, Little Father," Remo said. "Can't this wait?"

"We may be waiting hours or days before this one shows himself to us," Chiun said. "The hoodlum associates of our chauffeur will distract him until our arrival. There is nothing more for us to do, Remo. We may as well make the time useful. I have my phone. Perhaps you should come with me. Do we not need bottled water?"

"We have plenty of Oui Oui."

"Maybe it would lift your spirits to escape the confines of my home, which you find wretched and uncomfortable."

"I'm sorry I don't like your place, Chiun. Fine. Go ahead. I'll call you if something happens."

"Or have the chauffeur do so," Chiun said.

32

The last time that manager Luis Rand could remember a supplier visiting his store it was the guy who made gourmet caramel apples, begging for more store space. He couldn't understand that caramel apples weren't in demand. Candy apples were doing better, but they had a supplier of candy apples.

But Rand had heard stories of textiles suppliers sometimes dropping in to visit out-of-the-way Tarjé (Paris) Discount Superstores. These were fashion babes with flirty attitudes and sky-high expense accounts. They'd show a store manager a good time, according to the gossip.

The rep from Koh-Mo-Nos Enterprises was a major disappointment. Not female, not hot, not young. A little Asian guy so old he was probably going to drop dead at any second.

"I am interested in the sales success you have experienced with the fashionable Koh-Mo-Nos."

"Koh-Mo-Nos?" Luis Rand said.

The little man wore a fixed smile.

"Oh. Oh! Sure. The Koh-Mo-Nos. We're doing pretty well, now. Want to see the sales reports?"

"Yes."

It was against the rules, but it would be easier to print the sales report for the Koh-Mo-Nos SKUs than to go over the sales with the old man personally. "I've got a small fishing-tackle crisis in sporting goods. Be right back."

He left the little old man peering down at the print-out. He got only halfway to sporting goods before the old man was standing in front of him, as perfectly still as if he had been waiting in the aisle for an hour.

"Congratulations on your success," the old man said warmly. "You have achieved impressive sales of the Koh-Mo-No. Most impressive."

"Thank you," Rand said. It looked like the same little old man, but how had he moved that fast? Maybe there were two of him.

"I have visited many Tarjé stores, most larger and cleaner by far, but none have reported such grand Koh-Mo-No sales results."

"I see. Thank you."

"You have taken dramatic steps to achieve this success." The little old man was holding up the report, his glistening, long fingernails trailing down a column of dates and unit sales numbers. "I see here that you were experiencing marginal sales until this date, nine days ago. Something changed on that date."

Luis Rand was in despair of getting back to his inventory mess in sporting goods. "Well, yeah, we put up some new floor displays."

"With grand results."

"Pretty good, yes sir."

"Where other managers failed," the little old man insisted. "You must not be humble. I will ask you to speak of your success at a special gathering of Tarjé managers and executives."

Rand was stunned. "You mean, the shareholders meeting?"

"It is coming next week to an inconvenient locale, inaccessible by roadway."

"It's in Maui," Rand said.

"Yes. You shall be there?"

"I'm not invited. My store's not exactly a top performer."

"Then you shall come as my guest and you shall deliver the keynote address to all the attendees."

"I thought the former vice president was going to deliver the keynote."

"Plans are changed. Now, the speaker is you. The subject of your speech shall be thus, Strategies for Impressive Koh-Mo-No Sales: How to Raise the Status of One's Store with the Effective Marketing of a Single, Exemplary Product."

Rand nodded dumbly. He'd never delivered a speech in his life. He was trying to remember what, exactly, had been done to increase Koh-Mo-No sales.

The old man looked expectant. "You will explain all this to me?"

Rand touched his nose with his tongue as a stall tactic. "I'll do better than tell you. I'll show you."

The old man seemed very happy.

His happiness didn't last.

THE AIRSTREAM WAS starting to close in on Remo and he was boiling over with ripe energy. He went for a walk, but he didn't go far and the parking lot smelled bad.

Then he spotted the display window on the front of the Tarjé. It was a formal living room populated by a family of mannequins. There was nothing unusual about the way they were dressed, but Remo was struck by something odd in the vignette.

He got close and the ugly truth was revealed. "Oh, no."

The slipcovers on the easy chair were of a brilliant silk print. The tablecloth on the circular accent table was in a similar, colorful print on silk. So were the throw pillows. So was the bed for the stiff, plastic sheepdog. The furnishings were dressed in Koh-Mo-Nos.

As the door opened to allow shoppers to exit, the sound carried on the wind like the cry of a distant soul in purgatory. "Aieee!"

33

Chiun returned to the Airstream wearing, of all things, a look of satisfaction. That could not be a good sign. Remo stared. Chiun raised a questioning eyebrow.

"How'd it go, Little Father?"

"It went fine."

"Fine?"

"Sales at this outlet are quite good compared to those in most other stores in the chain. The Koh-Mo-No is a hit."

"That's great news." Remo was a man waiting for the second shoe to drop.

"Quite." Chiun nodded. "The manager was using some unorthodox methods to introduce the innovative style development, as he called it, to simple locals who are not usually setters of trends."

"What's that mean?"

"This junk merchant explained that the people in this vicinity are not what he called 'first adopters of new fashion heats.' They must be introduced to new styles in ways that are more gradual and suitable to their mundane tastes. He explained that they are much more likely to try a vibrant, original material to cover a decorative cardboard table or a cushion used to pitch about the home."

"A throw pillow?"

"I assume the reason for lobbing a pillow is to get the attention of fellow household dullards without risk of marring wall paint. Which is beside the point. What matters is that the Koh-Mo-No achieved a high degree of acceptance when sold as something a house wears."

"Housewares?"

"Please do not interrupt. Now that the community has had its eyes opened to the brilliant new style of the Koh-Mo-No, it is ready to be guided to the next level of acceptance of this fashion, which will be the actual *wearing* of the Koh-Mo-No. The franchise manager was motivated to come up with interesting suggestions for promoting the Koh-Mo-No as a garment."

"Like what?" Remo's voice trailed off as his attention was drawn out the window. He happened to see a pizza-face teenager emerge from the store in an reflective orange cart-patrol vest—worn over a shimmering Koh-Mo-No that flapped about his hairy shins. The kid looked as if he wanted to curl up and die in a corner somewhere.

"One idea is to change the store uniform," Chiun was explaining. "All employees will henceforth be required to wear the Koh-Mo-No at all times, and all employees shall be versed in the exemplary features of the garment.

The merchant promised me that every one of his personnel, from management to janitorial, will wear the Koh-Mo-No."

"Sounds like business is really booming," Remo said.

Chiun allowed the memory of some irksomeness to shadow his face for a moment. "I did not embark upon this venture to boom in business. Nor to see my investment in manufacturing and distribution used to enliven the pillows thrown by one household fool at fellow household fools. As I explained to the merchant, they will be worn, in public, or this effort is all wasted."

"I don't think you'll let that happen."

Chiun made his mouth hard and wrinkled like a year-old crab apple. "You are correct. I will not."

34

Remo felt cheap, like perfume from the Everything's a Dollar outlet next to the Tarjé, but it was for a worthy cause. Helping Chiun, he told himself, would help Remo. So really, this was a way of improving his own quality of life. All the rationale wouldn't make it any easier to lean against the brick facade of the Tarjé and start making eyes at young ladies.

Remo had a strange relationship with women. He liked women. A lot. And they liked him. Too much. The skills of a Sinanju Master constituted potent sex appeal that Remo never seemed to get under control for long. When he wasn't careful, he started attracting women like ozone attracted pesky, bloodsucking insects.

A foursome emerged from the Tarjé employee entrance, and one of them was still in her uniform Koh-Mo-No. One glance at this little group told Remo more than he needed to know about who was the flirt, who was the cheerleader, who was the smart one and who was the mousey, shy girl whose self-esteem the others walked on. It was the shy girl who was still in the Koh-Mo-No.

"Hi, girls," he said, propping his face up in the goofy grin that some girls seemed to like. Easy for him, since goofy was his regular grin. He gave them the bold, checking-you-out look that would have earned him a slap in the face when he was their age. This bunch of girls appreciated the attention—all except for the shy girl in the Koh-Mo-No. She didn't try to hide from Remo, because she never would have believed he would be checking her out.

"How are you doing?" he asked her directly.

She looked around at her friends.

"Yeah. You. I like that dress."

"You do?" She couldn't believe it. She forgot to hide.

"You like that uniform?" the flirty one demanded indignantly. "That's what we wear to work."

"You wear that to work? It's one hundred percent silk. That's hand embroidery on the seams. They're not even wearing this stuff in New York yet. How do you people rate?" He directed the question at the shy girl.

"They just had us start wearing them," she said, feeling uncertain.

"You a fashion guy or something?" the cheerleader asked.

"Advertising."

"Yeah, right," the cheerleader said.

"I have to tell you, I didn't know about this whole kimono rage when I started seeing them in Hollywood. Some people put them on and they just look silly. Others. Wow. Nice."

The shy girl smirked. "Whatever."

"You think I'm giving you a line, don't you?"

"Yeah."

Smart, too, Remo thought. Smarter than her friends. "Just wanted to say you look sweet in that thing. Maybe it's not the kimono at all." He walked away, which he thought was just the right thing to do.

It was. He had bowled them over—except for the shy girl who was his target. "What a jerk."

"Jerk?" demanded her friend the flirt. "He was totally hot! And he was into you!"

"He was into the dress."

"He was into *you,* girl."

"Who cares?" said the tomboy. "He was fine. You blew it, Phoebe."

"He was kind of nice," the shy girl admitted. "But he was a jerk."

"I'd take a hot jerk."

"Me, too."

An older, self-assured man with deep black hair strolled by them and slowed, growing a big smile.

"Afternoon, beautiful. Like the skirt." He looked straight into the eyes of the shy girl when he said it—and that was all he said. He kept on walking.

The girls were staring at Phoebe.

"Guys are such jerks," Phoebe said, but she was feeling fine.

Her friends had never seen her attract this much attention.

"I'm gonna start wearing my Koh-Mo-No outside work," the flirty one said.

"Me, too."

"Yeah. It's not so bad."

"THEY WAS NICE," Roy Candace said. "I could have stayed and talked with them all day long."

"You're old enough to be their dad," Remo said. "I just wanted to spread a little appreciation is all." He handed over the hundred-dollar bill and ushered Roy into the SUV.

Then playtime was over and Remo was back inside the Airstream counting the rivets in the aluminum. Chiun had retired to the meditation chamber in the rear, where he was monitoring shoppers entering and leaving the store.

The place was too still. Remo was alone with his body, feeling all the spots where the flesh was still tender. His mind raced, thinking about all the people who had died for the one and only purpose of drawing him, Remo Williams, into a trap.

And here he was, just waiting for it to happen again. More people would die, probably very near to where he was sitting at this very minute. There was nothing he could do to save those innocent, unlucky strangers.

But the next time he met up with Oscar Bedders and his gaggle of squid kids, it was going to be the last time. Whatever it took to put an end to it, *whatever it took,* he would end the slaughter. If that meant the world would be without Remo Williams, then, well, so be it. The lives of all the not-yet-killed were worth the sacrifice of one orphan from Jersey who had long ago been listed as dead anyway.

THE CALL CAME from CURE with news of a new attack. A church fish fry, of all things. The camper started rolling due west. They were on their way to meet Oscar Bedders's summons.

Chiun came from the meditation chamber and fixed Remo with a look.

"What?"

"You tell me," the old Master Emeritus said. "The walls vibrate with your tension, as if you are a man on the verge of a seizure. What troubles you?"

"Take a wild guess," Remo declared, his voice chill and hollow. "Next time we run into Bedders, I'm gonna make him stop."

"You have not tried to stop him when we met previously?"

"Next time will be different. I'll do what it takes."

"I see. Something foolish, you mean. Something that puts you at grave risk."

"Whatever it takes."

"An unwise determination. You may lead yourself to catastrophe without defeating the squid guardian. What then?"

"Then he's done. He did what he set out to do. Punished the rebellious Master of Sinanju. He'll go away."

"Or he will not. He will not be fully avenged while I live and breathe—I was party to your betrayal of Sa Mangsang."

"I think it's me he wants. I'm Reigning Master of Sinanju and I'm Avatar of Shiva. Shiva kicked Sa Mangsang's ass. It was Shiva who sent him back to the ocean floor."

Chiun shook his head sadly. "Remo Williams, there is so much you have come to acknowledge and so little you yet understand. I would tell you something that I have told you before."

"How unlike you."

"Hearken to these words, then, for I may never have the chance to speak them again to you," Chiun said tightly.

"Okay. Go ahead, Little Father."

Chiun looked away. "There is always a Master of Sinanju. Now, it is you, and yet it is me, and were we not here, there would still be a Master of Sinanju."

"I don't get it."

"Hush. There is Shiva. There is the Avatar. There is Remo Williams."

"So? What's the difference?"

"Wrong!" Chiun snapped.

"What? What did I say? What's wrong?"

Chiun glowered, letting Remo figure it out for himself.

"*What's the difference* is what is wrong?" Remo asked. "That makes no sense."

Then it did make sense.

"Uh-huh. Chiun, now it is you who's wrong. There is a difference. Me and Shiva, we're not the same guy. He just shows up without an invitation. Remo is not the Destroyer." He was rambling. He shut up now. He felt stupid and angry. "What does this have to do with anything?"

Chiun's eyes wandered out the window as they drove past a small, wooden church. There were police cars with lights flashing and bodies on the ground.

"That's what I care about, Chiun. That's what I can't live with. That's the difference between me and Shiva, see? That's what I have to make stop now. Do you get that?"

"I understand some."

"Well, then, I guess we're even."

35

Roy Candace was getting used to the way Remo would join him in the SUV from the Airstream, even when they were driving. No more violent starts when the door opened. He even gave Remo a friendly grin.

The grin went away.

Holy mother of God, what was this? Remo's eyes were on fire with something dark and endless and scary, like some sort of a monster that was going to start making lots of things be dead.

"Get a grip, Roy." Remo's voice sounded like rocks grinding together in a grave.

Roy was trembling. He hated this job. His phone bleeped and Roy yelped.

His hands were removed from the steering wheel and the phone was put in them. "Talk," Remo ordered, holding the wheel.

"Hello?"

"Candy, it's Lawr—we're on his ass," the caller said.

"Oh. Good."

"Where?" Remo asked.

"Where you at?"

"What's going on?" asked Sarah Slate from the dashboard.

"Shut up."

"Where you at?" Roy asked the caller as he rattled off a location.

"Bait shop. We're on the river. Look, this ass-bastard did a number on a bunch of folks at a goddamned church. You should have seen it, Candy. People all messed up, all over the place. They was having a picnic. Let me tell you, this guy has no class."

"So how'd you end up at the bait shop?" Roy asked.

"We, jeez, we just followed his lead. We thought he wouldn't be hanging around the fish fry at the church, you know, so we just kept driving and waited for news. Then we hear a disturbance-of-the-peace call on the cop radio, you know? I send a car to check it out, and there he is, the SOB. Killed the cop at the bait shop. Beat his fucking head in on the floor of the bait shop. My boys watched it happen, right through the door of the fucking bait shop! I got here right away. I can see the poor guy lying in his own blood. I see it wit' my own eyes, Candy."

"Okay, so *where?*" Remo asked Candy.

"Okay, so *where?*" Candy asked Lawr.

Uncle Lawr wasn't exactly sure. "We got on County Road 1, then Scruggins Road, then across this other road following the river and then a dirt road that kept going due west of that road."

"Wait, let me write it down," Roy said.

"I got it all," Remo said.

"Okay. We got it," Roy said.

"Tell them to keep their distance," Remo told Roy.

"You guys stay back," Roy advised the caller. "I mean, way back."

"All my boys are gonna be here quick," said Roy's business associate. "Lotsa muscle to take this up-fuck to the cleaners."

"Listen, Lawr, I'm begging you," Roy said, "keep back. For your own good."

The business associate from Jackson made a raspberry sound. "See you soon, Candy."

Uncle Lawr hung up. Roy looked at Remo. "They're a-goner, huh?"

"Not if we can get there first."

"Remo, please report," Sarah requested.

"That's a negative, HQ. I don't do reports," Remo said. "Keep your yap shut or I'm switching you off."

"There's no need to shut us out, Remo," Harold W. Smith cut in.

Roy went wide-eyed—he had never heard any voice from the dashboard except his female liaison.

"That's how you can tell she's pissed off," Remo explained. "She starts sounding like a really old, bitter, unfriendly guy. Nancy, there's nothing you can do to help. Just observe. Candy, how long until we get there?"

"You got me."

"I'd like an explanation, Remo," Smith said, his voice

like the growling of a sour stomach. "We locked on to your caller. You know you're consorting with a criminal?"

"Whoever they are, they've tracked down Bedders."

"What?"

Remo would have enjoyed Smith's dismay any other time. "Can you tell me how to get to where the call's from?"

"Wait a moment. We've got it. It's southwest of you, directly on the Mississippi River. We'll steer you in."

"Okay, Nancy. What's our estimated time of arrival?"

Sarah responded, "Maybe an hour. It's all county and unimproved roads. The going will be slow."

"Your buddies are going to be there way ahead of us," Remo said.

"That's the whole idea of bringing them on board, ain't it?" Roy asked.

"How many buddies are involved?" Sarah asked.

Remo ignored that—an hour until they reached Bedders? "Can't this thing go any faster?"

"We'll start fishtailing," Roy protested.

"Nancy," Remo announced, "alert Agent Moses. We're gonna jettison the battle camper. In ten."

Remo left the SUV. Roy grabbed the steering wheel just in time.

THE CAMPER'S WINDOW flapped open. "You would not dare, Remo Williams!"

Remo was flat on his stomach on the roof of the

SUV, reaching for the tow hitch as the SUV braked hard. "I'm in a hurry."

"My precious home will be left to be stripped by hoodlums and gangbangers!"

"It's slowing us down. You coming or not?" As the SUV came to a halt in the roadside weeds, Remo stiffened his hand and snapped it against the hitch. The metal clanged and fell into scraps. The chain popped and electrical cables snapped. Remo slapped the roof of the SUV to signal Roy and they tore onto the county highway. The spinning tires spit rocks against the aluminum camper shell as a farewell insult.

"Why do you hate it so much that you must kill it again and again?" Chiun demanded. He was now sitting on the SUV roof a foot away.

"It'll be fine," Remo said.

"You should hope that it is," Chiun sniffed.

"Believe me," Remo said. "I understand the consequences."

36

Oscar Bedders thought it was an insidiously cruel trick, making him care about the youngsters so much. His love for them was just one of the tools the squid daddy used. Bedders couldn't fight the compulsions that the squid daddy put in his head. The squid daddy wanted him to lure in the enemy and kill him. That was the only thing the squid daddy cared about.

But what Oscar Bedders cared about were the youngsters. Once the enemy was dead, and the little old man who went with him, then Oscar Bedders would be free to take the youngsters to safety. As much as he hated it, he first had to put them in danger to lure in the enemy.

Bedders laid the ambush carefully, luring him to this chosen battleground where escape would be easy.

The trail of killings would bring the enemy next to the church fish fry, then to the old bait shop on Fingoren Road. They'd have to come into the boathouse to find Bedders, and then they would be trapped.

The little fishing boat was puttering softly. From the

open deck hatch came the sound of splashing. The youngsters were nervous. Bedders could feel it. They were connected, him and the youngsters. They shared feelings. But what had the kids worked up? Was it just the tension of waiting and waiting, or was it something more?

He stepped off the deck and looked out the side window of the boathouse. He couldn't see much. The other window showed him the road and the entrance drive. There were a few cars, including a police car. The bodies of the car owners and the cop were strewed around inside the bait shop. Nothing else stirred.

Maybe this was a bad idea. He was too cut off. Lots of blind spots. What if they sneaked up on him?

But this boat was the ideal place to make a stand. The hated men would come, and when they got on the boat they were good as dead. The youngsters and Bedders, together, could not be defeated.

Bedders heard a pop. He bled from the shoulder.

A series of bangs come from the trees. A small hole opened in Bedders's head and the back of his skull bloomed.

"Just more cops," Bedders told the youngsters as he willed the back of his head to collapse and seal itself. "Anybody hungry?"

The youngsters thrashed impatiently. The kids made gluttons of themselves at the Baptist fish fry, and they hadn't touched all the free meat in the bait shop. Bedders had also charged his internal batteries as full as they would go. Still, it took a lot of juice to heal a head wound—maybe another sip of life energy.

But he wasn't going to bother with the cops. They were incidental. The hated men would be here any minute.

The trees erupted with gunfire. The fusillade punched holes in the walls of the boathouse and pocked the tiny deck cabin on the fishing boat. Bedders was shot a half-dozen times, but didn't let it distract him. He was peering into the darkness for signs of damage to the hull. No, the hull was safe from gunfire—it was below the concrete lip of the slip.

"Let 'em shoot all day," Bedders groused. The youngsters churned up the water in their tanks. "What's wrong?" he demanded.

The youngsters couldn't give voice to their worries.

Four men approached. They came into the boathouse without caution, only to find Bedders waiting for them.

"Hey! He ain't dead!"

Then came the shooting. Then came the clutching arms of the youngsters, and then the silence. Bedders sucked what energy he needed from the last dying gunner and examined the body. These weren't cops. Local vigilantes? Not with this kind of firepower.

Organized-crime enforcers of some kind? Maybe he had stumbled into a county under the control of a syndicate. Did that make a difference? No, Bedders decided. Who cared? They were just a distraction, and he couldn't afford a distraction.

Where was the enemy?

REMO WAS SWIMMING in green fog. Three feet below the surface and the sun was just a bright spot in the clouds of sediment. Eight feet down and there was only twilight. Remo relied on his ears to find his way, drawn by the slapping of the river water against the heavily laden wooden hull. He swam closer.

THE BUSINESS ASSOCIATES hadn't expected this. Four men killed just like that? Or were they dead? If they were dead, it gave the rest of the boys an excuse to get really angry and start firing indiscriminately into the boathouse.

"They must be dead," Uncle Lawr from Jackson decided. "Hose the place."

They triggered wildly into the wooden boathouse and advanced from their hiding place, firing on and on until entire eight-inch boards were removed from the boathouse walls. The man inside was visible, and he was still on his feet!

"Bastard," Lawr cursed. "Kill that fuck."

BEDDERS CROUCHED in the little deckhouse, ignoring the fragments of wood and rusty nails that rained down on him. A bullet gashed his arm. He never felt it. The enemy was close by and Bedders could feel him.

He rose up, peered out toward the highway. Was he out there, concealing himself among the gunfire? The sensation of his nearness felt as if it came from another direction.

The world exploded into whiteness when a high-powered round slammed into his temple and cleaved through part of his brain. Bedders roared in frustration, clapping his hands to his head. Crooked channels of yellow energy knitted the flesh together again, but Bedders was angry now.

He got to his feet on the boat, and the boat moved out from under him.

Remo felt the movement from the boat. Bedders was on his feet. A stroke of luck. Remo thrust his stiff fingers into the wooden bow, penetrating the wood, and he yanked on the fishing boat. It moved quickly, even without leverage, then stopped short on its ties.

Bedders flopped off the rear end and landed hard against the concrete lip, then tried to push up. The boat reversed into his legs, crushing them, and for a moment he was pinned and helpless. The boat eased off, and he clambered up as his legs healed. The boat was propelled from the slip with more momentum and the davits were torn free. The boat drifted on the surface of the Mississippi, then it lurched in the water.

Bedders felt the offspring shrieking; it rattled his bones. Tentacles shot from the deck hatch and groped over the sides.

Remo thrust his hand into the hull, penetrating the

wooden exterior and the metal lining of the holding tank, and he felt slime. He closed his fingers on a tentacle and dragged it through the gash. He felt the squid shudder and the tentacle twisted around him. Suckers lined with jagged barbs sank into his flesh. Remo put his feet against the hull and dragged the squid through the gash, tearing its flesh and compressing its winged mantle. More tentacles reached into the water from above, blindly churning the water to find him.

The tentacles from above began to sizzle. The extracted squid wrapped itself around his body in a vicious, bone-breaking embrace. It was time to get out of there. Remo pushed off the underside of the boat and the extracted squid was carried along with him. Sizzling yellow energy flashed through the water, reaching out for Remo—and the extracted squid. The others wanted to give the thing a boost of power.

The energy was too far away. Remo raced along the muck, then struggled onto the shore, carrying the extracted squid into the daylight.

Oscar Bedders came through the tattered boathouse walls, a berserker. Remo tore the limp squid down the middle and threw one jerking hunk of slime in Bedders's face. The exposed guts sparked with trickles of energy. The instant Bedders touched it the power magnified. Bolts of sizzling energy crackled across open space, trying to pull the two halves together.

The squid flesh tingled in Remo's hands. There was no pain. It wasn't directed at hurting him, but the half carcass was trying to pull out of his grip. Remo grunted as he tossed the half carcass as far as he could throw it.

It landed in the gravel with a sickening liquid sound, just beyond the flock of business associates from Jackson.

They were dumbfounded, but they had enough sense to part ways when the bolts of energy reached out from the carcass in Bedders's hands and sought out the other half.

Remo's foot slammed into Bedders's head with enough force to snap his neck, but the neck healed in an instant.

Bedders got better all the time.

Bedders tossed the half-squid carcass in the general direction of its other half and raised both arms to block Remo's next blow. His forearms snapped, folded, then straightened out and fused solid, but Chiun was there, coming down on his shoulders as if falling from the sky, and Bedders was driven down into the gravel in a spineless heap. Bedders pushed up, felt his head cleaved open and collapsed.

IT WAS the fish restaurant all over again, the hated men striking him like bolts of human lightning and then falling back before Bedders could raise his field of energy, but now they had lured him away from the youngsters.

Bedders felt the youngsters. Some were in a fury. Some were *dying*. The enemy had penetrated the walls of the holding tanks on the fish boat, letting good water out and letting river water in.

Bedders sensed the youngsters' anguish. The water was poison.

He didn't feel the critical blows that squashed him over and over, but he heard the gunshots. Another scream. On land, another youngster was being murdered.

"I DON'T *KNOW* what it is," Uncle Lawr choked, trying not to spew. "Just kill it."

The twin clumps of squid slime were exchanging dancing bolts of energy and crawling toward each other, until the Jackson business associates blasted them.

"Idiots," Remo shouted, loud enough to drown the gunfire. "Get out of here."

Oscar Bedders rose from the ruin of his own body, blowing a foghorn of despair. He pushed with both hands, creating a bowling ball of yellow energy that rolled toward the dying squid offspring.

"Eee!" Chiun was airborne.

"Don't!" Remo cried.

He couldn't stop the old Master. Chiun's sandals landed atop the ball of energy, deforming it, and then Chiun rebounded violently.

Chiun landed in a crouch, apparently unhurt.

Bedders chased after the quashed energy ball on all fours, absorbed it and kept moving, using exposed bones as arms and crushed muscle as hands. He tore into the business associates, a living nightmare, hacking at them, tearing them, throttling them, burning them with renewed energy, sucking up their flesh, sucking up the force that gave them life.

The only thing Remo knew was that Bedders was renewing himself with uncanny speed, and *that* had to be stopped. He flew at Bedders; Bedders sensed his approach and twisted himself and two of his victims, whacking at Remo with the bodies. Remo dodged gracefully and touched the ground again.

Roy Candace came to the rescue, dropping the transmission into gear as the engine revved.

"Lucky for you I came along!" he exclaimed.

"Get back," Remo thundered, but it was too late. The SUV struck Oscar Bedders, who flopped over the hood and smacked into the windshield.

For a moment, Roy Candace and Oscar Bedders were face-to-face, and Roy lost his nerve. Bedders reached around, into the open window, and extracted everything Roy Candace had to give him. Roy rolled his eyes up, began to smoke and then disintegrated like a wax figure in a museum fire.

Remo landed on his feet on the hood and punted Bedders into the weeds, and Bedders got up running for the safety of the water. Chiun made a grab for him. Remo grabbed Chiun first, keeping him from entering the river with Oscar Bedders.

As Bedders went under the water, a lightning storm erupted below the surface of the mighty Mississippi, and Bedders's body was jolted with the current even as he dog-paddled for the drifting boat. The squid had maneu-

vered the boat close to shore and their tentacles blasted
the water like dangling power lines. They hauled Bedders aboard. He was choking and laughing—a mad-
man.

37

"For a murdering scumbag, he wasn't that bad a scumbag," Remo said by way of eulogy as he hauled the steaming husk of Roy Candace into the weeds with the remains of his business associates.

"But a fool," Chiun added less charitably. "All of them."

"Yeah. What screwups. All I wanted them to do was stay out of it. Look, don't act. Why can't people just listen to good advice?" Remo brushed off the driver's seat and sat there, surrounded by the massacre. Another field of bodies left in the wake of Oscar Bedders. The interior was scorched and smelly.

"Is anyone there?" It was Sarah Slate. The dashboard still worked, anyway.

"We're here," Remo said. "Chiun and I, anyway."

"Roy?"

"Toast, honey bunch." Remo started the SUV.

The dashboard made very quiet noises.

"What's wrong with you?" Remo asked. "Are you crying? Hey, there's no crying in CURE, sweetie."

"Shut up, Remo."

He couldn't remember angry words ever before coming from Sarah Slate's pure little lips.

"What's happening?" Mark Howard interjected.

"We need a new chauffer," Remo said. "Check the IQs next time. Nobody under eighty."

"Where are you heading?"

"Downriver. No paddle."

"Take the next right onto an unimproved road," Sarah said, recovering in a hurry. "Coming up soon."

They were already on it. Remo spun the wheel and snapped through a rusty chain over the trail with a sign claiming the road was closed and that it was private property. The owners didn't use the trail anymore. The SUV mowed down weeds and inch-thick saplings.

"This will keep us close to the river?"

"For 1.2 miles," Sarah said.

"Remo, what's going on?" Mark demanded.

"Driving."

"There," Chiun squeaked, jabbing a finger at the flashes of muddy river that showed through the trees. "I see his craft."

The old vehicle path curved toward the river. Remo followed it, then slammed on the brakes, twisting the wheel and steering the SUV broadside into a clump of heavy undergrowth, bringing it to a hard stop.

"Road ran out," Remo explained before there were complaints from his passenger.

"So it has," Chiun sniffed. In fact, two tires now

rested inches from the crumbling soil drop-off that fell thirty feet into the muddy riverbank. A mile away was Bedders's fishing boat, coming alongside another vessel.

Tiny flashes of light came from the two boats, as if the sunlight was glimmering off of polished bright work.

"Crap." Remo closed his eyes momentarily. When he looked next, he was just in time to see a fisherman being beaten against the deck of his own boat by a writhing tentacle.

Minutes later, the boats drifted out of sight.

38

Remo Williams was drained. He felt tired. Defeated.

Theoretically, he could have slipped down the hill and then run across the very surface of the river to intercept Bedders. A hale Remo could have done it, or a fresh Chiun.

Chiun was weary, too, and with a pang of guilt Remo realized he had forgotten Chiun's wounded arm. The old man kept it hidden in his robe. How much was it hurting him and sapping his strength? Remo felt his own body trying to slump.

He drove back the way he had come.

"Is it me, Little Father? I don't see how this can end. Every time, he finds some way to beat us."

"You misremember," Chiun said. "He has never beaten us."

"We've never beaten him."

"These challenges cannot end in stalemate indefinitely," Chiun pointed out.

Remo didn't find that reassuring. "Somebody is going to have to lose eventually. And I hate to remind you, but he has too beaten me once. Remember, me in the hospital, high on dope, surrounded by lab coats?"

"My contributions are meaningless, then?" Chiun asked.

"Of course not. But you were not with me when he knocked my brains in."

"I am with you now, and I would appreciate not being dismissed as a useless hanger-around. I am no Roy."

"I never said you were Roy."

"You think like a man alone. Readjust your thinking to a more realistic plane, please."

Remo tried. "Little help?"

"You do not fight this thing alone. You have me, willing and able to enter the fray when your efforts are unsuccessful."

"Very encouraging."

"We do not fight Oscar Bedders. We fight Bedders and the offspring of Sa Mangsang, and we are winning. Time and again we have slipped past the powerful defenses and rid the world of these abominations. We whittled them down. Several of the monsters were annihilated just today when you poisoned them with water from the river. We are creating triumph through attrition, and now we have an advantage. He is on water. He thinks he is safe from us and yet he is not. We will find him on the shoulders of Old Man River and sink the vessel beneath his very feet, until the offspring of Sa Mangsang asphyxiate."

39

It was deep in the night and Oscar Bedders was losing the battle of wills. His entire body and much of his mind were determined to keep the boat on course down the middle of the Mississippi River. The sensible part of Bedders's mind argued that this was the most dangerous path imaginable.

"We couldn't be easier to find," he shouted. "We're sitting ducks. At least let me speed up the damned engines!"

Bedders didn't even know what or who it was he was arguing with. The squid daddy, that's what he called the thing—the one who dictated the destiny of the youngsters, and thus dictated the fate of Oscar Bedders. The squid daddy gave Bedders his orders in the form of compulsions that couldn't be ignored. Now his own will was forcing him to drive his boat right down the middle of the biggest river in North America.

The enemy would have to be a fool not to track him down, and soon.

The compulsion in Bedders's head had not even allowed him to switch to a better squid-carrying boat. How easy it would have been to pump the water from the holds of the old fishing boat from the bait shop into the holds of the fishing boat they attacked last afternoon. That boat was bigger, faster and probably stronger. But the squid daddy wouldn't allow it. Squid daddy wanted them to be obvious.

The enemy had punctured the hull in his attack at the bait shop, and one of the four holding tanks was opened up to the filthy water of the Mississippi. There were six youngsters in there—after the first one was extracted and murdered on land by the enemy.

Bedders's compulsions did allow him to stop the boat and dive over the side to inspect the damage. One of the dying youngsters was trying to cork the gap with his own arms. The damage was too big and irregular to be patched.

Bedders wanted to take the boat of the fishermen he and the youngsters killed, but that wasn't allowed. The enemy knew the boat they were in, and that was the boat he'd be looking for. Then Bedders tried to coerce the dying youngsters from the leaking tank to drag themselves on deck and into the good tanks, but there was no room in the good tanks. All the tanks were overcrowded already. Even Bedders experienced a jolt when he saw how thick the squid meat was in the three remaining tanks.

The youngsters sure were growing up fast.

He felt a twinge of paternal pride, then went through

the agonies of listening to the kids in the leaking tank slowly grow weaker from the loss of marine water and the inexorable trickle of filthy incoming river water.

Bedders hijacked a houseboat at the squid daddy's command. The compulsion told him to steer close to the shore and take the thing in tow, including the residents. There was a lot of shouting aboard the houseboat at first, but when the man with the hunting rifle tried to put up a fight he met Bedders and the long arms of the youngsters. Those youngsters could now reach all the way out of their holding tank and clear across to the houseboat. The ignored the rifle fire and had the man for a midnight snack.

Bedders heard the others wailing and moaning deep inside the houseboat He wasn't sure how many more were in there. He didn't even know the purpose of the houseboat. One of the houseboaters got desperate and tried to swim to freedom, but the squid kids reached into the river and snatched her up.

For hours, he prayed that the enemy would attack. Bedders was convinced that once the enemy, and the enemy's little-old-man companion, were dead, then the squid daddy would have no more interest in Bedders or the youngsters. Then Bedders could get them whatever boat would suit them, and maybe save the dying youngsters.

But the enemy had not attacked, and in the depths of the night the slow thrashing from the leaking tank grew slower, then stopped.

Then the tank started to smell.

Sobbing and enraged, Bedders tried to force the boat into a dock along the river. He was sure to find some boat better than this one. A good fast craft that could get them to the Gulf of Mexico in hours. Screw the squid daddy.

For a moment, his rage overcame the commands in his head, but only for a moment. It was no more than a swerve, and then they were back on the course set by the squid daddy.

Oh, how he hated the squid daddy, second only to his hatred of the enemy. He couldn't touch the squid daddy, but he could and he would meet the enemy again, and when he did, the enemy would pay for all the misery Oscar Bedders had endured.

Not even two in the morning and the smell was ungodly. Not only did the youngsters grow fast, but they also fell apart fast when they were dead. The stench was being pulled into the houseboat, and the hostages were choking on the fumes.

The little fishing boat's autopilot consisted of a couple of rope loops that went on the knobby steering wheel, and it was good enough to allow Bedders to walk the deck almost constantly, listening into the water for any sense of the enemy. Bedders could feel the enemy's presence when he was near—even feel him from a few hundred paces away—but there was nothing exact about the sense.

Would the enemy come over the water or under the

water? Maybe hire a helicopter to attack from above? Doubtful. Would he send the little old man to initiate the attack, taking Bedders by surprise?

Easiest thing in the world would be to find the boat and send in some sort of aerial bombardment. Once the boat was sunk, the youngsters would simply die—then Bedders understood the reason for the houseboat. Human shields. The enemy wouldn't blow up a bunch of innocent people.

What would he do? And when?

Come on already. Let's get this over with.

It was after three in the morning when he felt the glimmer of the presence of the enemy. Close enough, but not too close.

"Get ready, youngsters," Bedders announced. "He'll be here soon enough."

The Mississippi River was wide and peaceful. The shore was dark except for the glimmer of lights a few miles down on the eastern shore. That had to be the enemy.

Bedders cried out when he felt the presence of the enemy escalate, quickly—the enemy was closing in at fantastic speed. But the water was still! No one could move that fast under the water. The sky was empty of aircraft. The enemy was almost here but where was he?

Bedders made a small sound when he spotted something ghosting over the surface of the water. Running on water! How could he? The youngsters were already thrusting their arms out of the deck openings—ready to grapple with the enemy.

THE ARMS REACHED into the water, guided only by whatever mystical Remo-waves were coming off of him. The offspring arms were strong and huge, but they were slow. Remo danced around the arms and never slowed. He stepped off the water and turned his body, putting all his momentum into a horizontal kick. He chopped open the hull of the boat, then snatched the upper rail in both hands and vaulted almost straight up.

Bedders yelped as the boat canted dramatically under his feet.

Remo was thinking about elephants, rocks, boulders, mountains. Big heavy things. When he came down it was like a mountain coming down—and he came down right on top of Oscar Bedders, who was driven down through the deck, into the hold, into the squid. Bedders's broken body cracked the plastic lining of the holding tank and punctured it. The squid youngsters' aggressive response was to attack, and they pummeled the place of the intrusion.

Remo pushed up and out, flying out of the tank with squid arms constricting all around him. He could only imagine what they were doing to Bedders. With any luck, Bedders would stay lodged in the hull.

Remo knew better than that. Bedders was the ultimate bad egg.

Remo bounded across the deck and landed on a tightrope of steel chain that led to the houseboat. The eyes of the houseboat dwellers were on him. He ignored them, bent and tapped a link of the chain with one finger. The welded steel link was just welded steel, after all, and it had inherent weaknesses just like any other substance. Remo's tapping created the precise resonance needed to magnify the weakness, and the steel link crumbled like stale bread.

The chain popped apart and the tension yanked it across the deck of the fishing boat. Remo ran across the flying chain, using it momentarily as a bridge, then stepped off as it looped around a mass of protruding squid arms like a cowboy's whip snatching a tree branch. Remo grabbed the chain and gave it a yank.

Two squid were extruded from the deck opening, slimy, grotesque and heavy. The tilting deck lurched back to center at the moment the squid flopped on it, and Chiun stepped aboard.

"For you," Remo said, waving grandly.

"Feh." Chiun stepped lightly into the mass of invertebrate slime and set upon them like some sort of mincing machine. Each of the Knives of Eternity, the deadly nail on each of his fingers, sliced off chunks of squid meat and sent the pieces arcing off the boat. The squid began to flicker with yellow energy bolts that snatched for the missing pieces as they flew away, but the pieces were being left behind in the river.

Remo cut in from behind, his hand stiff enough to pass into the muscular flesh like a butter knife dragged through grape gelatin. "One day they're just caviar, next day they're big as Clydesdales."

One of the squid was taking all of Chiun's damage, but Remo's victim tried to drag itself to the deck opening to the holding tank. Remo moved in close and took the creature by the wings of its mantle, which was now as big as Remo himself.

Remo hoisted the squid out. The mantle splashed into the water, but the arms were grasping the rail and the deck davits. Remo stomped the arms and pulled them apart, but the squid was pulling the severed pieces back together with flashes of energy.

"Chiun, did you poke a hole on your side?" Remo called.

"I did not fail in my duty. Does the boat not sink?"

"Not fast enough." Remo's squid was healing quicker than Remo could tear it apart. It turned its energy against him, and Remo knew this battle was a waste of his time.

"I'm going under."

"Foolish!" Chiun snapped, then stepped into the soggy mass of the squid he was battling and sliced its mantle into shreds, which he whipped off the boat. The shreds sizzled with energy, then dissipated in the murky Mississippi.

By then, Remo had gone overboard, too.

THE SQUID REMO WAS battling didn't want the fight to end. It spread out in the water, eight great arms plus two tentacles that were even longer and deadlier. Remo did a serpentine dance under the surface. It kept his ankles out of its grip for the moment, but Remo was unpleasantly aware that the squid was nearly intact, in spite of the punishment he'd just delivered it.

The boat sank deep enough to stall the engine, then it drifted with the current. The squid moved more slowly, immersed in poison, until the current carried it out of reach.

It was now clear that they weren't going to defeat the squid young in armed, so to speak, combat. There were many more still alive on the boat. The only choice was to put them on the bottom, boat and all, and let the river water kill them.

Or would it? Maybe they were strong enough now to survive a dunking in the mighty Mississippi. Maybe they could even get themselves to shore—but what then?

It wasn't worth considering. Right now Remo Williams had a plan and he would follow that plan. He would bring these slimy, murderous monsters into the Mississippi muck. They had to be stopped.

He thrust his hand into the hull, breaking through wood, meeting with the plastic liner of a holding tank, and scored it with his one extralong nail. Like Chiun's Knives of Eternity, the nail was steel sharp and scalpel strong, and the plastic opened up. Remo thrust his hand in and yanked out a fistful of squid flesh.

He gagged on the cloud of putrefaction that blossomed around him. He'd cut into the holding tank with the dead squid—it was the same tank he broke into when he attacked the boat at the bait shop this afternoon. The bits of flesh had to be the remains of the squid in the tanks and they were rotting in a big hurry.

Remo felt the boat sinking above him, but too slowly. Chiun had kicked open one side and Remo opened another, but the boat was still too buoyant. He clawed along the underside, put his hand against the wood and felt the vibrations of heavy movement above him. An intact holding tank. He thrust through the wood, cut the plastic and withdrew more squid flesh. This time, the squid flesh fought back.

Remo ignored the tentacles that extruded into the water and wrapped around his body. He had to enlarge that breach in the hull. He thrust both hands into the gash, forcing them past the tentacles, mangling the edge of the break. A piece of the support frame snapped and the shell burst open. River water flooded into the hold, and it wanted to carry Remo in with it. The tentacles were dragging on him, too.

Remo reached out, found a ridge to dig his fingers into on the outside of the hull bottom, and dragged himself away from the gash. The tentacles refused to release him, even as the squid giants in the open hold writhed in agony. Remo squirmed away and found himself staring at a flesh protrusion from the hull. They were human legs and feet, dancing with energy. Oscar Bedders was re-forming himself, even as he remained lodged in the boat bottom.

Remo did an underwater log roll, unfurling some of the tentacles from his body too swiftly for the squid to react, then he grabbed the longest of the arms and whipped it at the feet of Oscar Bedders. The squid latched on to Bedders and dragged the squid keeper out of his place in the hull. Bedders yowled and waved his arms, clinging to the hole—but it was too late.

He had been serving as a human cork, his body keeping the river water from entering the hull, and now the river water rushed in to another holding cell. More squid arms shot from the hole, snatched at Bedders and tore off an arm, a shoulder and a head and dragged them into the opening. The remains were insufficient to plug the hole.

Remo could feel the mass of the boat sinking. It was going to press him into the mud of the river bottom in seconds. He swam to the side of the hull. Squid arms fought to hold on to him. Remo slashed them, pummeled them and grabbed them in his hands. He ripped them apart. More squid arms came. Six or more squid in a holding tank, ten limbs each. He couldn't keep fighting that many squid arms—even if they weren't re-forming in shimmering flashes of yellow energy. They dragged Remo Williams to the opening in the hull that was no longer plugged by Oscar Bedders.

His body was yanked to the opening, pulled across the hole, sloppily plugging it like a wad of oilcloth. He could feel his backbone bending. The pressure was intense and the slimy hull was pressed hard against his face. He kneed the hull, weakly, with little leverage, then fought to get his arms inside. The squid tentacles pulled him harder against the opening, and Remo used his fists to batter the plastic and wood. It cracked and weakened, and his spine was grinding from the unbelievable pressure. His fingers clawed at the hull. He had to break it or he would break against it. Pieces of the hull floated free. He was tearing off only small fragments and that wasn't fast enough.

Teeth closed on his fingers. Human teeth. Remo couldn't see inside the hull but he knew what it was— Oscar Bedders, nothing but a head and an arm, inside the tank trying to stop him from tearing open the tank.

Remo thrust his hand inside the mouth. His freakishly thick wrists forced the mouth open too far. The jaw shattered. How many times had Oscar Bedders' face been broken since this all began? Remo Williams could think of nothing he'd rather do than break it some more. He wadded his fist deep in Oscar Bedders's gullet. The squid keeper struggled to escape, pounding Remo with one fist, until Remo used Bedders as a club. He pounded the inside of the squid tank again and again until the plastic was coming apart—and Bedders with it. The tank opened around Remo, and he was dragged inside.

Bedders lit up like an ugly yellow Christmas tree,

and the squid went into throes around Remo Williams. The river was rushing in around them. They were dying. They had nothing to lose. All they had left to them was to kill the hated enemy.

The bolts of energy impaled Remo. He felt the penetration into his core, like iron spikes. His breath was forced out and water flooded his lungs. All he knew was the endless reality of impalement.

Then he moved, somehow using a reserve of will he didn't know was in him. It was just enough to interrupt one bolt of energy with the fist that was still buried in the throat of Oscar Bedders. He moved the bust of Bedders *into* the energy bolt.

Bedders went into throes of agony, his fist beating on Remo's arm. The energy bolt fell off. Remo thrust Bedders into a second bolt. Bedders was broiled. The bolt dissipated. Remo could feel his strength coming back even as more bolts of energy continued to fry his insides.

The squid were slowing. They were weakening. The water was killing them. Remo felt the roof of the holding tank bang the back of his head. That meant the boat was submerged.

He felt—satisfaction.

The squid's grip was less powerful, but there had to have been thirty tentacles wrapped on his body and legs, and they adhered to his flesh with suckers and sucker barbs. Who'd give out first? Remo wondered. The squid, or him?

He never found out. A thin, bony human arm grasped

him around the back and pulled him through the deck hatch into the open air, while the squid tightened their suckers and barbs all over him in a last, defiant gesture. There was a moment in time in which Remo was caught in the middle.

This is gonna hurt, Remo Williams thought, when the bony arm dragged him out of the grip of squid suckers and squid barbs.

And hurt it did.

40

The celebration was in its final, climactic hours. The riverside site was rented out until eleven the next morning. Nobody wanted the party to end—and there was no reason it should end. Why not just keep it going all night? When the band started packing up, the kids passed the hat until they collected enough to pay for one more set.

There were a few thousand young adults dancing on the riverside when the band stopped playing, midsong.

"What the fuck, man? That wasn't a full set." Thirty-three-year-old Pete Hotter was the organizer of the event. Every year was a raging success and a big moneymaker—until now. Why had everything come to a screeching stop?

The crowd got quiet. The assholes in the band weren't listening to Hotter—they were watching the river. Oh, great, a river accident? Right in the middle of his party? Wouldn't that just be his luck.

"What's going on?" he demanded, pushing through the quiet crowd. One second the place was ringing with beautiful noise and the next was so quiet you could hear the damned crickets in the weeds.

The crowd opened a big gap in the ring around the bonfire. A little old man was standing there in a wet robe. He looked like he was steaming, but he hadn't got close to the bonfire yet. His smile was forced.

"What event is this?" asked the little man.

"Why?" demanded Pete Hotter. "Who wants to know?"

"I do." The man grasped him by the elbow. "What event?"

Pete thought that alcohol was supposed to dull the pain. He'd had lots and lots of alcohol and he could still feel lots of pain. The old man had his elbow in some sort of a kung fu nerve pinch. Pete didn't try to speak, but gestured dumbly at the collapsed banner in the weeds.

"Ah. I believe I have heard of this Bogunhurst Bayou Bash." The old man nodded. "This is an event for young adults? You have much alcohol here. The air is redolent."

Hotter pointed at the kegs and the table full of bottles of hard liquor.

"Are there young females who are encouraged to remove their garments and display their upper bodies at the shouted demands of the males?"

Hotter waved at a girl from Baton Rouge, her eyes half-closed while she swayed to music that no longer played. She wondered why everybody was looking at her, then realized she was naked above the waist.

The old man seemed displeased. "It is unsavory."

"What did you expect?" asked a second man. Hotter hadn't noticed him before—where'd he come from? He was covered in red scar welts and bloody scrapes. "I told you it would be unpleasant," the younger man said.

"It is more than unpleasant. It is quite repulsive."

"Yeah." The younger man had something tucked under his arm. It was a human head. A human shoulder. A human arm. People started screaming. Several staggered into the bushes to purge their poisons.

"Not a solitary sober human being among them," Chiun said, at last releasing his elbow-hold on Pete Hotter. Hotter ran away, tripping drunkenly, then running some more. "Disgusting."

"Yeah. Yuck." Remo placed Oscar Bedders into the glowing heart of the bonfire. The peeling remains stirred to life. Bedders's eyes shot open. He tried to scream as the flames bubbled his skin, but without lungs he couldn't move the air through his unhinged mouth.

"I knew he was playing possum." Remo helped himself at the booze table. "Tequila," he explained to Chiun.

"I see."

"For Oscar."

Remo held the bottle over fire. The liquid glugged out over Oscar Bedders and the flame roared to life, trying to climb up the waterfall of liquor. Bedders vanished in the cleansing fire, but spider legs of yellow energy reached out, seeking any living thing to give life energy.

There were only charred coals and rocks for it to feed off of. When the fire dissipated, Bedders was only a blackened skull and bones. The Masters of Sinanju were alone amid the untidiness of the Bogunhurst Bayou Bash.

"Better safe than Bedders," Remo announced, tossing in more booze.

"We will leave this place now," Chiun said.

"In awhile."

"I am revolted. Whites are as degraded a race as I ever dreamed they could be. It is impossible that I could attend such events as this. It is all vomit and filth."

"I think that's the name of the band," Remo said, trying not to inhale the stench of hot agave and cooked flesh—and, yes, vomit and filth.

"It is dead, Remo. Let us leave here."

"Just want to be sure."

"I shall go without you."

"Go ahead."

Chiun lingered anyway. Remo emptied the remains of more liquor bottles over the fire. It burned and burned.

"He is now incinerated," Chiun said at last.

"The part we found," Remo said, poking the crusty ashes with his ruined Italian shoes. "We didn't get most of him. We didn't get his heart."

"It is a large river. We will not find the rest of him. But you retrieved and destroyed the head, where the intellect dwelt. The human pawn and the offspring are destroyed. That is all that can be done."

"There's no way those squid kids could survive all the way down to the Gulf," Remo said to assure himself. "They didn't last ten minutes once they sank in the river. There's nothing you-know-who could have done to save them."

"Of course not."

"And Oscar Bedders is charcoal."

"You have seen to that."

"Yeah. But what will come next? They were just the tools of Sa Mangsang, right, Little Father? Sa Mangsang will have other tricks up his sleeves."

"The gigantic squid of Illinois was in an opportune place from which it might strike to attract the attention of the Master of Sinanju. There are no more such oversize squid on display, anywhere in the world, from which *his* children might spring. Smith would have known if there were."

Remo frowned into the firelight, his face red and pockmarked with bloody scrapes and circles. "There's other squid in the ocean."

"Yes."

"Who knows how you-know-who might come at me next time."

"Exactly, no one knows how. Not me. Not you. For what purpose would you dwell on this subject? Are you simply adding scraps to your compost barrel of self-pity?"

Remo shrugged. The fire had burned so hot that there was nothing left in the ring now except powder and few glowing coal remnants.

"Where'd we leave the camper?"

Chiun looked suspicious. "It is abandoned on a county road in Misserippi. Why?"

"I could really use a nap," Remo said, with a crooked grin. "Let's go home."

Epilogue

The famous and irate marine biologist Philip Sylvie
blasted the media, vilified the Chicago Aquarium and
disparaged the City of Chicago. Political correctness be
damned—he was mad as hell and he didn't care whom
he told about it.

· "You're a horrible, awful, evil man," said the caller
on the Chicago radio show.

"Don't be an idiot, madam. I'm a considerate scientist exposing the work of inept scientists. The fact is, the
aquarium did a miserable job of keeping that unique
creature in a proper environment. They did everything
wrong. They gave it improper food. They kept it at a
temperature that was too high for its normal metabolic
function, and they interfered with its natural rhythms by
lighting the tank."

"Better to put it in the dark where no one can see it
then feed it live dolphins and whales?"

"For a start."

"You are an evil man."

"Dr. Ordonez wrote the creature off too soon—I'm

guessing that the *Mesonychoteuthis hamiltoni* specimen was *not* dead when she thought it was. When she entered the tank it caused the squid to lash out in self-defense."

"Can you expand on that?" asked the radio host. His job was to egg this lunatic on to greater extremes of outlandishness. The heartless old bastard was a guaranteed ratings spike, and this whole morbid business with the deaths at the aquarium was big news. City officials were still not coming clean on the nature of the events that killed all those people, starting with Dr. Ordonez.

"Squid are marvelous survivors. They have incredible regenerative capabilities. For example, a squid can lose an arm in a battle with a whale and regenerate it entirely. Some squid are thought to go into a comatose state to recover from illness or trauma. What I'm saying is, Dr. Ordonez should have known better than to get into that tank. She was a victim of her own incompetence.

"Did you know that a squid has three hearts? One primary heart and two hearts for pumping blood to the gills. There is some evidence that a squid can survive a terrific mutilation—even if its primary heart is damaged. The other two hearts can work harder to compensate. Did you know that?"

"I did not," the radio host admitted.

IT COULDN'T SEE or hear or smell, but it could feel. It was in the water, covered in muck. It had one hand and two feet. It crawled with its hand and pushed with its feet.

It felt turbulence in the water—a boat rumbling nearby.

It crawled into more shallow water, where it could feel the temperature changes caused by the rising and setting of the sun, and for survival's sake it crawled only at night. It crawled for nine long nights.

Finally, it found what it had been waiting for. Something splashing in the water nearby. The shifting of feet in the shallows. The gentle plop of a baited hook landing in the water. The fingers came in contact with a rubber-clad boot. Fisherman's waders.

There was a fisherman standing inside of them.

The hand grasped the foot and the fisherman tried to pull away—but the lightning show had already begun.